THE

FINAL

DOOM

This is a work of fiction. All of the characters, organizations, and events portrayed in this novel are either products of the author's imagination or are used fictitiously.

THE FINAL DOOM

Published by Damn Fool Press
www.damnfoolpress.com

Cover illustration is a public domain image from U.S. Centers for Disease Control and Prevention—Medical Illustrator.

ISBN 978-0-9950434-3-5 epub
ISBN 978-0-9950434-4-2 mobi
ISBN 978-0-9950434-2-8 trade paperback

First Edition : January 2017

This is for Lynn and the cats.

CHAPTER ONE
Into the Big Smoke

Rain washed blood off the truck as I drove down the highway, but couldn't touch the memories of the horrors I had left behind. The sight of bloody remains of people, both neighbours and strangers, continued to haunt me. The werewolves had begun to purge humans from the rural areas north of Toronto. No doubt the city would be next. I had survived the purge, but didn't know what to do other than run.

The fucking werewolves had ruined everything. Smashing through them with the truck didn't bother me, to be honest.

As I lost myself in remembrances, the wheels touched the unpaved shoulder and I struggled to fight the truck back onto the road. Losing focus was dangerous, given how tired I was. Speaking of which, it couldn't hurt to pop another mild stimulant—it was only my second of the day. I washed it down with some coffee from a thermos and a couple bites of bread. It all served to settle my stomach as well as my nerves.

It was a long drive to Toronto, and I couldn't afford to stop. My friends were waiting for me, and needed the new information I was bringing. Assuming one considers werewolf corpses to be "information". The werewolves were changing into something different, something deadlier than the world had been seeing these past few years. And that was in addition to their greater than normal numbers. No-one understood why.

Just before the purge, I had discovered that the Change

1

Plague was actually a series of yearly plagues that emanated from Toronto. The how and why were more unknowns that needed answers. Hopefully my friends could help me figure it all out.

The rain began to let up the closer I got to Toronto. Fortunately, it had managed to do a decent job of cleaning pieces of werewolf off the plow and pickup. A pickup with a plow was odd enough at this time of year. One with blood and body bits on it was sure to attract attention.

Rolling down Highway 400, I was struck by the paucity of traffic. It was noon-ish, and so past rush hour, but it should have been busier than this on a week day. Maybe I had just got lucky and hit a break between traffic pulses. It was about time that I caught a break.

Speaking of which, the plow was bouncing up and down rather more than I would have liked. Ramming through those cars hadn't done it any good, nor had slicing through werewolves. I worried that the support struts were knocked awry or broken, and having the plow drop to the ground at the speeds I was going would be a Bad Thing for sure.

Spotting a roadside gas bar coming up, I pulled over into the exit lane. After turning into the facility, I parked as far as possible from the building, with the plow facing away from it. No point in advertising my problems.

Turning off the engine I sat there in the sudden silence. It all seemed so unreal. Here I was sitting in a gas station, cars whizzing by me, and everything seemed so normal. I had escaped an attack from the legions of Hell, and I wanted to rush out and yell at everyone to run and hide because Armageddon had arrived. Though why should they believe me? Heck, right now I was having problems believing it, and I had just escaped it.

Well, there was still work to do and problems to solve, Hell on Earth or not. I got out of the truck and walked somewhat stiffly to the front to look at the plow. There were numerous dents and scrapes all along it, the worst damage being to the edges of the wings on either side. The edges were folded back and there were a few chunks missing. Slashes of paint of

2

different colours were embedded into the blade. Thankfully, the little blood that remained just kind of blended in. Hopefully the rain would finish cleaning it all off before too long.

Looking along the support structure, I could see that a couple of struts were bent, and the lift mechanism on the one side was broken. A closer examination showed that the struts themselves were fine. The problem was that the main connecting bolt in the lift mechanism had sheared off somewhere along the way.

My choices were to fix it or remove it and leave the plow here. The latter was not the best of options, considering that the damage and blood might cause serious questions to be raised by the police. Besides, I was loathe to abandon an expensive piece of gear. Fixing the problem turned out to be a relatively straightforward, if profanity-laced, process that took longer than it should have.

After completing the task and putting the toolbox away, I celebrated by eating some bread and drinking coffee. That sat so well I decided to have a protein bar for extra nourishment. Sighing contentedly, I listened to the rain thrumming gently on the roof of the truck.

Soon I was feeling a little too warm, so I shrugged out of my vest and tossed it to one side. Remembering the data keys stored in there, I took a couple sets out of the vest and stashed them around the cab in different spots. After that, I just sat there for several minutes, soaking up the gentle solitude. It surely did feel relaxing.

Sitting up with a start, I shook off my lassitude. Those data keys reminded me that I had promises to keep and miles to go before I could sleep. Not to mention several werewolf corpses and assorted body bits that needed to be delivered before they degraded even further. With a sigh I resealed the coffee thermos, took a swig of cold water from another thermos, and got my sorry ass into gear.

I started the truck and prepared to leave. Then I noticed what they were charging for gas, and realized that it was actually a damn good price. It never failed to amaze me how highway gas bars often had the best prices. The truck was only down a quarter tank, but best to keep it topped up. What with the end of the world coming, and all. Of course, I paid with my credit card. If worst came to worst I wouldn't have to pay it.

I was about to pull away and continue my trek to Toronto when it occurred to me to check for cell phone service. All phone service—cell and land line—had been cut off to my house for so long that I'd simply turned my phone off to conserve battery life. Rather than calling while sitting at the gas pumps, I pulled over to the parking area again. Pulling out my phone, my fingers clumsily tapped at the touch screen. To my surprise, service was available.

Somewhat hesitantly, I dialled Lee's cell number. It had been so long since I'd actually spoken to anyone that I was bit nervous. The phone rang and rang, and finally I heard Lee's breathless voice say hello. I was so shocked that I couldn't speak until she said my name a couple of times. I snapped out of my temporary paralysis and explained that I was in a gas bar on the 400 just south of Highway 9.

Lee started to cry and said it was wonderful to hear from me. I managed to calm her down by assuring that I was all right and had a truck full of goodies, including the specimens Gail wanted, and where did she want them? She blew her nose, and said something to someone else before she started speaking to me again. She told me to use the rear entrance, and gave me the street names and the best route to get there. She assured me that it was used by trucks all the time, so my pickup shouldn't have any problems.

No problems for professional truck drivers who do it all the time, perhaps. Not so much for an old man used to driving on empty country lanes. Ah, bugger, but such was life. I assured her that I would find the way and not to worry.

Did she believe me? She did not. In fact, she insisted that I program the GPS unit while she was on the line (wasting my air time minutes) and wanted to hear the unit speak out the route. Only then was she satisfied. Kids these days.

She asked how the trip had been. I said that things were fine, and I got out fine, and I'd be there in an hour or two depending on traffic. I pointed out that Toronto drivers had been known to panic if a single raindrop hit their windshield. She laughed and wished me well, and we ended the call.

It had been damn nice to hear her voice. I sat there for a minute until my breathing steadied. And I'll admit that I wiped my eyes once or twice. Putting the phone into the seldom-used holster on the front dash, I paired it with the hands-free system, and prepared to head out.

It occurred to me, that if the cell phones were working, maybe the regular radio was as well. I'd gotten so used to the solar storms wiping out both the FM and AM stations (not that reception at the farm was ever that good) that I hadn't turned the truck's radio on. Well, that and the fact that I had been listening for werewolf howls.

I tuned to one of the Toronto all-news stations to catch one of their regular traffic reports. While listening, I pulled out onto the 400, merged with traffic, and stayed at the speed limit in the right-hand lane. It was damned seldom that anyone drove at the speed limit on the 400, of course. Still, given that it was drizzling and I was out of practise at driving in traffic, it seemed prudent.

The news was depressing, with talk about the possibility of an impending depression and trade embargoes. There was nothing about werewolves. The traffic report came on, and it proved to be interesting, if puzzling. Apparently southbound traffic volume was lighter than normal due to the unexpected fewer number of commuters. There were a few scattered reports of power failures, so perhaps the inclement weather had downed some lines.

Uhm, hadn't anyone noticed fewer cars on the roads because people were being frickin' slaughtered outside the cities? Apparently that wasn't a news item. As accustomed as I had become to the media ignoring anything outside of Toronto, this was hard to understand.

I seethed about that for some minutes until I calmed down. The analytical side of my brain kicked in and I realized that there were several possible explanations for this. Maybe the government was censoring the news. Or just maybe no-one knew about it yet. That latter possibility started to sound better and better the more I thought about it.

The purge of humans in my area was recent. The whole social system that tied us all together was already strained to the breaking point and getting kind of frayed. Small OPP detachments in the boonies that didn't report in on time were no longer much of an issue. Nor were small towns that hadn't been heard from in a while. Give it a few more days and, yes, questions would start to be asked.

Toronto had always been insular and the past few years had made it more so. Everyone was more insular, in fact, keeping their heads down and just trying to get by. Keeping up the pretence that nothing was wrong. Well, I couldn't argue that that wasn't a valid response. But only up to a certain point—and that point was long past.

Thinking on such matters began to give me a headache. Actually, the headache had been building in the background for a while, but I was only now truly conscious of it. In fact, it almost felt as if I might be coming down with a flu or something. On the other hand, it could very well be due to the fact that I was exhausted and on the run after barely escaping with my life. On the run with information that my friends in Toronto needed, data and insights that no-one else seemed to have. My headache was getting worse, and I began to feel rather sorry for myself.

Enough of that maudlin nonsense. It was time for me to do my own bit of pretending everything was normal, and that meant cruising music. I switched to a music station that played the classics—the old stuff by Bach and such. I'd have preferred music from the 1950's and 60's. Alas, no-one played the real classics any more. Sigh.

In any event, concentrating on driving while listening music seemed to mute the headache, and made life seem sweeter. Something about that bothered me but I decided that lack of pain was better for driving, and focused on the music.

And so it was that I rolled on down the highway, reaching Steeles Avenue, then Finch, and finally the turnoff to the 401. Now came the fun part. I exited onto Highway 401 and headed east. With a minimum of slowdowns (minimum for Toronto, that is) I arrived at the 404 and headed south, and onto the Don Valley Parkway. Or Don Valley Parking Lot, as many people called it.

To my surprise traffic wasn't too bad, for Toronto. Damned scary for an old man used to driving in the country. I told myself to suck it up 'cuz the worst was yet to come. That is, when I got off the DVP and went into downtown Toronto. I had once thought of that as Hell on Earth, and even now it ranked a close second for that title.

The less said about that trip the better, I think. I followed the soothing voice of my GPS unit, and came to loathe it. Turn here, turn there, it would say. However, it didn't have to deal with onrushing traffic and idiots who honked at me. Damn punks who thought they owned the damned road. Piss on 'em. I went where I had to go, and if they wanted to waste their pretty cars on my built-like-a-brick-shithouse pickup, well that was their call, wasn't it? Fortunately none of them did, although it was a damned near thing a few times.

Eventually I got to the rear of the ROM, just like Lee had told me to, and I backed up into an empty slip in the delivery area. Turning off the engine with a heavy sigh, I rested my head on the steering wheel for a few seconds. Stifling a groan, I sat up, reached for the cell phone, and called Lee. She answered after the first ring and yelled out, "He's here," to someone.

I was wondering how to respond to that when I heard the big delivery door on the building roll up. Glancing in the side mirror I saw Lee holding up her phone and waving. I gave a small wave back, and disconnected the call. No sense in wasting air time or battery. I was about to climb out of the truck when suddenly I was confronted by a crowd of smiling faces. It was everyone in The Group.

Damn, but it warmed my heart to see them. I stumbled out of the cab and hugged and shook hands with them all. It must have been allergy season, 'cuz everyone had the sniffles, even me.

CHAPTER TWO
The Prodigal Son Returns

"Sorry to be so late," I mumbled after clearing my throat. "Had a bit of bother along the way."

Dixon was gaping at the battered state of the plow. "No shit, Sherlock. Damn. What the hell did you hit?"

Clio swatted him none-too-gently on his arm.

"Ow," he exclaimed, with a hurt look. "I was just asking."

"Let Felix catch his breath," Clio said with a frown. "Dammit, Dixon, you've got to work on your empathy skills. We've talked about this."

With everyone's attention drawn to the exchange between those two, I took the opportunity to wipe my eyes while no-one was looking. A man's got his pride, after all.

Lee came up, laid a hand on my arm, and asked gently if I wanted to rest up. I noticed Gail turning away from the squabbling duo, and her amused smile became a querying look.

"Nope," I said, "I've got some...cargo that needs taken care of right away. Those...ah...specimens that Gail asked for. They're at the bottom of the pile in the back, so we'll have to decant everything to get at them."

Upon hearing that, Gail dashed forward to peer into the back of the truck. "I'll get some of the labourers to help us with this."

I held up a hand to stop her.

"Uhm, there's some other cargo there that we don't want to show around to strangers," I said.

Gail just looked at me with a quizzical expression for a

moment, then slapped her head. "Oh damn, Felix, sorry. You bugged out, didn't you? Ah, that means you brought some guns, I guess?" She had lowered her voice as she said the last bit. Even so, everyone's head turned toward us.

"Yeah," I replied, drawing out the word. "Was kinda hoping to keep that quiet, you know? Need to know, and all that."

As I said that, I could see Stan, Jack, and Clio exchange glances. The two men looked as if they wanted to say something but were too embarrassed. With a snort, Clio came up and asked quietly, "Got anything you could spare? All we've got is my skeet shotgun, and that's only useful against clay plates."

The rest of The Group had moved forward, and leaned in to hear the exchange.

"Are things really getting that bad here in the city?" I asked. "Last I heard, things were quiet here and firearms were being actively discouraged."

Stan spoke up. "Officially, that's still the case. The reality is that a lot of people have been quietly stocking up these past few months. And not just because of the werewolves, either. I figured that my crossbow would be all I needed, along with Clio's shotgun. But after hearing about the earlier attacks you had, we got a bit antsy. After seeing those recent videos, well, we all realized that we were nearly defenceless."

"On top of that there's the increase in general violence," added Jack quickly. "Robberies, home invasions, and break-ins are all on the rise. Officially, reporting on those has been suspended. And, no, that suspension isn't allowed to be reported, either. Still, people talk. And everyone knows someone who's been affected."

Lee piped up, "That's one of the reasons I wanted Gail to move in with me. High-rises are simply less safe than the smaller apartment buildings like mine where people know everyone."

After a quick look around to ensure that it was only The Group here, I said quietly, "I've got some spares of guns and ammunition. Couldn't bring everything, but managed to find room for more than I expected."

Turning to Clio I said, "How about a 12-gauge pump-action shotgun with some boxes of No. 4 buck and deer slugs? That the sort of thing you were looking for?"

Her look of relief was gratifying to see. These were my friends, and I would do my damnedest to help them.

"Stan and Jack," I said, looking at them, "I can't spare another shotgun. Would a rifle help? I've got a couple of three-ought-threes and a couple boxes of cartridges for each."

The two young men exchanged glances and nodded gratefully. Both had been raised up north and had grown up hunting for food. I had no qualms about their ability to safely used firearms.

"Dixon, how are you two set?" I said turning towards the young man. Dixon blushed and looked down at his feet for a moment before looking up. "I'm fine, thanks. My contacts have set me up." "OK," I said. "Stick around anyways. I brought something for you." He gave me a quizzical look, but he was obviously pleased that I'd brought something just for him.

"And," I said looking at them all, "I've got a shitload of frozen meat to divvy up amongst you lot. I used it keep the ... specimens ... cold." Well, from the way their faces lit up you'd have thought it was Christmas.

Lee was the first to speak up, "We hadn't wanted to say anything to you ... decent food is getting damned expensive here, and sometimes hard to get. That'll help us all—a lot."

Ever-practical Gail added, "And serve as inducement to smooth the way here amongst the staff."

We all turned to look at her.

"We're going to have to move these specimens to the labs, and store them there, and arrange for people to look the other way. Not to mention get the testing done in a timely fashion. How much food are we talking about, Felix?"

The others just nodded at this, as if agreeing to something that had slipped their minds.

"Excuse me?" I blurted. "Have things been reduced to using bribes to get things done? Holy shit."

The others just looked at me and nodded.

"It's just the way things are, Felix," said Dixon. "You can get things done slowly or you can help speed things along. And it is called tipping. Better remember that—people get really upset if you call it a bribe."

Oh, hell. This indicated a level of social deterioration that I hadn't been expecting.

"Felix?" Lee's gentle voice brought me back to the here-and-now.

"Uhm, yeah, sorry. Two layers in the back are frozen meat. The 1- and 5-gallon containers are dry goods like flour, rice, and beans. Miscellaneous stuff tucked in here and there. Like those imported chocolate biscuits you like, Dix—I brought a couple of tins for you. And some chocolate to spread around for the rest of you. Oh, and quite a few small potatoes and carrots that I salvaged after the last attack. No sense leaving it for the damned werewolves."

The looks on their faces told me that I'd chosen well.

Clio piped up in a slightly stunned voice, "Damn. That's ... that's ..." She rushed forward to envelope me in a hug. Clio was a great hugger, but this was more like a drowning person holding on to solid ground. Although I heard a couple of muffled snuffles while her face was buried in my shoulder, when she raised her head she was smiling. When I looked around at the others, they were smiling as well.

After clearing her throat, Gail spoke up, "Wow. Well, don't forget we need to set aside a fraction of that for tipping. Still lots to go around. Speaking of which, we may need to get the frozen stuff to the freezers."

"And distribute the weapons," I added. "I've got some spare knapsacks and tote bags that I was using as padding. How about we start divvying up from the top down, so we can see everything we have. That way everybody here will get what they need."

Clio spoke up, "Much as I hate to grab and run, some of us need to get back to work. And we've got to get the frozen stuff home before it completely thaws, don't we?"

"Excellent point, love," said Jack. "Uhm, Gail, maybe you and Lee could ensure a bit of privacy for the first part of this?"

The ladies in question just smiled and nodded their

agreement. They told the rest of us to start working while they sealed the area for the next little bit.

With that, we started unloading the truck. I hadn't realized how much stuff I'd managed to pack in, and was mighty glad to have help getting it all out. The day's efforts were beginning to wear on me, and I was feeling somewhat droopy. Dix came up to me with a portable chair that he'd found in the loading bay.

"Take a load off, old man," he said with a smile. "It's our turn now."

I smiled my thanks at him, too tired to do my usual "why, in my day ..." spiel. After watching for a couple of minutes, I went into the truck's cab and grabbed the coffee and a snack. Heading back to the chair, I leaned back with my eyes closed and sipped the warm-ish coffee and nibbled on a protein bar.

Damn it felt good to be among my friends again. Thoughts of the horrors that I had fled from began to seep into my mind until I forced them into the background. Time enough to deal with that later. For now, it was time to focus on the important things in life.

A loud crash of opening doors and rattling wheels from behind me interrupted my reverie and I jerked upright in the chair. The coffee would have spilled if there had been any left.

"Hey, Doc, whatcha got for us?" enquired a loud voice.

I turned around in time to see Lee wave over a pair of large men who were pushing a cart toward us. As they got closer, Gail pointed to one side of the dock area and said, "Those bags hold specimens that need to be put into the big freezer in my lab. When that's done, this other lot under the tarp needs to go into the freezer, too."

Judging by the neat piles of sorted items off to one side, it appeared that I'd dozed off. The specimens were laid out neatly in a row, there was a pile covered with a tarp that had to be the frozen meat, and finally the containers of dried food were neatly stacked off to one side. My personal stuff was no-where to be seen. The tailgate of the truck was closed, so I took that to mean everything was all safely locked away.

"Well, Doc, you know how it is. There's all that paperwork that needs to be filled out before we can put specimens in the freezer," said the larger of the two men, rubbing his chin thoughtfully. "Not at all sure that there's space for these. Might need to move some stuff around. You know how it is."

"I do, indeed," said Gail with a smile. "And don't forget that you'll need to make room for the second lot of specimens."

Lee was standing next to the pile of what I assumed to be the frozen meat, She lifted up a corner so that some of the butcher-wrapped packages could be seen. She, too, had a slight smile. This was obviously familiar territory for the pair of them.

The large man's mouth twitched upwards at one corner. "Yes, ma'am. I'm thinkin' that the second lot won't be sitting around too long, will it?"

"No, indeed, Fred. Just till the end of today, or tomorrow at the latest, I'm sure," Gail replied brightly.

"OK, Doc, we'll get right on it. Oh, there's a couple of guys downstairs that don't eat meat."

Gail glanced at me, and I made a brief motion with my chin towards the dry foods and vegetables.

"Not to worry, Fred, we'll see that they are taken care of."

Fred's posture radiated relief, as he and his partner gathered up the specimens and trundled off with them. Waiting until the labourers were gone, Lee and Gail motioned everyone over to the remaining piles. Gail suggested that we divvy everything up for ourselves before there were any more interruptions, and the others quickly agreed. I enquired if they'd found the spare knapsacks, and Dixon gestured at the back of the truck.

"I'm pretty sure I brought enough of everything for everyone, but you might want to double check that," I said. "Should be roasts, hamburger, bacon, chops, and whole chickens. Oh, and some fish. Don't forget the veggies, too. And the rice and beans and flour."

Everyone ended up taking a knapsack of food, with a fair selection of everything. Dixon got his special biscuits—he'd found them, and was obviously hoping that he'd get some. To his surprised delight I gave him both tins with a whispered, "Great job on getting that data, lad." He beamed broadly.

There was still a lot of food left, though the girls and I hadn't packed up our share yet. I noted with approval that they had kept the guns and ammo well hidden in the back of the truck. I emptied one of the duffel bags that held various electronic goodies, and put the spare shotgun and rifles in it for Stan and his group. No sense in advertising what they had while riding the subway. I wrapped the weapons in a blanket to further disguise them, then tossed a couple of small bags of rice on top. Clio would already have a cleaning kit, so there was no need to include one.

There was a quick exchange of hugs as everyone left for home or work, leaving the girls and I standing on the dock.

"That went well," I said with a bemused smile. "It was fantastic seeing everyone. I really needed that."

Gail had a worried look as she turned to me and said, "You need to talk about what happened, Felix. No, don't give me that stubborn look—that hasn't worked on me for years. We'll get all this straightened away here, head home, have a proper supper, then you can tell us how you've been keeping. We've got some whisky, so there'll be no excuses."

She said that with a smile, as her normal good humour returned.

Lee put in her own two cents worth. "Damned right, old man. Now, let's figure out what's for us and what's for trade goods. I'm goin' to need some of this to grease the wheels for gettin' stuff done." She knew it always irked me to hear a woman swear, and enjoyed tweaking me.

The smile on her face grew thoughtful as she added, "Best to keep any excess downstairs in the lab. It'll be locked up and safe there, and be at hand when we need it. Our ratty old fridge at the apartment won't hold much of the frozen stuff, anyway. We can take some of the veggies and dry goods home with us. Keep in mind, though, that the veggies especially will be better than cash."

Gail nodded slowly before speaking up. "And we'll need to arrange parking permits for Felix's truck both for here and at the apartment. With a little of this stuff, we can get that done today with no questions asked. Oh, Felix, while I think of it, do you need that plow attached for some reason? It'll be awkward to drive around town with it, and could draw unwanted attention."

I shook my head. "Don't see it as needful any more. Is there a place to put it, though?"

"We'll check with Security when we get your parking permit. Won't be a problem—with the appropriate tips," replied Lee.

Gail chimed in, "Why don't you and Felix go to Security to sort that out while I arrange for all this to be taken downstairs?"

"Smart idea," answered Lee.

"Uhm," I interjected, "will the truck be safe just sitting here? There's some, uhm, special gear in there in addition to that food."

The girls just looked at me blankly.

"Guns? Remember?" I asked gently.

They looked at each other, then shrugged.

"Should be fine, actually," said Lee. "Just lock the truck. Security here is top notch, given the sorts of things stored and on display here. So long as it isn't out in plain sight it'll be OK."

That didn't seem fine to me—no, not at all—but there wasn't anything I could do about it. With a sigh I looked around, shrugged, and said, "Well, if you two say so."

That got them both giggling, as they both knew full well how much I hated not being in control of my environment. Nice kids, though with a twisted sense of humour. Perhaps they got that from working with me for so many years? Nah—being girls they had always been that way.

With that happy thought I tossed the truck's keys to Gail, while Lee and I went off to square things with Security.

CHAPTER THREE
Sanctuary

By the time Lee and I finished with Security, Gail had completed moving the stuff to her lab. She phoned Lee to let her know that she'd even arranged for someone to remove the plow and put it off to one side out of the way. It would need a tag to show that it was allowed to be there and wasn't waste, which was in the works. Yes, there were tips involved, but I got the distinct impression that those were icing on the cake. The respect and trust that everyone placed in the girls was quite impressive, and I felt sure that such twisting of the rules wasn't done for just anyone, tips or no.

Lee assured me—again—that the truck was safe where it was, so despite my worrying we headed to Gail's lab. As we walked down the hallway towards it, we saw a small procession of people coming out, each carrying a bag. Lee smiled and greeted each one in turn, and was rewarded with big grins. I guess they liked the tips that Gail was handing out.

With the doorway finally clear, the two of us walked into the lab. Gail was now wearing her white smock. Her demeanour was subtly different—almost like the change that occurs when an action character puts on the super-hero costume. I wasn't the only one who had noticed that about her, either.

Right now she had a satisfied look as she said, "Yes, the truck is locked. Yes, it is safe. Stop looking so damned worried, Felix. Everything is properly stowed away down here, so we're just about ready to begin a preliminary inspection of the specimens.

Damn, this is exciting."

"Uhm, sure, but what about the tips for Security?" I enquired in a somewhat numb voice. Things were moving more quickly than I was used to.

"Ooh, good point. Lee?"

"No problem. I had a quiet word with Chief of Security Thansworth, and he'll be down a little later. He wants to make sure that the goodies get distributed fairly."

I looked askance at her. "Yeah, right."

Lee took some offence at that remark. "Yes, really. He's a good man and takes care of his people. Demands a lot from 'em, and puts a lot of trust in 'em. He does right by 'em, and don't you forget that. That's the way we do things here, old man. You took care of things, for lo those many years, so sit back and let us take care of things now. In fact, see that comfy chair over there? Sit."

I meekly took the indicated chair. A man's got to know when to pick his battles, especially when a woman gets it into her head to take charge. In truth, though, it felt delightful to take a load off my feet. It had been a damned long day, and it wasn't over yet. To top it off, my headache had returned.

Gail, bless her heart, put a cup of hot coffee into my hands. After pulling up a chair, she opened her notebook and demanded details of the specimens. For the moment, they were in the freezer. She hadn't unwrapped them and wanted some idea of what to expect.

I blew on the coffee to cool it before taking an appreciative sip. "Sorry, kiddo. I really needed a hit of caffeine. OK, now let me think. Oh, yeah—the longest cylindrical one is the Priest. The most intact one I could find."

Unbidden and unwanted, memories came back to me, forcing me to pause. Blinking furiously, I forced my thoughts to focus on the here-and-now. To cover my lapse, I took another hurried sip of coffee, scalding my tongue slightly in the process.

"Uhm, the slightly smaller ones are Drones. One is the regular sort of Drone I've been seeing for years. The other is the new type of Drone—the ones I've taken to referring to as

Uber Drones. This one has had markings carved into it, similar to the ones the Priests have. The smaller bags are bits and pieces from as many different bodies as I could easily find. The one bag has whatever I could find, and the other is just Priest bits, including some spare heads. Figured the more the better for building up a DNA database for these things. Dunno if that will give you anything useful. Seemed like a good idea at the time. Things were somewhat rushed."

The memories and images came back again, and I scrubbed at my face with my free hand. When next I looked up, both girls were looking at me with worried expressions. I assured them that I was fine, just tired. They recognized it for the partial truth that it was, but let it go for the time being. Good people, the both of 'em.

"Smart thinking, Felix," Gail said in a soft voice. "I hadn't thought to ask you for samples from multiple sources until after you'd left."

"So when do you plan to unpack and start in on them?" enquired Lee. "It's nearly quittin' time. That means no-one around to help us lug those heavy bodies around. You really want to do that sort of heavy liftin'? 'Sides, a night in the freezer will put a halt to any further degradation."

She gave me an apologetic look before adding, "I know you did the best given the circumstances, but they'll have begun the decomposition process."

Gail nodded thoughtfully. "Yes, you're right, Lee. A fresh start in the morning is the way to go about this. We'll get here early, then get the biopsy samples ready to be shipped out to the DNA labs in the morning's pickup. This isn't something that requires a chain of custody or anything—we just want quick results."

Turning to me she added, "I've taken a look at the pictures that Stan downloaded from your system. Only a couple dozen, though we could see that more were on the server."

I slapped my head. "Oh, shit. I've got data sticks with all that stuff and more on it. Even made duplicates to pass around The Group. With all the excitement I forgot about them. Sorry about that, kiddo. They're in the truck."

She waved me back to my seat when I started to rise. "Nah. I've got the keys, so just tell me where they are and I'll get them."

It took me a few seconds to remember where I had put them. "There's a couple places. There's a set in my vest, so you could just bring that with you. The next easiest one is the laptop case that's on the floor on the passenger side. There's some crap on top of it—the case itself is right on the floor. Just bring the whole case rather than digging through it. And, yeah, there's pictures you'll want to see. Close-up shots of the mouth and hands, that sort of thing. From bodies left after the various attacks."

Gail had a large grin as she headed off upstairs. She was a woman who thrived on data—it's just that her data came in the form of cadavers.

Lee, on the other hand, was favouring me with a sour expression.

"OK, kiddo, what's the problem?" I asked with a sigh.

"You are, Felix. You're worn down to a nub, aren't you?"

"Could use a nap," I admitted.

"You OK to drive? Although it might be easier just to leave the truck here overnight. Way more secure than my apartment building. I don't think any of us are up to moving all the stuff you've got in there tonight."

"Yeah," I sighed, "you're probably right. Still, I'd feel better if we pulled the laptops and guns out of the truck. Any chance of leaving the guns here in the lab? Don't think we'd want to be caught transporting those things around on the subway."

As it turned out, we were able to leave all the sensitive stuff in Gail's lab with no problem. And we could leave the truck under the watchful eye of Security. Quite frankly, I was too tired to argue. It seemed easier just to trust the girls on all this. Life was so much simpler when I lived on my own up at the farm.

All in all, we stayed at the ROM for nearly two hours before leaving, what with one thing and another. The girls emailed some of their contacts to pave the way for the many samples being sent out the next day for DNA analysis. After that, Gail wanted to take a quick peek at some of the pictures of the werewolves. "Research prep for tomorrow," she insisted.

Finally we packed up and headed back to their apartment. Each of us had a knapsack. In addition, I had a duffel bag containing some food, personal effects, and my revolver. To tell the truth, I felt kind of naked without the reassuring heft of the revolver at my hip. Which was a strange realization for a man who had no use for guns of any sort up until a few years ago.

I was afraid that we'd be conspicuous carrying such a load around, but needn't have worried. There were a lot of scruffy types, and not-so-scruffy types, shuffling around with knapsacks and duffel bags on the subway. It looked as if half the city were on the move—or on the run. The girls ignored it all, of course, as being normal. I hadn't been to this part of Toronto for several years, and the differences from before shrieked out to me.

It all jangled on my nerves. A vague memory of something teased at the back of my mind until just before our stop. I remembered some photographs of the Great Depression of the 1930's. The ragged clothes, the hopelessness staring out of sunken eyes. And most of all, the ground-in dirtiness that covered everything.

Toronto had begun to resemble that era of hopelessness and gradual breakdown. Like the old allegory about boiling a frog. You put it in a pot of cool water, then brought it up to a boil so gradually that it never realized it was being boiled alive. Our society was like that frog, adapting to a degrading situation until the day it all fell apart. Or maybe what I needed was a proper night's rest. The headache I'd developed was getting worse.

We got to the apartment just before nine, and the girls decided to check in with the building super to arrange for a parking permit. Quick, easy, and all it cost was a small roast, and some fresh veggies to pay for the next few months of parking. I found myself clucking my tongue at how far things had fallen. On the other hand, in the countryside we routinely did the same sort of bartering. Maybe this was a sign of improved civility, rather than degradation. Now wasn't that a thought?

20

Anyway, we got into the apartment and dropped our loads with relief. Lee put away the perishables, and Gail put all the dry goods into their pantry. Not much of a pantry, from my point of view. I'd forgotten how much smaller everything in the city was. It was a bit late to be making a fancy dinner, so I fried up some bacon, potatoes, and carrots—fast, easy, and tasty. There was even some of the bread left, and girls gobbled it down despite it being not all that fresh. We finished the meal with cups of cocoa. From their happy sighs, I knew that I had chosen wisely. The chocolate was carefully put into the fridge—to keep it away from mice and cockroaches, they explained.

Lee took my laptop and configured it to use their Internet connection. Almost immediately my email inbox started filling up, to the surprise of the girls. "Don't get too excited," I told them, "dollars to donuts most of it's spam."

Turns out I was right, of course. There were a couple of emails from The Group—one from Stan, and the other from Grant—saying that they got home OK and thanks again for the food. As expected, there was nothing from Dix. Still, I was worried about him. He had appeared to be kind of flushed when I saw him earlier. Ah, hell, he was probably just a bit flushed from rushing around, not being in the best of shape.

We sat up for a while chatting about inconsequential things for a bit until I started nodding off. That got the girls fussing like a pair of hens around a chick, setting up the couch for me to use. I started to protest, but realized that I was weary to the bone and beyond. So we said our goodnights, and I fell asleep even before my head hit the pillow.

CHAPTER FOUR
Into the Breach

I awoke the next morning when the sunlight hit my eyes, and jumped to my feet with a start. It took me a few seconds to get my bearings and realize where I was. I dropped down on the couch and scrubbed at my face.

"'Bout time you woke up, old man," teased Lee, peering around a corner. "Give us five minutes to finish up in the bathroom, then it's all yours."

To her credit it took less than that. Seeing that they were going to boil some water to make instant coffee, I put a stop to that and pulled out some coffee beans. They had no working grinder—hence the instant coffee—but a few passes with a rolling pin ground it well enough. Leaving them to make the coffee, I hit the bathroom to shower. Damn, the hot water and soap felt refreshing.

I made it a quick shower, as the drain wasn't working and the water level was rising. Getting out of the shower I grabbed the toilet plunger, removed the metal strainer at the top of the drain, and rammed the plunger up and down a few times. Several large chunks of gunk came flying out, and with a shudder I tossed those into the toilet. The water drained out of the shower much better after that, so I re-installed the strainer and did a quick wipe-down to remove any remaining slime.

After drying myself off and getting dressed, I went out to join the girls for breakfast.

"Fixed your shower drain," I mentioned while drinking

coffee and munching cereal.

"Oh, was that what those horrible sucking noises were? We thought the water pipes might be acting up again."

It sounded as if they were serious. I just shook my head and affixed them with a baleful glare. "You young folk with hair need to realize that it can and will clog your shower drains. Just use the toilet plunger whenever the drain gets slow."

I may as well have been speaking gibberish for all they seemed to understand. These were bright kids. It's just that sometimes the most basic things seemed to flummox them. If it didn't have a touch screen or Internet connection, they got lost.

"Uhm," said Lee, "yeah, it's been like that for a while, now. Sorry. Thanks for fixin' it. By the way, the kitchen sink faucet kinda leaks real bad. Maybe you could look at it tonight when we get home?"

I sighed, drained my coffee cup and carried my dishes to the sink. Sure enough, the faucet was dripping at an alarming rate.

"Your water usage metered?" I asked.

"Uhm, yah. Been meaning to fix that leak for a while now," Lee replied with a guilty look.

"Got any tools?" I enquired. "Mine are in the truck."

"Yep," said Lee. "Remember that tool kit you gave me for Christmas a few years back? I'll go get it." She scampered to her bedroom and hurried back with the toolkit. Ah, yes, now I remembered it—it should have the wrench that I needed. After a quick look under the sink, I turned off the water valves and opened up the tap to drain the remaining water.

"Look, Felix, this is great and all, but we really should be going to the lab. You can take a look at that later," said Gail in a somewhat strained voice.

"Yeah, OK," I said, and kept working. After peering at the faucet for a few seconds, I loosened a bolt, tugged on the appropriate piece, and it all came apart to reveal the washer. I plucked out the washer and examined it—it actually seemed in not bad shape except for being covered in slime. Wiping off the slime from the washer and inside the tap, I put everything back together and turned the water back on. No more leak, though now the pressure coming out seemed low. I unscrewed the cap on the end of the tap, cleaned the filter screen was covered in crap, reassembled everything, and the water came out at a much better rate.

"Gotta clean those things out once in a while," I explained, as the girls just stood there gaping.

"OK, I'll just brush my teeth, then I'm ready to go," I added. "I thought you said we were in hurry?"

I will admit to enjoying the look on their faces as I headed to the bathroom. It felt good to be useful.

A few minutes later we were all ready to go, but I halted our exit just before the door.

"Uhm, what about the guns? Keep them all here or take some with us?" I asked.

Lee and Gail exchanged glances, and agreed that leaving them here was the best option. I collected the knapsack and duffel bag that held the weapons and ammunition, and we decided to toss it into the bottom of the hall closet towards the back. Better than nothing, as hiding places go, just not great. Would have to sort that out later.

I wasn't too pleased about leaving without weapons, and had no qualms about saying so. Both girls rolled their eyes and said they were fine. Each carried the heavy fountain pens I had made them a few years ago. The pens wrote like a dream and made dandy weapons. I went to my duffel bag and pulled out a couple of multi-tools, and handed one to each.

"Wear this on your belt. Not too bulky, easy to pull off, and legal. Even damned useful. The knife can be extended with just a slight flick of your thumb. Like this ..."

I showed them trick to opening and closing it. They mastered the process after a few seconds of practise, then slipped the tools onto their belts.

Appropriately armed, we were now ready to roll.

★ ★ ★

The trip to the ROM was uneventful, yet educational. I got a closer look at what the city looked like in the daylight, and it didn't impress me. My mind kept returning to my boiled frog imagery of the previous night. If anything, what I saw reinforced that. Everything, almost without exception, looked shabby, worn, and dirty. No-one seemed happy—although that was normal for Toronto, to be honest.

I wasn't one to give a flying fart about Toronto, but this was not right. Even the subway seemed to creak and groan more than I remembered from years ago. And yet everyone was carrying on as if nothing was wrong. Where was the panic? The werewolves were slaughtering everyone in the countryside, but there were no news bulletins or government warnings or anything out of the ordinary. Just a dirty, grimy normality.

For that matter, The Group's attitude concerned me. They seemed to have accepted the news only as interesting facts to investigate, not as something to take action on. I was burnt out and suffering from shell shock—after even a short time with The Group I was beginning to realize that—and was just too numb to initiate action. Besides, after seeing all this I was wondering who in authority I could even tell about what was happening outside of Toronto.

No, something wasn't right. I needed to figure out what it was before I took any action. Werewolves weren't the only dangerous creatures around these days. As plans went, it made perfect sense, and fit in well with my current mental numbness. Besides, I was beginning to develop a killer of a headache, again. It only eased when I sat quietly and didn't think about anything in particular.

We got to the ROM, and entered through the employee entrance. The security guard there gave me a baleful look, so Gail got that sorted out. I was now on their records as a field consultant, but hadn't yet been issued a pass. No big deal—it would be ready before noon, the nice young man said. Both Gail and Lee favoured him with a smile as we went on our way down to Gail's lab. Lee worked in another part of the building, but she came with us out of curiosity. She said she'd call her supervisor from the lab to let him know she was in, and where to reach her if needed.

Once in the lab, Gail started preparations for the biopsies and autopsies. Without a word, she waved Lee and myself over to one of the empty desks before continuing as if we weren't there. With a smile at each other, Lee and I began setting things up to suit our own brand of investigations.

I had brought both of my own laptops, so I gave one to Lee.

"Hey, I've got one in my office," she protested.

"You can get to it later," I replied. "Besides, don't you want to get started right away?" I think it was my big-eyed innocent look that persuaded her. Some things never got old. We settled easily into old work habits as I pointed out what types of data lived where on the laptop. She nodded and took notes, only interrupting with an occasional query.

The lab was divided into an office area and an examination area, separated by a wall with a large window. A dull tapping sound interrupted us. Gail had been tapping at the window trying to get our attention. She motioned for us to join her, so we got up and went in.

The sharp coolness of the room matched the clinical look. Which was not surprising, considering that the room was used to examine bodies. In most cases the bodies were rather more ancient, but it was set up to handle fresher specimens if required.

It turned out that Gail needed some help in moving the various specimens around, and had decided to make use of us rather than calling in one of the labourers. Fair enough, and a sensible idea from a security point of view.

There were three examination tables, so we put each of the bodies on their own table. Gail had decided that it might be useful to have all three laid out, to make comparisons easier as she went along. We put the bags of parts on the same table as the smallest body. After finishing, Gail stood there, hands on hips, surveying the bounty with a smile. She took one last careful look around before declaring that she was now ready to begin.

"Oh," she added, "it might be useful to have another pair of hands available as I do this. Any volunteers?"

Lee blanched, shook her head, and backed up.

I sighed and nodded. Lee gave me a concerned look, and asked me if I was sure. She worried about me too much, sometimes. Gail was, at this point, in full-on researcher mode and quite indifferent to what the living thought.

Lee declared that she was going to get back to checking out the data on the laptop. She wanted to re-run the analysis I had done with that fascinating new data that I had somehow obtained from somewhere. I just shrugged and asked Gail for a smock and gloves. While I was putting those on, Lee went back to the desk.

Once we were ready to begin, Gail turned on the UV lights and we again sprayed the specimens with a strong disinfectant spray. The Change Plague, for all its nastiness, was never terribly contagious. In fact, the rate of infection was so low that no-one understood how it survived. On top of that, either UV-A lights or mild disinfectants quite effectively killed it. The combination of the two seemed to offer a perfect defence for anyone who had to come into contact with victims of the Change Plague. And yet somehow a fresh crop of victims would arrive each spring.

The first thing we had to do was to remove the coverings from the bodies. The specimens, I hurried to correct myself. Cold and time had helped to congeal the ookie stuff, and that made it a bit easier for me. With all three of the bodies in view, Gail directed me to operate the HD video camera as she performed her initial surface examination. At this stage she wasn't going to clean the specimens, just record and comment upon what she could see. As Gail dictated, I recorded, zooming in or out as she pointed out features—jaw structure, teeth, hands, limbs, and feet.

The next step was to take biopsy samples to send out for DNA analysis. This consisted of samples of tissue, blood, and hair—Gail insisted that we do that for each of the specimens, including the bits and pieces. Each sample was labelled to indicate which specimen it had come from. She was quite pleased with the variety of what she had to work with.

From her point of view this was all great stuff. It wasn't every day that she got to work with leading-edge specimens of this sort. For me, though, it was difficult to be so detached. These were vicious creatures who had been doing their level best to kill me a short time ago, and I still viewed them as dangerous enemies to be exterminated. It was going to take a while before my scientific detachment kicked in.

This preliminary examination and collection of samples for DNA analysis took several hours. I quite pleasurably lost track of the time as I assisted Gail. I had never had an opportunity to work like this with her before, and I'd always enjoyed watching a true professional at work. Finally she stopped and straightened up. Putting her hands on the small of her back, she began a series of loosening-up exercises, punctuated with small groans as a joint popped or a muscle resisted moving.

"Oh, stop your grinning, Felix. You do the same thing," she snapped with mock seriousness.

My smile broadened as I answered, "Heh. Just wait till you get to be my age, kid. Seriously though, you need to start worrying about proper ergonomics and posture when you work. You're not getting any younger."

Most times my cracks about getting older got a smartass retort out of her. This time she just grinned wryly and grunted in agreement. Neither Lee nor Gail was particularly old, mind you. It's just that sooner or later we all had to take better care of how we moved around.

"Fair enough," she admitted. "Say, how about we wash up and grab a bite to eat? Time to feed the inner nerd, as you like to say."

The latter was said with a quick glance at my waistline. Hey, it wasn't that I was overweight or anything. It's just that as one ages, things begin to settle, that's all.

With a sniff indicating hurt feelings, I helped her pull covers over our works-in-progress. After washing up, we went to join Lee at her labours in the office. Gail and I grinned at each other as we observed her staring at the screen, lost in thought. We weren't taking any pains to be quiet, mind you. Lee tended to get lost in the problem at hand. A wicked smile played on Gail's lips as she moved her head to the side of Lee's, then puffed into her ear. Lee started with an incoherent exclamation, which turned into a heartfelt curse at both Gail and myself.

I held up my hands and stepped back. "Twasn't me! I'm just an innocent bystander in all this."

Lee favoured both of us with a glowering frown, and her right foot began tapping. Gail just stood there with a look of innocence spoiled by her grin.

"Time for lunch," I interjected. I wasn't one to interfere—certainly not without an excellent reason—but I was both hungry and eager to get back to the examination. "So, do we make do with rations here or do we go to the cafeteria or what?

The ladies interrupted their staring contest to look at me, turned to look at each other, and shrugged.

"The caf promised a soup for today," suggested Lee.

Gail's eyes lit up and she nodded agreement. I made it unanimous, and off we went to the cafeteria.

"Hope you ladies have some money," I sighed. "I seem to have left my wallet back at the apartment."

This was a standing joke for us, and managed to get a snort out of the two of them. I would end up paying, of course. I always did. Well, except for that one time years and years ago, and they never let me forget it.

Along the way we dropped off the container of samples at the shipping office, and let them know who to contact for pickup.

★ ★ ★

The food turned out to be pretty tasty, I had to admit. It wasn't the sort of thing I'd have made for myself, mind you. Rather, the fancier sort of thing that city dwellers seemed to enjoy. The three of us enjoyed the soup and sandwiches in friendly silence. The ladies were focused on the food, but I couldn't help scanning around as I ate.

Finally, Lee kicked my ankle and whispered, "Dammit, stop lookin' so damned feral, old man. You're startin' to attract attention with all that furtive lookin' around."

Gail nodded her agreement and added in a soft voice, "You're safe here, Felix. Sit back, relax, and enjoy the food. We won't let anything happen to you."

I closed my eyes, took a deep breath, and slowly exhaled. Followed by a soft, self-deprecating snort. "Sorry, kids. You're right. Just not used to being around so many strangers, I guess."

Glancing around the room I added with a smile, "Or being in a room larger than my living room."

A young man, who looked to be in his late twenties and wearing a worried expression, walked up to our table. "Hey, Lee. Hey, Gail. Who's your friend? Something wrong with him?"

After seeing the look on my face, Lee hurriedly made introductions. She added that I was a field investigator, and was just back after being out for some time. With that, the mood of the young man—Timothy, his name was—brightened right up and he insisted on shaking my hand. He started going on about his own field trip, and it took several throat-clearings and a glare from Gail before he wound down.

"Sorry to interrupt you, Timothy, but Felix brought some new items that we're in the middle of cataloguing. Just taking a quick break for lunch."

Gail put a slight emphasis on "quick" that wasn't lost on Timothy. My estimation of his survival skills went up as he quickly, but politely, excused himself and rejoined his friends. Their worried expressions and furtive looks in my direction became much sunnier as Timothy explained what he had learned.

"He's a good guy," explained Lee as we finished our meal, "and a new-ish postdoc. Had the typical know-it-all attitude of that sort until he went on an extended field trip into the Northern bush a couple of years ago. Back then, there were no werewolves or Changed of any sort north of Kenora, and still lots of useful work that needed doing. A few weeks of living rough wore the edges off of him, and revealed him to be a good guy to have around. Now he loves to talk about field work with anyone who does it. I think he wants to go out again, though with funding cuts—not to mention the spread of the Changed—that seems unlikely for the foreseeable future."

That bit about the funding cuts was news to me, and I made a mental note to ask about it later. Maybe after they'd had a drink or three—talking about funding cuts always raised bad feelings. For now, though, we had work to do, so we got up and got ready to head back down. I was about to pick up my tray to place it in the waste area, when Lee stopped me. "We've got people doing that, now. Rather than downsizing they decided to open up some low-wage positions. Better low pay than no pay."

I nodded and we headed back down to the lab. When we got there Lee went back to the computer, and Gail and I headed to the autopsy area. She passed me a smock, but continued to hold on to it. "Felix, you gonna be OK doing this? I mean, it's not going to be pleasant." She seemed quite embarrassed to have to ask this. I guess she'd seen one too many unhappy reactions to autopsies.

"Gail," I replied in a quiet voice, "I'm the guy who put them here. Gathered them up. Dealt with their remains. I'm fine with this."

The stare she gave me signalled worry and sternness at the same time. "Felix ..." she began.

"No, I'm fine. Truly. The past couple of years have been bad. And, yes, worse than I've ever let on to you or anyone. This needs doing, though. I need to know what it is I've been fighting." I sighed softly before adding, "But I think I'll be needing a drink or two when we get home tonight. Brought some whisky. The real stuff."

Her mood lightened with that. She gave a brief snort as she tossed the smock at me, then donned one herself. There was work to do.

The work turned out to be both as icky as I expected, and as fascinating. Humming to herself, Gail made the decision to work on the Drone body first, as it was a variant of the "normal" sort of werewolf and would give her a baseline for studying the Priest. As before, I was both the cameraman and extra pair of hands. Together we got the body—which Gail insisted on referring to it as "Specimen 1"—fully decanted from the wrappings and began cleaning it. The rinsing hose made short work of getting the dried mud and blood and whatever off the body, revealing the werewolf in more detail than I'd ever seen before.

Oh, I'd seen them—far too many of them, actually. Just not cleaned and stretched out like this. Gail continued a running commentary as she examined the body from top to bottom. She only paused a couple of times when it came to commenting on the various wounds. My improvised munitions had done their work well. She matter-of-factly referred to them as wounds of such-and-such a description and size.

For my part, I stared in fascination at the creature before me. It had been human once, with hopes and dreams and a life. Then he—it—had become infected and the infection had modified it. Through no fault of his own, he had been transformed into a monstrous thing. When he attacked me, I killed him.

No. Killed *it*. No longer a human being. No longer a sentient creature with a future, or even a past. Just a monster whose existence I had terminated. I became aware that Gail was speaking to me. Had, in fact, been speaking to me for several seconds.

"Felix, are you alright? Felix?" This was Professional Gail, not Friend Gail, speaking to me.

"Uhm, yeah. Sure. I'm fine. Just never had chance to study one like this."

She looked at me with concern, not saying anything.

"Look at the mouth," I said after clearing my throat and giving my head a shake. "That's changed over the years. This one is the most wolf-like I've ever seen on them, yet it still looks like a human mouth that's been pushed out here and there. Except for canines." I pointed to the mouth, and Gail turned the head to one side and pulled open the lips to better examine the teeth.

"Notice how the canines appear to have been somewhat extended," I continued. "The gum line has receded somewhat, which emphasizes the teeth overall. The incisors and the teeth to either side, though, are longer than any normal human teeth I've ever seen. The extended teeth are something I've always seen in them, although this is approaching that of a dog or wolf."

Gail nodded. "I agree that this specimen's canine teeth have developed more that any I've had a chance to study or read about. We'll have to look at the heads you gathered for comparison. Dental impressions might be in order, too, after we've done the preliminary autopsy. Perhaps we can get some estimates of these changes over time by analysing the photos you've sent us over the years, as well as any other photos in our records."

She said the last as if speaking to herself, before looking up at me with a questioning look.

"Yep, an excellent idea," I agreed. "Something for Lee to look at. She's better at image analysis than I ever was."

Gail grinned as she said, "And who was it that taught her?"

"Introduced her to it, perhaps," I responded with a grin of my own. "She has a special talent for it, though, and this is the sort of challenging problem that she thrives on."

Our momentary interlude of amusement was short-lived, alas, as we bent down to examine the body once more.

"What about the hair?" she enquired, "Would you say that this one's pelt is more or less developed than normal?"

"Hair or fur?" I asked. "Was that question ever definitively answered? I thought the jury was out on that."

Gail nodded before answering, "Good point. We'll take samples for analysis. Early victims had enhanced growth of their existing body hair, though there were some reports of fur-like growth."

I had to snort at that. "They've gotten hairier over the years, I can tell you that for a fact. And not just from their existing hair getting longer. Definitely got looking more like a pelt every year. Whether it was hair or fur or a mixture, I'll leave to people like yourself to argue over. For me, they just got hairier."

I paused for a few heartbeats to gather my memories and keep them at arm's length. "And the hairier they got, the more feral they got. More wolf-like. Speaking of which, what about the feet?"

She frowned a bit as she moved to examine the feet of Specimen-1. "Well, there is definite extended callousing on the feet. Which is only to be expected, given their lack of footwear." Her frown deepened and her brow furrowed as she continued, "However, you'll notice that the toes appear somewhat elongated and the nails more claw-like than previously seen."

She poked and peered at the foot. "This callousing is more extensive and thicker than normal. In fact, it almost looks like it is in the shape of a pad, like that found on a dog or wolf. Not a true pad, to be sure. Almost as if the body were attempting to emulate one as best it could."

"Like the changes in the mouth," I interjected.

Gail nodded as she replied, "Exactly. Doing the best it could to emulate ... what, exactly, and why? That is strange, Felix, very strange indeed. The human body can be tweaked only so far to match the template imposed by the Change Plague, physically or mentally. Past that point, the changes turn into cancers. In fact, historically that is the leading cause of death in the Changed, in the first couple of months after they appear. This specimen is changed physically just about as far as I suspect it can be done."

"Look at the genitalia," I suggested. "That doesn't look normal to me. Shrunken beyond the norm, I'd say."

Gail did a brief examination and allowed as I was correct. "Almost as if the genitalia were beginning to atrophy." She looked up at me and added, "Looks like your characterization of them as drones was correct."

"And look at the markings," I said. "These symbols carved into them are similar to the symbols on the Priests, though much less complex."

"Hmm, you could be correct, Felix. 'Carved' being the operative word here. My initial impression was that the markings were scratched in. Closer examination indicates that it was made with a single motion. Suggesting cutting as opposed to a series of repeated scratchings. That would imply something rather stronger and sharper than a human fingernail. Although this specimen's nails are somewhat more talon-like than a normal human's, they don't match what made the marks."

"Check the hands on the Priest over there," I suggested. "They've got real claws. I could see that even through the dirt covering them."

Gail glanced up and gave the other specimen a thoughtful look. With a slight shake of her head, she said, "No, we'll finish with this one first."

She glanced at the clock on the wall before turning to me. "We'll take some close-up pictures of this one, then do the autopsy, I think. That shouldn't take us more than an hour, unless we find something bizarre. From the looks of this one, it is just a regular Changed, albeit rather more wolf-like than normal."

We actually finished in just over half an hour. After making the traditional Y-incision, Gail took a quick poke around, but found little of interest. She took a few samples for the sake of completeness. The spleen and kidneys were somewhat enlarged, so she removed those for storage and later analysis. After a moment's hesitation she decided to removed the brain and store it as well. The type of tests required to properly examine the organs and brain were beyond her equipment and expertise, though she knew someone who might be interested in them.

When done, she stepped back and declared that it was time for a break. Without waiting for my answer she grabbed me by an elbow and hustled me out of the room. We de-gowned and de-gloved, and had a bit of a cleanup. As we were washing, I could feel her eyes on me.

"You OK, Felix?"

She sounded so serious that I chose my words with care. "Yep. The science of it all is quite overwhelming the nausea factor. More interesting that I was expecting, in truth."

Gail just shook her head, "Not that. I expected that from you. No, what I meant was are you OK with ... how you obtained the specimens?" Her eyes locked onto mine, and gazed deep and hard at me. "I saw how you were looking at it when we started. Like you were thinking of it as a human. I had the same look when I was first exposed to a human cadaver—everyone does. This is something different, isn't it?"

A chill tingle ran up my spine and wrapped around the base of my skull. I'd never discussed the battles, aside from clinical descriptions, and never ever discussed the cleanups. Never discussed with anyone how I felt about it all. It just wasn't the thing one talked about on an open circuit, or email. I found

35

that my breathing was getting ragged, to the point where I needed to close my eyes and run through a quick mindfulness exercise. Gail waited without judging, without interrupting.

I got my breathing under control, and was thinking about opening my eyes but found that I couldn't. I just wanted to stand there, shutting everything out and not having to deal with anything. I felt tears dripping down my cheeks, and I wiped them away. I had to be strong. This was a dangerous time, and there was too much work left to do. My left hand rubbed my mouth, rasping on the short growth of whiskers that had grown since I'd shaved that morning. I wiped my eyes again using my right hand. My left, now stationary, was covering my mouth.

Drawing a ragged breath, I let it out in a controlled fashion. My next breath was much more controlled, and I felt my emotions stabilize. I turned to Gail and said in a quiet voice, "It got damned bad, yeah. Like something out of one of those old zombie movies, in some ways. Surrounded. Cut off. Makes a man go numb inside. It's either that or just give up. Gail, it wasn't like here in the city. Here, things are somehow normal despite the shortages. At the farm, it was a war of survival. Started out as vague, intermittent threats, gradually ramping up worse and worse each year. This past year, though, it was one damn thing after another. The escalation was so gradual that it all seemed like a new form of normal, I guess. I ... I kinda knew what was happening. It's just that there was nothing to do about it but hang on. So I kept hanging on. I do that pretty well, you'll recall."

Gail smiled softly and carefully put her hand on my arm. Hanging on till the bitter end, and damn the consequences, described many of my jobs, as she was well aware. She'd been there at one of those jobs, and seen first-hand just how stubborn I could be.

"The worst of it was *how* it got worse. The Changed started out like classical zombies—shambling about, easily neutralized. Over time they got nastier, more feral, more dangerous. Now they're pack-like. Intelligent. Scary intelligent. As in planning and executing army-like maneuvers. As in capturing and herding human women, and taking them off somewhere. That latest data I got, the stuff that Lee is analysing now, shows that the Change Plague is a series of planned events. Someone is creating a series of plagues, each one worse than the last. We've got to figure out what is going on, and we have to fight it and stop it. Yeah, I feel bad about killing them. They were people once upon a time. Not anymore, of course. I'm really sorry about that. And I'm really sorry that I had to kill them, though it isn't like I had a choice. Aside from a handful of damn fools at the beginning, nobody chose to be Changed. And no-one chose to be attacked by them. Their attacks are increasingly deadly, especially now that they are attacking as soldiers instead of animals. I don't hate them, Gail, and I only killed when they attacked me. Hate is for losers and fools. But right now I hate the ones who are causing these plagues. I want them stopped, and I really don't care how."

My head was pounding, and I felt myself shaking with emotion as I hissed out those last words. Despite my own headache, I noticed that Gail was rubbing her head and grimacing. A glance out the window showed that Lee, too, was rubbing her head as if in pain.

Something was not right.

I guided Gail out to the office area, collected Lee, and herded them out into the hallway. Neither of them resisted, which got me really worried. I herded them to the loading dock area to get some fresh air. My headache was receding to a dull ache, and I found it easier to think straight. The ladies, on the other hand, still seemed groggy. As if it was too much effort to think clearly. We stood in the loading bay, shivering in the cold. I put my smock around Lee's shoulders, and she smiled her thanks. A wan smile, but a smile nonetheless.

They both seemed a bit dazed and confused, so in an effort to get them focused I asked them about the latest gossip. Stuff that wouldn't have made it into the emails or Net Night discussions. It took a bit, but in fits and starts, they seemed to rouse and be more like themselves. Within ten minutes or so, they were pretty much back to normal as they chatted happily about how the various members of The Group were doing.

Neither of them seemed particularly disturbed about what

had just happened. After another few minutes of this, I interrupted their happy chatter to enquire how they were feeling. Both felt fine, their headaches were pretty much gone, and it was time to get back to work.

"Uhm, kids, you were both ready to keel over a few minutes ago with splitting headaches. You sure that you're OK? Was it something in the air?"

"No, no, Felix, we're fine. Everyone gets these now and again," explained Lee.

One of the labourers had been keeping an eye on us, and began to wander over with a concerned look. Before he could speak, Gail called out, "Brain cramps. Better now, thanks."

The labourer gave a sympathetic grin, waved goodbye, and went back to his job.

"Excuse me?" I asked, none too politely. "What the bloody hell?"

"Brain cramps. Everyone gets them," said Gail in a patient voice as if speaking to a child. Or a senile old man.

"No they don't. That's not normal," I replied somewhat more tartly than I'd intended.

"Yes, they do. And, yes, it is," explained Gail impatiently. "Just time for a break, is all. A quick break and back to work. That's normal, Felix."

Something about the circumstances and her reply bothered me, and I wasn't sure exactly what it was. I wasn't given time to puzzle over it or ask any more questions. Both ladies pushed at me to get back to the lab, so off we went.

As we walked back, Gail outlined to Lee her idea to analyze photographs of the Changed to quantify the changes over time, focusing on the faces and hands. Lee got excited about the analysis, as she always does about a new challenge. I could see the visions of algorithms dancing in her head by the time we got back to the lab. We left her to her work, then returned to the examination room.

We gowned up and went to the table that held the Priest body—Specimen-2, as Gail designated it. We cleaned off the dirt and such, and stood there in silence contemplating it. It was even more frightening when cleaned up. The face, which

I'd always seen as constantly in motion or barking or snarling, was revealed to be something non-human. We could see that, even with the damage my weapons had done to it. Gail peeled back the lips, and it was obvious that the teeth were those of a strict carnivore. The face was in the form of a muzzle—truncated compared to a dog or wolf, but a carnivore's muzzle nonetheless.

The eyes were somewhat larger than a human's, and seemed to reflect light like a dog's or cat's. That would explain how they could get around in the dark so well.

The proportions of the limbs, although similar to a human's, were markedly different. The joints themselves were different, too. They appeared larger, as if designed for stronger muscles. However, a formal autopsy would be required to see if that was actually the case.

The fingers and toes were definitely not human, and ended in actual claws—long, sharp claws.

There were no external genitalia, and no obvious internal ones. No nipples, either.

The entire body, except for the palms and soles, was covered with dense hair or fur. Although my own inexpert opinion tended to the latter, as it did look and feel like dog fur.

The symbols on the body were quite extensive and intricate, more so than I had suspected. What was truly puzzling was that the symbols didn't appear to be carved into the body. Instead, they seemed to have been pushed out or grown from within.

We'd been examining the body together, pointing out features as we went along. Finally we finished and looked at each other without speaking. Gail seemed to be struggling to say something but failing to find the words. After a few moments she turned away, rubbing at her head.

"Gail," I asked in a quiet voice, "You OK?"

"Yeah, uhm, the UV lights and disinfectant sometimes give me a headache. Gimme a minute, OK?"

I stood without speaking to give her some space. She didn't seem to be getting any better.

"Hey, Gail, how 'bout we call it night?" I suggested.

She just nodded and was now rubbing her head with both

hands.

"I'll put the specimens back into the storage locker, and we'll get back to them tomorrow. How would that be?"

Again, she just nodded.

I took her by the elbow and steered her out of the room. A suspicion was growing in the back of my mind, though this was neither the time nor place to worry about it. I rolled the carts holding the specimens back into the cooler, shut down all the equipment, and made sure that everything was secure in the lab. I de-gowned and de-gloved and washed up before going into the office. Gail was leaning against a desk, and Lee had a supporting arm around her shoulder.

"Hey, you OK?" I asked in a quiet voice. "Lemme take the gown and gloves off you, and toss them into the lab, OK?"

Between the two of us, Lee and I got the stuff off of her and planted Gail in a chair. She looked flushed, with a light sheen of sweat on her brow.

"She need anything for the headache?" I asked Lee.

"No, she'll be fine in a minute. The usual headache pills don't work on brain cramps."

That was an interesting piece of information, and pretty much confirmed my hypothesis. I'd worry about that later, though. It was time to wrap things up here.

"Lee, Gail, how about we call it a day? It's damn near quitting time anyways, and no sense in working overtime, is there?" I tried to keep my tone light and normal.

Lee nodded, and after a few seconds so did Gail. After about five minutes, Gail decided that she needed to wash up, and off she went to the sink in the lab. Lee and I sat waiting for her to finish. It didn't take long, and she came back looking wan but refreshed.

"Ready to face rush hour on public transit, or should we maybe grab supper around here and head back home later?" Gail enquired.

Before Lee could say anything I interjected, "Supper sounds lovely, and my treat. Don't forget that I've got a truck that I can chauffeur you home with."

The ladies looked at each other, and perked up.

"That sounds like a plan," decided Lee.

"A quite delightful plan," added Gail.

As it was spoken, so it was done.

★ ★ ★

The drive home later that evening was notable only in that the ladies seemed to perk up more the closer we got to the apartment. Despite the night's chill I kept the windows down the entire time. The breeze created by the truck's motion made the rank city air seem fresh and invigorating. I wasn't impressed with the smell, though the ladies just sat back with their eyes closed and seemed to drink it in. No-one said anything, and I was glad for the time to sit and think my own thoughts.

To my relief, I didn't get lost along the way—backtracking due to a missed turnoff doesn't count as "lost". And I didn't have to use the horn (or invective) at all. Truly a magical interlude.

By the time I arrived at the apartment and parked at the designated spot, both Lee and Gail were sitting up and taking notice of things. After a brief discussion we decided that it would be prudent to take all the remaining stuff in the truck up to the apartment.

In truth, I have to admit that I was quite adamant about no bloody way was I going to leave my stuff in the truck. Not in this damn city, thank you very much. The girls both made sounds of disgust and rolled their eyes, but didn't disagree with me. We each grabbed a couple of duffel bags or knapsacks and headed up to the apartment.

It took a couple of trips with the three of us schlepping to get everything transferred. It helped that Lee was able to snag a dolly from the superintendent—and without a tip, which surprised me. That wide-spread practise of small-scale bribery was beginning to both annoy and worry me.

With my bug-out supplies carefully stashed—that is, piled up out of the way—we dropped ourselves into the living room chairs. It had been a long and exhausting day, what with one thing or another.

Gail waggled a finger at me and said with feeling, "Earlier

41

you said something about whisky, Felix. Give us wee dram, would you?"

Lee turned to her with eyes wide. "He promised you whisky? Damn. Didn't say a thing to me about it." She turned to look at me with soulful eyes and a face full of hurt. "You always liked her best, old man." She punctuated that with a mournful sniffle.

Gah. Women.

Double *gah* for women who knew how to push my buttons.

Nay, *enjoyed* pushing my buttons until I yielded to their unreasonable demands.

Much as I disagreed with their methods, in this case I had to agree that whisky was called for. I rummaged through a couple of duffel bags and one of the backpacks until I found the bottle I wanted. Should have been able to zero in on it right away, though. Brain still felt a bit fogged up. Which was disturbing, but fit into the hypothesis I was forming.

Grabbing some ornamental glassware from the cupboard (if one can call branded glasses from a fast food chain "ornamental") I poured a generous helping of whisky for each of us. Although my supply of whisky was rather limited, now was not the time to be chintzy.

We sat in companionable silence as we sipped. From the contented looks on the faces of the girls, I knew that I'd done the correct thing. It would appear that decent whisky was yet another thing in short supply, or else they would have grabbed a drink from their own stash. This meant that luxury goods, as well as staples, were running low. That wasn't an encouraging sign in any city, and especially Toronto. As I tried to process this new data, my head began to throb. This was a confirmation of my theory that I would rather have not had.

"Hey, Lee, how did your analysis of the photos go?" I asked, trying to sound casual despite the rising aching and fuzziness in my head.

She babbled with enthusiasm about the algorithms she was going to use, and which languages she'd be using for which stage of the analysis. My brain was too fuzzy to follow much of it. I just waited for her to wind down and take another sip of her drink before asking her about her analysis of my data. She frowned a bit as she talked about looking at my analysis and trying to replicate the results. Her tale started out well enough, but she soon wound down and shortly thereafter stopped in mid-sentence. Her expression indicated both confusion and pain, as she rubbed her temples.

Gail was looking at Lee with concern, when I asked about the specimens and the new morphology. What did she think that the symbols meant? How could they appear on the torso without being carved in? Gail looked nonplussed, then began an increasingly technical discussion of how scarification might occur. I interrupted her to ask, again, her opinion of what the symbols actually meant. Gail started murmuring something, trailing off mid-sentence as she started rubbing her head.

OK, that was all the confirmation I needed. Time to get them ready to hear about it.

"Hey, girls, remember this afternoon when you were telling me about all the latest gossip about The Group? Are you sure that Stan and Jack and Clio are an item?"

Both Lee and Gail gave me a puzzled look. After a brief hesitation, they began to each chime in. Within a couple of minutes they were both laughing as if nothing was the matter. I interrupted their recitations by waving my hands in front of me.

"Kids, you've been infected with something. All of us have, though the two of you have it worse."

The looks they gave me started out incredulous, then changed into dismissive. Gail opened her mouth to say something, but I interrupted her.

"This is for real and for serious," I said. "Something is horribly wrong. Please please please hear me out."

The expressions on their faces were incredulous, but they listened.

"Look, something is wrong here. Hell, with the whole damn city. No, no, hear me out *please*. These 'brain cramps' that everyone seems to be getting, those are pretty recent, yah? Like within the last year or so, yah?"

They glanced at each other, then nodded.

43

"Lee. Gail. This is important. My recent analysis showed that the Change Plague is actually a series of plagues, with a new one coming around each spring. Right, Lee?"

Lee nodded, although her face showed signs of distress. Her right hand began rubbing at her temple. Gail looked at Lee with concern. She seemed about to speak, then began showing signs of distress as well, and started massaging her head.

"Remember the Net Nights?" I enquired in a gentle voice. "How we use to pass all the latest gossip and pictures back and forth. Those pictures with those silly poses and outfits?" I kept my tone light, with undertones of amusement.

Both of the girls stopped massaging their heads, although their faces were still pinched as if fighting pain.

"I think I've got something that'll deal with those headaches of yours," I said with forced confidence. "Got it from a medical friend of mine a few years back. Prescription-only stuff. It'll do the trick, I think."

I headed for one of the duffel bags, this time quite sure of the one I needed to go to. My head was clear—this was a standard problem and I knew what the solution was. I reached in and pulled out one of the medical bags, the one with the prescription drugs in it. I got it open and grabbed the necessary vial—everything was colour coded—and confirmed that it was what I wanted. I tapped out two pills into the unwilling hands of each of the girls, and tapped out a pair for myself.

"Swallow 'em down, ladies," I instructed in a firm voice. I swallowed my own pills, and washed them down with the remainder of the whisky. Not the preferred medical procedure, I'll admit, but needs must.

I gave the girls a baleful stare until they somewhat reluctantly swallowed their own pills and washed them down with the whisky. The shudders and looks on their faces as the foul taste of the pills interacted with the whisky would have been comical if the situation hadn't been so serious. Well, OK, I did manage a small snort of amusement, which got a foul glare from both of them.

"Not feelin' better, old man," belched Lee, still wagging her tongue about in an attempt to remove the taste of the pills. Gail nodded her agreement, as she made small "Bleh" sounds.

"Drink a few cups of water," I advised them. "It will help, I promise you."

Both of them were shaking their heads, as if attempting to break loose from the fog within.

"Go to bed. You'll feel better in the morning. Honest."

I helped them to their feet and pointed them towards the bedroom, and they wobbled off. None too steady on their feet, but under their own power nonetheless. For my part, I took my own advice and swallowed several glasses of water. After a quick jaunt to bathroom to make use of the toilet, I made the couch ready for my evening slumber.

My thoughts were clear, with just a touch of fog. Or maybe it was just normal fatigue. Whatever the cause, I fell asleep quickly.

CHAPTER FIVE

By the Pricking of My Thumbs

I woke up the next morning at my usual time, just before dawn. There were no sounds indicating anyone else was up, so I went to the bathroom and did a hasty wash-up without bothering to shave. I opened the door of the bathroom, and jumped back with start. Lee was standing there in the doorway, giving me a baleful glare. It was a clear-eyed, no-nonsense look that I knew all too well.

"Now would be a damn fine time to explain, Felix Kurtsius."

Oh, dear. She had used my full name. That meant that she was irked—at the very least. Best to tread with care.

"How are you feeling?" I asked. "How did you sleep?"

Her visage grew stormy. As she opened her mouth to speak I interjected, "Not being polite. This is important. Truly."

That got her to close her mouth with a snap, and she got a thoughtful look. After a moment she replied, "Feelin' OK. Better than OK, actually. And slept well. Felt a bit flushed when I went to bed, and it took a while to get to sleep. After that, though, I slept real well. Better than I have in ages."

She said the last with a hint of puzzlement in her voice.

"What *exactly* did you give us?" she demanded.

Ah, good. Back to her normal self. With luck, her old normal.

"Uhm, there's something of a story you need to hear about this. Want to wait until Gail wakes up?"

"I'm right here. So spill it," said Gail with a hint of frost in her voice, standing in the doorway of the bedroom with her arms crossed. I was gratified to note that Lee jumped just as much as I had at the interjection.

"Uhm, OK," I muttered. "Maybe coffee would be nice?"

"You talk. I make coffee," commanded Gail as she strode off, leaving no room for discussion. Lee and I exchanged glances—we both knew when obedience was the better part of valour.

So off we went to the kitchen in Gail's wake. Besides, the idea of coffee sounded real good about now. My appetite was sharper than it had been for a few days.

It turned out that I wasn't the only one with a healthy appetite. Both of the ladies expressed an interest in food (or rather, their growling stomachs did). I fried up some bacon and eggs for us, while Gail made the coffee and Lee made toast. It was all quite tasty, except for the toast made using rather old store-bought bread. Blah. Still, the rest of the breakfast made that sorry excuse for toast acceptable. In fact, everything seemed a lot ... "brighter" was the only word that came to mind.

The happy moment ended as the girls first glanced at each other, then turned their basilisk glares upon me. With a sigh I drained my cup and began.

"OK, starting the story from the end, the pills I gave you were anti-viral drugs."

Lee just shook her head. "No, no. Those are under strict rationing. Only available at hospitals. Always under strict controls."

It was my turn to shake my head. "I got these a few years ago, before the rationing and controls. Available by prescription only, yes, but I had a medical contact who worried about me being out in the boonies on my own. And knew that I wouldn't abuse anything."

"A...medical contact?" Gail said, with a hint of a smile.

"Just that," I said in a no-nonsense tone. "Not gonna say more. It was a stretch to give me that stuff, and could cause real problems now. That topic is off-limits."

Both girls nodded in agreement with that attitude. Personal contacts were more important than ever these days, and protecting them was considered a sacred trust. Hard times can cause improvements to society, not just problems.

"OK," I continued, "on to the serious issue at hand. I'm convinced that those brain cramps are related to the Change Plague, somehow. The timing is just too close to be coincidental. They started appearing last year, right?"

Both ladies nodded.

"Widespread, yes," said Gail in a quiet tone, as if recalling a long-forgotten memory. "It first started showing up, oh, maybe a year ago?" She looked to Lee for confirmation, and Lee agreed with a nod.

"Right, and consider how it manifests itself," I continued. "So long as you do whatever is normal, whatever that may be for you, everything is fine. Once you start doing something outside of your routine, the headaches start. If you keep doing the new thing or thinking new thoughts, then the headache gets truly hellacious. On the flip side, once you revert back to your routine the headache not only goes away, you start feeling giddy with happiness. I first noticed that yesterday when we took that break on the loading dock. Remember that?"

Lee and Gail exchanged glances before nodding. They looked not quite as fresh as they did a few minute ago.

"Beginning to feel a little off, aren't you," I suggested. It wasn't a question. I could see from their expressions that I was correct.

"But not a full-fledged brain cramp," said Lee. Gail nodded.

"That shows that the anti-virals are having an effect, and proves my hypothesis about the virus. Think about it. Everything is fine as long as you stick to your normal routine. Change your routine, and pain follows. Return to routine, and reward follows."

"Pavlovian conditioning," breathed Gail, her eyes growing wide. "It's bloody Pavlovian conditioning. Holy fuck."

Both Lee and I just stared at her, aghast. Gail rarely swore.

Lee turned to me, pointed to Gail, and said in a deadpan voice, "What she said. Doubled."

Gail was still standing there, staring off into space. Her right arm was raised, and her index finger extended as if to make a point, and the hand was slowly wagging. This was her "deep thinking" mode. Lee and I waited without speaking until Gail turned to us and said in a brisk tone, "Can't be done. Too specific."

"Hah," I replied. "So is the Change Plague. Dollars to donuts this is a variant of that, aimed at control instead of change."

That returned Gail to her deep thinking mode for another minute. She snapped out of it with a shake of her head.

"Damn. Getting a bit of a headache trying to think about this. Not a full brain cramp, thankfully. What's the dose frequency of those anti-virals, Felix?"

"Every twelve hours. It's been a little less than that. Should be alright to take the next dose?" I queried.

Gail pondered for a few seconds, then nodded.

I gave us each another pair of pills, and we washed them down with water. They still tasted kinda rank, so we drank the remains of our coffees, and that seemed to help.

"How much of that drug have you got, Felix?" asked Lee. "Enough to finish our treatment? And how about the rest of The Group?"

I passed the vial to Gail who grunted her approval, adding, "This is good stuff. The Change Plague is brittle enough to be contained with UV lights and mild antiseptic—that's why we don't worry about catching it when we dissect any specimens. No known cases of contracting it from the Changed. If this Control Plague is based on the same virus, a couple of doses of this stuff should be sufficient. Especially given how much improved we are after a single dose. Got more of it?"

"Three more vials like this one," I replied. "Some more back at the farm. Although that's out of reach unless we get desperate."

"That's enough for The Group," Gail decided, "and maybe a few more. We'll have to see how we respond. We'll need to get this out as soon as possible. Tonight, if we can. Lee, can you start contacting people after we get to work? They'll all have left home by now, so no sense calling them until then. Hmm, just phrase it as an urgent need for a meeting. Don't give details. Heck, we've got enough news to share with them even without this. So, yeah, that's the way to arrange it I think."

She said the last almost to herself, her head bowed. With a start she jerked herself erect, glared at Lee and myself. "Well, what are you two waiting for? We need to get to work. Felix, you clean up here. Gail and I will hit the bathroom first. You can finish up after us. And, yes, you have to shave. Don't sulk. It's not a suitable look for a man your age."

I wasn't sulking, actually, just thinking. "Gail, speaking of work, how much do you remember of our autopsies yesterday?"

Gail frowned. This wasn't a question she had been expecting. She thought for a moment before replying. "Well, I remember doing the first specimen, then going out to the loading dock, then coming back and starting on the second specimen. It gets fuzzy after that until we got back to the apartment."

By this time her frown deepened, and Lee was frowning as well. "Yeah, that timeline matches my own points of zoning out."

"Why, Felix? That's an interesting side effect of that Control Plague thing, but there's more to it, isn't there?"

Both ladies were aiming questioning looks at me.

"Yeah. It kind of defines what we need to start working on when we get back to the lab. That second specimen? It wasn't human."

★ ★ ★

We decided to take public transit to work that morning, it being rush hour and all. After an initial disorientation at the apartment, both Lee and Gail were quick to adapt to normal awareness. They both had first-class minds and a large measure of common sense, so neither of them was panicking about the discovery of their mental fog. Disquieted, to be sure, but keen to discover the extent of the Control Plague's interference with their memories and perceptions.

The ride in the subway was their first real wake-up to the extent of that interference. Our brief discussion about the non-human specimen just made them eager to get back to work. The nasty grittiness of the streets and subway system was like a slap in the face, and their faces showed it. For my own part, I was glad to be rid of the damn headaches. And grateful that my perceptions of the run-down nature of the City were verified.

Their minds no longer filtered their perceptions into "everything is normal" ruts. Now it filtered through a much broader range of memories and expectations. Neither of them said anything during the trip. They spent the time taking sharp notice of everything around them. It was only during our walk from the subway station to the ROM that they spoke.

"This is how you saw things when you got here the other day, isn't it, Felix?" said Lee in a quiet voice. "I just assumed that you were being your usual grumpy anti-city self."

"Harrumph," I replied. "Nice to know that your default view of me is as a cranky old fart. Maybe not far off the mark, I'll admit, but I *had* hoped for better." This got the expected smile from both of the girls.

"What strikes me is the most is the run-down look of everything," said Gail. "I mean, I always saw it. It just never struck me as anything other than the same-old same-old. Maybe an impression that it was time for the street crews to do a cleanup, though never as being much worse than normal." She gestured with her chin, "Look around. It has never been this bad, even during the garbage strikes. This is awful."

Lee took my arm and gave it a squeeze as she smiled at me. "Sorry to have doubted you, Felix. Should have followed your advice to always trust the old fart. And remembered that you have the most irritatin' habit of being right, far too often." She leaned over to bump her head against my shoulder, and squeezed my arm again.

Gail noticed my glum expression and lack of gloating about being proven right. She gave a small sigh and asked, "I gather that you think that there's more to all this, eh, Felix? You've got your thinking face on."

That got a small snort of amusement out of me, and a wry smile. "Yeah—though damned if I know what. Too many questions and not enough data. Hell, I don't think we're even asking the right questions, come to that. Though now with the

51

two of you up to speed and ready to rock and roll, I'm confident that we can start to science the shit out of this problem."

That got everyone's mood swung over to the happy side, and we entered the building with smiles. Passing through the various security checkpoints on the way to the lab made those smiles somewhat forced, though. The girls began to take serious notice of the dilapidated state of the building that had once been a shining highlight of Toronto. They began to notice, as I had, the cracked paint and the ever-present dust and grime. We finally arrived at Gail's lab and went inside. We dumped our bags on the floor next to one of the desks, and Gail got the coffee brewing.

It was fortunate that I had thought to bring some of my own coffee, because the stuff she had there was awfully foul-looking. When the girls realized that they had been making coffee for weeks with that crap, they blanched and shuddered. At least keeping the pot and machine clean was an ingrained habit, so everything had been sanitary. While the coffee was brewing the girls each sat at a desk to check their email. I decided to power up and check my emails using my smart phone. An unladylike expletive from Lee got our attention, and we looked up to see her grimacing at her screen.

"Crap. Crap. Crap. Gotta run, guys. Manderpootz is raisin' hell with my boss about my not bein' around to be at his beck and call. I gotta deal with this back at my own office. I'll try to meet with you for lunch. Gimme a buzz 'bout eleven thirty or so. Oh, and use the office phone so it sounds important."

With that she got up, grabbed her bag, and with a look of deep longing at the brewing coffee she prepared to head out. Gail stopped her with an upraised hand, grabbed a cup, and filled it from the still-in-progress coffee. It wasn't the best way to get a good cup of coffee, but better than what awaited her. With a nod of thanks, Lee took the cup and headed out at a brisk pace.

"Don't forget to send an email out to The Group for tonight," Gail called out. Lee raised the cup in acknowledgement as she exited.

"Is she in some sort of trouble?" I asked, becoming concerned.

"Nah. Manderpootz has a somewhat inflated sense of self-importance and sometimes throws his weight around. Unfortunately he has solid connections to senior management, so we usually try to make time to listen to his requests. Not that we always take action, you understand, but we have to at least listen. Besides, he's the one that found those strange artifacts we told you about before your escape. It probably is his turn for access to Lee's brilliance. Still, enough of that. We have our own issues to deal with. Starting with getting a cup of coffee. Damn, it smells good."

I had to admit that it wasn't bad coffee, despite the beans not being at their peak of flavour. And that coffee machine would never make great coffee. Nonetheless, it sure hit the spot. We sat in silence sipping our coffee, each dealing with our email. My own included a couple of status reports from my farm's security system, as well as the usual junk.

According to the reports, everything was OK and there had been no breaches or catastrophic events. The timestamps on the messages were over a day old, and there should have been more of them. Guess that meant that all the communication links were acting up again.

My allergies seemed to be acting up, because my eyes were watering a bit. Enough that I had to give them a quick wipe. I looked up to see Gail favouring me with a questioning look, and I waggled my hand to show that nothing was wrong. She wasn't buying it, and raised one eyebrow to tell me so. I sighed and said, "It's nothing. Just a couple of status messages from the farm's security system. Everything seems fine."

I paused for a moment to make a snort of amusement. "Fine. Yeah. My home has become the front line for Armageddon and I had to run for my life to get away. But all systems are green and go."

"You miss it."

I sighed deeply and nodded. "I miss what it *was*, Gail. After all those years of being kicked around, I'd finally managed to create a little spot of happiness in this stupid world. Wasn't much, but it was my home. Finally, a place that I could call a real home."

She said in a kind voice, "There's still a chance that it'll survive, you know. With you gone, maybe they'll leave it alone."

"Maybe," I replied. Then my tone firmed up, "The wolves were moving into other houses, so who knows. The farm has a chance, though. We all do. And we can increase our chances by getting to work."

Chins up and eyes clear, we looked at each other, drained our cups, and got to work.

★ ★ ★

The autopsy of the Priest answered some questions and raised a whole lot more. By the time we finished, even Gail was referring to it as a "Priest ", not "Specimen-2". What we found was not just puzzling, it was downright scary.

The eyes, as we had discovered, weren't human. Rather, they were predator eyes adapted to night vision. The muscles were denser than human muscles, and Gail suspected that they were closer to those found in apes. That is, kilo for kilo the Priest was stronger than humans—a lot stronger.

Also, it would have been capable of a reasonable range of vocalizations despite their larynx not being as developed as that of a normal human. That much I had seen for myself during their attacks at the farm, but it was nice to get verification.

The Priest was a true neuter—no sexual organs of any sort external, internal, or vestigial. There was an anus, which was used for the excretion of both solid and liquid waste. The extra space inside the body was taken up with a larger stomach, liver, and kidneys. Those organs seemed different than normal, even ignoring the size difference, so Gail removed them for further study by experts. The lungs were were larger than expected. We hypothesized that was for holding its breath for long periods, or to extract more oxygen for increased strength and endurance. Those were just guesses on our part, of course.

A surprise discovery was of what seemed to be scent glands located in the armpits and groin area. Gail removed and saved those. The fur or hair or whatever it was covering the body turned out to be true fur, not hair at all. And it was a lot denser than any human Changed victim on record. More like an ape or a wolf, according to Gail.

The real shocker concerned the markings on the body. They were a lot more extensive, and much more intricate and complex, than they appeared at first glance. Almost like a three-dimensional pattern. They appeared to have been grown into the skin in some fashion, rather than being created through mechanical means.

We stood there contemplating what those markings might mean, but by this time our minds were overloaded. Too much raw data, and not enough solid information. After gazing at the extracted organs, Gail decided to give those a closer look.

"Felix, take some pictures of the organs on the scale. That way we'll have a pictorial record of the weights."

As it was spoken, so it was done. Gail wrote up a brief tag to be included in the picture. When we completed that task she said with a sigh, "I'd love to do a proper series of cross-sections of those organs. Something isn't right about them. Unfortunately, those are our only samples and I'd rather them be properly examined by experts."

"How about the brain?" I suggested. "We've got two more intact samples that could be extracted from spare heads." Damn—now she had me talking about the damned monsters as if they were specimens.

With precise movements, she set up the extracted brain on a cutting board. After each slice with a sharp knife, she had me take a picture of both the slice and the exposed part of the brain.

"This is just for a quick examination of gross features," she explained, "something even I can do. The overall shape isn't right, and maybe I can see something ..."

She paused as she examined the slices arrayed before her, then grabbed a magnifying glass for a better look. She focused on the samples, moving from one to the other, for a minute or so before motioning me to examine them.

"See those dark threads here and here on this slice?" she

asked.

"Yep. Hmm, they appear to be intertwined with the rest of the tissue. Is that normal?"

"Not in the slightest. And yet they don't appear to be a pathology. In fact, they have the appearance of something normal for this brain. Notice how the lines run throughout the brain. Notice anything strange?"

"Are you kidding, Gail? To me this is all strange."

She seemed taken back by that, as if she'd forgotten that I wasn't a medical colleague. Giving her head a small shake, she began pointing out various structures within the brain. I gathered that these weren't something she'd been expecting to find. Those strange black threads went snaking between those new structures and normal structures.

"If this were a human brain, or even a normal mammalian brain, I'd say those new structures were somehow wired into the speech and vision centres of the brain."

"Uhm, OK," I replied, "but what does it mean?"

"Damnifiknow, Felix. This is way beyond me. Beyond anything I've ever heard of. OK, we'll package these slices up and send them along with the other brains. This is so cool."

I wasn't sure that was the way I'd describe it. This wasn't a human being who had been Changed. This was something based on the human template, with strange modifications.

My ruminations were interrupted by Gail dropping another pair of heads onto the examining table. She looked up at me with a grin as she said, "It occurred to me that we've got a spare head of each of the two types of Drones. What say we check out their brains?"

I opened my mouth to protest, then closed it with a snap. That was an excellent idea. With some excitement, we both set about the task at hand.

It was uncanny to watch her slice the new specimen brains with cuts that seemed to duplicate those made on the first. We soon had the slices of all three brains laid out before us. The strange lines were the most dense and complex in the Priest brain, less dense and complex in the Uber Drone brain, and minimal in the regular Drone brain. I looked at Gail for an explanation, but all I got from her was a baffled shrug.

At this point, Gail decided to take some more samples to try a DNA analysis with her own equipment. It would be a lot cruder than what the outside lab could do. On the other hand, she could get results a lot faster. With any luck that might give us a hint to explain what we had discovered.

Switching gears from brains to a full autopsy, we examined the Uber Drone in detail. We suspected it to be a Changed human, and the full autopsy proved it. As was hinted at from the initial examination, the testicles were no longer functional. Similarly, the larynx was atrophied to the point where normal human speech was impossible—at best limited to grunts and howls.

Gail and I had stopped our work to step back and take a breather. We had been going flat out for several hours, and were starting to wobble. "Not my finest work," said Gail with a grin, quite pleased with herself. "Just a step above a field autopsy. More than sufficient for what we need, though." To my untrained eyes, the lab looked like something out of a horror movie. There were bodies flayed open and plastic tubs with various ooky bits in them.

A buzz from my phone startled both of us. I removed my now-messy gloves before digging out the phone. It turned out to be a text from Lee, telling us meet her at noon for lunch. The time stamp on the message indicated that it was almost noon. That meant that we had forgotten to contact her. Oops.

Gail and I exchanged guilty looks as I read the text to her. We covered the bodies with opaque plastic sheets and cleaned ourselves. As we headed out to the cafeteria, locking the door to the lab behind us, we exchanged grins. We could hardly wait to tell Lee about all the interesting stuff we'd found.

When we got to cafeteria entrance, we were greeted by Lee sitting at a table and waving at us to get our attention. Giving a small wave back, we headed over to her and sat down. "You'll never guess what we found," we all said in unison. With a start, we each sat back and waited for the other to speak.

Gail broke the silence. "The autopsies turned up some quite fascinating information ..."

Lee interrupted her, "Nope. Nope. Not at lunch, thank you very much." She waved both hands to emphasize the point, and grimaced. Gail was startled by the response. She sometimes forgot that most people didn't share her love of ick, ook, and things that go squish. I interjected, "OK, Lee, you seem a lot happier than you were this morning. I guess things turned out OK with that meeting you had to get to?"

To my surprise, Lee was actually beaming with excitement. "Yep. Turns out that Manderpootz actually had some new artifacts that he wanted me to look at. Well, actually to scan and do image enhancement on. The old coot, no offence Felix, had been doin' his trick of dolin' out information in dribs and drabs to make himself seem important. Remember those fragments that I told you about before you had to escape from your farm? Well, turns out that not only hadn't he shown us all the contents of the crate, he actually had another crate of them tucked away. Idiot. Well, anyway, he had given me some more of the pieces from the original set to scan and analyze. That went quickly enough, because I could use the same algorithms developed for the original stuff. It was obvious from the images that these were part of a larger grouping, perhaps a fresco.

"I sighed and did the "oh, dear, you know that this might actually mean somethin' if only we had the remainder of the set" thing. And the old fool, no offence Felix, actually puffed out his chest and allowed as he had some more. A few minutes later he came back with the entire crate, and that allowed me to scan the rest. They all actually were part of the same larger figure. Manderpootz managed to recreate that larger figure from all the different images, in almost no time at all. He really does have some talent, you know, even if he does hide it under that bluster of his. To everyone's surprise, it was obvious that this was actually part of a larger piece.

"Manderpootz was so excited at this point that he was almost dancin'. The man truly does love his work. Told us all to wait right there and he'd be right back in flash. A minute later he was back luggin' yet another crate. His hands were shaking as he opened it, but damned if they weren't surgeon-steady when he handled the fragments. We scanned the lot, and again managed to do the image analysis right quick. Manderpootz once again amazed us all by recreatin' the complete fresco from the images of the various pieces. He was amazin' to watch, mutterin' to himself and pointing out the images he wanted me to move and where. Took maybe ten minutes—and that my friends is truly impressive, given what we had to work with."

This was all very interesting. However, by this time both Gail and myself were beginning to fade from a lack of food. We were saved by the arrival of a waiter, who took our orders and went away. In truth there was little to choose from—no soup, and only a couple different types of sandwiches. A few seconds later, a busboy came by and poured out water and coffee, dropped off a few buns, and left. We each grabbed and buttered a bun, then spent a minute or so munching and drinking in silence.

Alas, all good things come to an end. Gail forced herself to enquire, "So, Lee, you were telling us about the images and stuff." She was so polite. To a fault, I'd always felt.

"Yah," Lee said, her voice low so that only we could hear. "There are gaps in the final fresco or whatever it is, and Manderpootz *swears* that he's got no more bits stashed away. It seems to somehow link those original symbols with some new ones. Real interestin' stuff, too. Here, take a look at these pictures I brought. None of us can figure out what they mean, or how they're related to those original symbols."

She passed over a sheaf of pictures to us. The top one showed the completed fresco thingie. I peered at it, and parts of it teased at the edge of familiarity. There just wasn't enough detail to be sure. I passed that picture over to Gail. As she examined it, I shuffled through the pictures of the individual pieces. Something was causing my intuition to itch.

In a quiet voice, Gail snapped out, "There. That set of symbols there," and she pointed to a section of the fresco surrounded by gaps. "Gimme your magnifier, Felix," she commanded.

I always keep one or two small plastic Fresnel magnifiers on me—they were just so damned useful. I dug one out and handed it to her, and continued shuffling through the pictures as Gail peered at hers.

"Just as I thought," she muttered. Looking up, she turned first to me, then Lee. "Those symbols there are the same as those on the specimens that are in the lab."

Lee blinked and looked startled. "Wait ..." she began.

"That's not all," I interjected, holding up a picture of one of the pieces. "Some of these other symbols seem familiar. I think I've seen them on other Priests during the last attacks at the farm. Would need to verify that, though."

At that moment the waiter arrived with our sandwiches, and we retreated from conversation to eat and collect our thoughts. The sandwiches weren't too bad, though meagre fare. They didn't take long to finish, despite our slowness in eating. I was still a bit peckish. Looking around, I realized that it seemed to be the allotted ration for lunch, so didn't say anything. Now I understood the excitement about having soup in addition to the sandwiches.

Both of the girls were looking as if they wanted some more as well. I got their attention with a look, and signalled that we should leave with a small jerk of my head. We drained the remains of our coffee (which wasn't bad, just not as good as mine), gathered up the pictures, and headed back to Gail's lab. Lee made a token protest about having to get back to her own work, but the mention of snack bars in my pack assured her compliance.

We got back to the lab, Gail unlocked the door, and we trooped inside. There was some coffee left, enough for a half-cup for each of us. Gail poured as I dug into my pack and pulled out a snack bar for each of us. They were my home-made efforts, and meant to be filling as well as nutritious. Both the girls had always been modest nibblers as far as snacks were concerned. Now, though, they scarfed the bars down in no time at all. Both had guilty looks as they sat sipping their coffee.

"It's a normal post-infection case of the munchies," I assured them.

Lee gave a snort before replying, "A lie. But a beautiful effort, and I thank you, kind sir."

Gail was looking thoughtful. "I rather wonder how much the Control Plague kept our expectations in check. I seem to recall always hoping for more, though being satisfied with what I did get. Except soup days—every soup day seemed like Christmas."

A sudden realization came to me. "That might help to explain why everyone in the city is so accepting of the many shortages. No-one ever seems to complain, so long as a certain minimal level is maintained. Might be part of that Pavlovian Control Plague, or maybe yet another variant."

Lee made a small gasp, then exclaimed, "Speakin' of control, I gotta get back to my own lab. Oh, and I can't leave those pictures with you, either. Manderpootz would have a shit-fit if he knew I'd shown them to you. I'll have to email you copies."

"We need to talk more about all this, Lee," Gail said, a note of insistence in her voice. "This is getting too big and too strange."

"Save it for the meetin' with The Group tonight," Lee replied. "I talked briefly with Stan, and he's goin' to do an email blast and textin' sometime after lunch to set it all up. Didn't tell him any details, of course. Just told him that it was urgent that we together. Tonight if possible. He was fine with that—more than fine, actually, so expect to get that invite any time now. Gotta run. Thanks for the snack bar, Felix. Good coffee, Gail." And with that she gathered up her pictures and trotted out.

Gail nodded as if Lee's leaving completed an item on an internal checklist. "We have work of our own to do, Felix. Why don't you help me to finish up with the autopsies until Lee emails those pictures. Then you can focus on those." It was not a question, but I didn't mind. My friends were back to their no-nonsense, ultra-competent normal, and my world seemed a lot brighter for it.

★ ★ ★

It had been a busy afternoon for us, and looked to be a busy evening. As promised, Stan did his usual brilliant short-notice organizational thing, and set up a meeting at his house for that evening. The ladies wanted to work late, then head straight to Stan's place. It was left to me to be the voice of reason.

"We need to pick up some more anti-viral pills, not to

mention copies of all my data and the analysis I did with it."

Gail shook her head, "There's still so much we could finish up here, Felix. Besides, you brought that almost-full container of the drug with you in case one of us needed an extra dose. That'll be enough if we give everyone a single pill. And Stan and Dix are downloading the data from your servers."

"Not if everyone shows up that we want to be there. Besides, a half-dose isn't of much use. We have enough for two full doses for everyone, and we are going to need everyone up to be full mental strength. As for downloading, I'm not getting any more status emails which means that the comm links are down again. It'll be easier, and safer, to drive to Stan's house from your apartment than to take transit from here." Both girls grudgingly accepted the latter argument.

"And besides," I added with the absolute clincher argument, "We need to have a proper meal. Let's take a small roast out of the cold storage locker in the lab, and slice that up for quick-fry steaks. After what happened at lunch, it's obvious that we need to pay extra attention to adequate diet." More than anything else, that convinced them, I think.

So that's what we did. Left work at the usual time, headed to the apartment for a decent, if quick, supper. After a brief discussion we decided not to get into what we had each discovered that afternoon during our individual researches—too much chance of getting lost in the discussion and missing the meeting at Stan's. It's good to be aware of one's weaknesses.

As we gathered up the supplies to take with us to the meeting, out of habit I grabbed a shotgun and pistol. Lee and Gail weren't pleased with that, and told me so in no uncertain terms. Being Torontonians to the core, they were fundamentally opposed to guns. I could even sympathize with them. However, there was no frickin' way that I was driving around a werewolf-infested city without weapons.

After a brief, intense, and sometimes acrimonious discussion, we compromised. I'd take the weapons, but make sure that the girls couldn't see them. Whatever. So long as I could protect them from any threat, I was satisfied. My friends were important to me. However, their reaction got me to thinking. This was in stark contrast to their reaction when I arrived and had handed out weapons. I shrugged mentally and chalked it up to the effects of the Control Plagues.

The drive to Stan's house started out in chilly silence, but thawed out along the way. It helped that there were a lot of street lamps burned out, especially in the residential areas. That made for a rather desolate and sometimes threatening appearance the further we went. The shimmering of shadows added to the general creepiness. In better times, it would have made for a fun sort of spookiness. These days, not so much.

We arrived at Stan's house a few minutes before the scheduled start time. Stan was a stickler for starting on time, and late-comers were lucky to get a cup of coffee, much less a warm reception. We got out of the car, each carrying a bag or knapsack. Besides my knapsack, I was carrying a duffel bag that contained the shotgun and pistol, plus a few other supplies. The ladies made a point of not looking at it as we marched towards the door. For my part, I kept it unzipped and kept my head moving around to survey the area as we walked the few dozen metres to the door. Neither of the ladies made any comment about my alertness level.

Stan only kept us waiting a few seconds after we knocked, and greeted us with enthusiasm as he ushered us inside. A broad smile came to my face. We'd had so many get-togethers in this place, and just seeing it again made all those happy memories flood back with a warm tingle. The only off-notes were all the extra bolts on the door, and the care that Stan took in ensuring that they were all set back into place. I gave him an approving nod. He was a good lad, and it was reassuring to see that he was serious about security.

"Go on into the living room," Stan said as he took our coats and began putting them into the hall closet, "You're the last ones here. The tea is all ready, and Jack made some cookies. Go, go."

The three of us shuffled into the living room and into a cacophony of greetings. These were my closest friends, and aside from the brief meeting a couple of days ago, I'd not had physical contact with them in the better part of a year. I felt awkward and out of place as the noise level decreased to silence and everyone looked at me. My smile was now more than a bit forced and I made a little wave with my free hand.

Clio broke the spell by rushing up and giving me a big hug. When she pulled away I could see tears on her cheeks. "Welcome home, Felix. We were all so worried about you."

Bless Clio—she always did know how to break the ice and make a person feel welcome.

After that things felt a lot more normal, and we shook hands and exchanged hugs all around. All the Group was there—Felix, Stan, Jack, Clio, Dix, Lee, Gail, and Grant. Damn, it was nice to see them all. It was a glorious happy anarchy for fifteen or twenty minutes before Stan called the meeting to order. Actually, he announced that the tea was getting cold and the cookies were getting stale. That was sufficient to get everyone's attention. Cups got filled, plates heaped with cookies, and we all found places to sit.

Stan stood up and thanked everyone for coming on such short notice. I wasn't impressed by that so much as filled with pride at being part of a group of such fine people. He then turned the meeting over to Lee, saying that she had some important things to discuss. All eyes turned expectantly towards her, as she stood up.

"Hey, guys, thanks for comin'. We've discussed a lot of stuff in our recent Net Nights, and Felix managed to collect a lot of new information before he had to escape from his farm."

There were murmurs of concern as she mentioned the escape. She quieted them with a gentle waving of her hands. "No, no, he's perfectly fine. And I know we're all glad that he managed to bring some fresh food with him." They all applauded at that, as I blushed and had to clear my throat.

"Stan, Dixon," Lee said, raising her voice to override and silence the applause, "how's the downloadin' of data from Felix's server comin' along?"

Stan said, "Stalled. Got some, though". He nodded at Dixon who continued the tale. "Comm links are all down, Felix. We only got a few dozen pictures, one short video, and some small analysis files. If I had to guess, maybe twenty percent. At best."

"Don't worry about it," I said. "I brought copies of all the data. Should I pass them out now or later?"

The consensus was to do it right away, so I passed around the data sticks. Luckily I had enough for each household, though not every person.

With that done, I continued, "Since arriving, I've had a couple of emails from the security system at the farm indicating that everything was OK. Nothing recently, which meant that the comms were down. From what you're telling me, that's a safe assumption. Dix, any thoughts on where the problem might be?"

Dixon shook his head. "Land line links to your farm crapped out weeks ago, so those are probably down for the count. The ham repeaters are starting to crap out faster than we expected and not getting fixed. The remaining ones are being increasingly taken over by jammers. Solar activity is acting up again, though not enough to affect the satellite links. Sorry, Felix."

"S'OK, Dix," I replied, "I didn't expect any better. In all likelihood the satellite dish got knocked out of alignment or trashed. Either way, the farm is going to have stand or fall on its own devices for the time being. Speaking of which, did you manage to download a copy of the enhanced security measures I installed just before I left?"

Dixon shook his head.

"No problem," I said. "Details are on those data sticks I passed out. The important thing to keep in mind is that I gimmicked the house and barn with some extra nasties. Some are tied into the security system, and some are mechanical—for example, caltrops on the floors. The object was to make life hard for any werewolf or casual looter who broke in, not make things impenetrable. There's still a lot of useful stuff stored there, so keep that in mind if things get bad. The freezers are full and will keep until the backup power systems fail, and those should last for many months if not years. There's non-perishable food and useful items like tools and books. The barn has lots of machine shop tools plus various mechanical goodies. Weapons and the remains of my ammunition are in both locations. If you need to get into them, follow the instructions. And be careful."

The mood was somber as I finished. No-one here would dream of breaking into my farm while I was still alive, I was confident of that. I just needed to ensure that they were taken care of in case anything happened to me. These people were my family. Not by blood, it's true—just in every way that counted.

Gail stood up and took up the narrative at this point.

"Listen carefully, please. Felix discovered something terribly important after he arrived here. You're all aware of the brain cramps that have been going around for the past year, yes? Anyone *not* getting them?"

There was some muttering and looking around at each other, but no-one spoke up. A few people began rubbing their foreheads.

"Right. Turns out that those are caused by another virus. We can discuss more about it later. First I want everyone—and I mean *everyone*—to take a dose of anti-viral pills that Felix is going to pass around."

By this point everyone except Lee, Gail, and myself was showing varying signs of distress, from wicked headaches to sweats. The three of us passed around a pair of pills to each person, and ensured that they swallowed them along with a large swig of tea. Lee was having problems with Dixon. I waved her away and took over that task.

"Hey, Dix, you gotta take these," I said in a quiet, even tone. "Bad shit is happening. Screwing with your head. These'll help clear that up."

Dix just sat there shaking his head, beads of sweat gathering on his forehead. I remembered that he had seemed a bit flushed when I had arrived. I just squatted on my haunches in front of him, making sure not to touch him or get too close. This wasn't like him at all, and I wasn't sure how to deal with it. With a jerk, he raised up his head and looked straight at me.

"Can't, Felix," he croaked. "Against the rules. Gotta stay with the program."

Program? What "program" was Dix talking about? Ah, shit, what had the dumb kid gotten himself into this time?

"Dix, buddy, ya gotta trust me on this. I've never lied to you, or steered you wrong. Right?"

He nodded slowly.

"I'm not gonna let anything happen to you, Dix. You're family."

Dixon lowered his head and averted his gaze. I held my breath. This was way more touchy-feely than either of us was comfortable with, to tell the truth. Needs must and all that.

After a few seconds, Dixon raised his head, wiped his eyes on a sleeve, and held out a hand. I put a pair of pills into it, and he popped them into his mouth. I picked his cup of tea off the ground and told him to take a big sip, which he did, keeping hold of the cup. I watched him until his breathing evened out and he took another couple of small sips from his tea.

Satisfied that he was back to something resembling normal, I stood up. Then became aware that squatting was not the best of ideas for a man my age. I had to put my hands on my thighs and push before I could straighten up. Oof, how embarrassing. Taking a quick look around (Vanity, thy name is Felix) to see if anyone had caught my decrepitude, I was mortified to realize that everyone was watching me. Crap. So with a sigh I hobbled back to my chair and dropped into it. Everyone looked from Dix to me and nodded with approval.

Gail looked around the room and spoke, "We'll take a break for half an hour before continuing. By that time you should all be feeling a bit better, then quite a bit better pretty quick. Be prepared to be a bit hungrier than usual tomorrow morning." She said the last with a smile and a nod to me. I was expecting some pushback about taking a break. Perhaps not so surprisingly, there was none. Lee told everyone to stay sitting while the three of us made some more tea. Again, there were no arguments—though the offer did get some weak smiles of gratitude.

The three of us gathered up the now-cool pots of tea, and took them into the kitchen. As we waited for the water to boil, I washed out the pots and prepared them for fresh tea. Lee and

Gail were standing there with concerned looks on their faces.

"Is this going to work? Is a half hour going to be enough, do you think?" whispered Lee.

"They'll be fine," I assured her, "They're taking the pills with food and fluids, like they're supposed to. And no alcohol, which will help them a lot."

Gail closed her eyes and made a disgusted sigh while shaking her head. "Yes, you're undoubtedly correct, Felix. Damn. I should have realized that."

"Hey, kiddo, stop beating yourself up," I said. "I've had more time to think about this and learn about this drug." Gail was the sort who demanded perfection of herself, and got upset if she failed to meet that high standard.

Lee patted her shoulder and rubbed it as she said, "The old man is right. This time. Hey, it's not like it happens often."

My honour had been insulted, so I clutched my chest and said, "I am shocked. Shocked and horrified that you would say such a thing, Ms. Neilan."

The byplay got the expected smile out of Gail, and everyone's mood was brightened. The kettle came to a boil, so we busied ourselves preparing the tea. Once that steeped, we took the pots back out to the living room and placed them on the side table to steep. No-one, aside from myself, liked their tea too strong so we were able to start pouring within a couple of minutes. Between the tea ritual and some meaningless conversation, we managed to kill almost three-quarters of an hour.

By this time most of The Group seemed a lot better, as if they were bouncing back after a bad headache. Despite looking a bit iffy, Grant claimed to be on the mend in spite of his flushed appearance. Dixon concerned me—although not as flushed, he was still sweating a bit. I suggested waiting until the next day until we started serious discussions, but no-one would hear of it. There was too much to do, they insisted—and they were correct.

As our medical expert, Gail once again took the lead. She explained what we'd deduced and managed to observe about the Pavlovian conditioning exerted by the Control Plague. It didn't take long for the others to grasp the implications. I think both Lee and Gail were a bit miffed that the others grasped it more quickly than they had. Gail went on to suggest that perhaps there were several types of Control Plagues, each exerting different subtle influences. Influences that made us accept the way things were without questioning them. Again, the others were all quick to grasp the implications.

"Wait a minute," said Jack. "How is it affecting so many people in such a short time? Besides, there are always going to be people who are naturally immune to any bug. What about them?"

I held up a hand. "I'll answer that, if you don't mind, Gail. Taking the last question first, yeah, there are going to be a lot of people who are immune for one reason or another. Just think about that. We're wired to be social creatures. If a large fraction of the population, not even a majority, exhibit some behaviour the tendency is for the rest to more or less follow suit. Also, note how the Control Plagues play into normal city behaviour. Go along to get along, don't make waves, just do your normal stuff and live your own life. No new behaviour patterns are being introduced here, just enhancement of specific existing behaviours. As for the first question, I don't have any solid answer yet. Wait a sec—how many of you besides Lee have had a chance to look at my most recent analysis?"

Only Dix raised his hand. Oh, dear.

"OK, well, my most recent analysis using some new data showed that the Change Plague isn't a single virus or even a virus that is changing over time. The implication of the analysis is that a whole new Change Plague is released each year at the start of spring. That's why a new crop of werewolves springs up after the winter die-off. That's why each year the werewolves get nastier and more dangerous. Each crop of werewolves seems to have been an experiment, an attempt to come up with a new and improved werewolf while getting rid of the failures—until this year. This last winter, the werewolves didn't die off, at least not to any great extent. That means this year's crop was reinforced by a large number of last year's. Which allows the new crop to build on the experiences of the previous year's crop. To organize. To take more effective action against us."

I decided to stop there for a moment to let everyone catch their breath, and come to terms with the new information. By this time only Dixon was still showing signs of distress. Still, even he was focused on what I was saying.

No-one asked any questions, so I continued. "There's more to this. From what Gail and I have discovered analyzing the specimens I brought down with me, the Change Plague seems to have reached its goal of creating an Ultimate Werewolf. Well, ultimate in that it modifies humans about as far as they can be modified without destroying them. I call them Uber Drones, and Gail has come to agree with that term."

Gail nodded, and motioned for me to continue. I hadn't planned to talk this much about this, as this was her field of expertise. She seemed to be content to let me take the lead, though. I licked my lips and took a sip of tea before continuing.

"OK, this drone form is kind of what you'd expect. The mouth is still a mouth, with the beginnings of a muzzle. Extra hair—and it is hair, not fur. The larynx is atrophied to the point where real speech is impossible and all that remains are basic grunts and howls. The sexual organs are atrophied to the point of uselessness. I called them drones because of how they acted, but the term seems to apply physiologically as well."

As I paused for another sip of tea, Stan piped up, "OK, if they've been turned into drones like you say, who is controlling them?"

Gail and I exchanged a look, and she indicated that I should continue.

"That's the other thing. Remember those werewolves I called Priests because of their markings and how they seemed to be in charge? Well, it turns out that they are physically different. To the point of being not human. Never were. They aren't victims of the Change Plague—they had to have come from somewhere."

Now *that* got a reaction. Not fear or panic—these were rational people, after all—just expressions of surprise. Next came the questions that I couldn't answer. Like where these non-human werewolves came from. I resorted to waving my hands to get their attention and quiet them down.

"Look, I don't have answers to anything right now. Just data. And there's still more data that you need to know about." In other circumstances the incredulous looks on their faces would have been a glorious sight. I emptied my tea cup and Clio, bless her, filled it up again. I smiled my thanks before continuing.

"OK, the Priests aren't human, or so it appears from the autopsy. We're still waiting for a DNA analysis. Gail can do a quick and dirty DNA sequencing, though it won't have much in the way of resolution to it. Possibly not enough to tell us anything useful. She's got it cooking away, though, and we might have something by tomorrow afternoon. We've sent out samples for proper analysis. Unfortunately, that'll take days, if not weeks."

Clio raised her hand, and asked Gail where the samples had been sent. Gail's answer made Clio snort and curl a lip in disgust.

"Those idiots will take several weeks to get back to you. And don't count on them not mixing up your samples or contaminating them."

Gail was taken aback by that, "I've used them in the past with good results."

"Not recently, say within the last year?" Clio queried.

"Well, no, it was nearly two years ago," Gail replied.

"Yep," stated Clio. "That'd be about right. They got sold just over a year ago to an American management fund, and their quality has been going down the toilet ever since. Lost a lot of excellent people, too, who got replaced by lower-cost new grads. However, quarterly profits are up, I hear. After making big bucks for the next year or so, they'll lose all their contracts that they've pissed off with their poor quality. On the plus side, we've picked up most of their best people for the labs at a couple of the hospitals."

We all just stared at her in amazement. Clio was such a motherly type, fussing about and making people comfortable that we always forgot that she was a force to be reckoned with in her own field of lab management. When she said something was so, that was the end of the argument.

She turned to Gail and said, "Send any samples you want analyzed to me, and I'll send them off to a lab that'll do the job right and do it fast. This is too important to fart around with going through proper channels. Is it just a sample from that Priest thing you want analyzed?"

Despite being taken off guard (a rare occurrence) Gail was quick to snap back into professional mode. "No. There's a couple dozen sets of samples to sequence. There's the three complete cadavers, Priest and two types of Drones, plus a number of fragments that Felix collected from different individuals. We were hoping to build up a DNA database to see what sort of commonality, if any, we could spot."

Clio nodded thoughtfully before replying. "Good thinking. And good job, Felix. I hadn't realized that you'd been so thorough in your collection of specimens."

It warmed me to hear her say that. She offered hospitality at the drop of a hat, but praise was a much rarer thing to hear from her.

She went on, "Yes, the database idea is an excellent one. I'll have to spread that many samples over two or three labs. But, yes, leave it with me and I'll get it done. Be sure to mark the priority samples, though. I can't guarantee that I'll be able to get that many samples done right away. So, by all means continue your own sequencing efforts. I thought you got some decent new equipment for that a few years ago?"

Gail made a rueful smile. "Equipment, yes, but no service contract or budget for on-demand servicing. The wretched thing is just so much junk taking up space right now. I'm reduced to using the decade-old sequencer. Better than nothing, though not by much, I'm afraid. Management decided they had the budget for getting the analysis done by an outside lab, but not for fixing our own equipment."

Clio looked as though she had bitten into something sour. A poorly-run lab, and especially a quality lab allowed to degrade through poor management practises, offended her greatly. "Hmm. If I remember correctly, that new one was a PSX-9700, yes? Do you know what the problems are with it?"

Gail nodded, "Yes, that's it. The 9700TR9, actually. Burned

out a couple of the modules and the spectroscopy lamps."

Clio sighed. "That sounds normal. It's an otherwise excellent piece of kit, just prone to those issues. The replacements aren't all that expensive, so labs tend to keep a stock of them on hand and replace them as needed. I'll see if I can find you some replacements. I can try beating up our sales rep, too—she owes us."

Gail blushed and opened her mouth to say something. Clio just waved her to silence. "No, forget it. I just wish you'd have let me know about the problem long ago—although I understand why you didn't. Anyway, just send the samples to my office, and marked to my attention and with your name plainly visible. I'll alert reception and receiving to be on the lookout for it. We'll get this done for you, never fear. It is obvious that this is 'shit hitting the fan' time, as Felix likes to put it."

She favoured me with a friendly smile at the last bit. Not a big fan of profanity, she tolerated my language so long as I made an effort to control it in her presence. Which I did—and usually succeeded.

I cleared my throat before speaking. "There's more to all this, actually."

"Holy fuck, Felix, are you shitting me?" exclaimed Jack. Clio gave her spouse a soft look and a sigh, then held onto his hand. She didn't like profanity, though allowed Jack to speak for both of them when the occasion demanded it.

"Remember those markings I mentioned in my emails while I was still at the farm?" I asked. "Well, it turns out that the markings on the Drones were created by mechanical means, like cutting. Simple markings, with a few different designs. The Priest we autopsied, though, its markings were both extensive and a lot more complex. And those markings weren't created by mechanical means. It appears that they were somehow grown into the Priest's body."

I paused, and Gail nodded to show her agreement as well as to encourage me to continue.

After taking a deep breath I continued. "The markings on the Drones we have, aren't identical to those on the Priests we have. However, I reviewed some of the pictures that I've taken over the past few months, and I think that the markings on the Priests match the markings on some of the Drones in the pictures. Perhaps to indicate clan affiliation or ownership."

There was a brief discussion about the implications of that, especially given how well organized the attacks on my farm had been.

"Were specific Priests leading specific groups of Drones, Felix?" asked Grant.

I sighed before answering. "Can't say. Those attacks occurred at night, and the video cameras didn't pick up that sort of detail. Regardless, there's more about those markings that you need to know about."

With that I nodded at Lee, who motioned to indicate that I should keep going. I sighed and took a large swig of my now-cool tea. It had been a long time since I'd done any lecturing, or indeed talking at length, and my throat wasn't used to the strain.

"OK, well, you might recall a few months ago Lee talked about some ancient artifacts with symbols and such on them. She's analyzed some more of them, and one group of symbols matches the markings on our Priest specimen. After looking at pictures of other Priests, I think there's a match with some of the other symbols on those artifacts."

"How old did you say those artifacts were, Lee?" asked Stan.

Lee answered, "At least eight thousand years, perhaps more. Pre-Sumerian, for sure."

"So," said Jack, "we've got markings on a non-human creature that match symbols that haven't been seen or used for thousands of years. Right?"

Lee nodded.

"And," he continued, "we've got a Change Plague that is actually a series of plagues that seems designed to transform humans into drones controlled by these non-human creatures with the ancient symbols that are grown into their bodies. Right?"

Gail and I nodded.

"On top of that," Jack went on, "there's yet another type of plague, a Control Plague or series of plagues, that seems designed to control or influence us to keep us from worrying about the gradual degradation of everything. Hell, that could even explain some of the societal degradation. Right?"

I nodded.

"Well, why hasn't anyone noticed this? The Control Plague stuff? The multiple plagues?" Jack had leaned back into his chair, sweating a bit and breathing a bit hard.

No-one else seemed inclined to answer, so I jumped in. "They have. Someone has seen all this. People in positions of power. Had to have. Can't miss it."

Everyone stared at me, with their jaws dropping to a greater or lesser extent. Having gotten their attention, I continued to press the point. "Still, what could anyone actually do about it? No-one seems to know where the plagues are coming from, just that Toronto appears to be ground zero for it all. Why here? There's nothing special about Toronto, the Mayor's boasting to the contrary. Hell, nothing special about Ontario or even Canada, if it comes to that. We're not major players on the world stage in any sense. Why here?"

Dixon was rubbing his face and head, wiping off the sweat that was building up. He shrugged off all offers of assistance, but did accept a glass of water that I gave him. Something was eating away at him. Something beginning to surface now that the effects of the Control Plagues were receding. In truth, though, everyone except Gail, Lee, and myself seemed to be a bit under the weather. Too much new information to process before the Control Plague had fully been flushed out of their systems.

Looking around, Gail insisted that we call it a night. After a token protest, everyone agreed that was the best course of action. I gave everyone a pair of pills for a second dose to be taken in the morning. Before coming over, I'd taken the time to fold paper into twisted packets for each pair of pills. Simple, sanitary, easy to dispense, and easy to store until the morning.

After a bit of discussion about what to do next, I suggested that everyone review the data and data analysis I had given them earlier. I pointed out that images of the ancient artifacts were on there as well, so they could take a look for themselves. Maybe they'd spot something.

We decided to keep in touch via email or text, and planned on getting together on the weekend. Those few days would give us time to get some of the DNA analysis results if nothing else. Getting together on the weekend would allow us to spend a couple of full days discussing things. Everyone agreed with that as a working plan, so we broke up and began heading home.

Stan, Jack, and Clio declined offers of assistance in cleaning up, insisting that we all go and get a proper night's sleep. Grant had come by car, and was feeling a lot better so he decided to leave by himself. That seemed a bit strange, since he and Dix normally drove together. Maybe they'd had a falling out. It wasn't my business, I figured. Grant was Dix's friend, and not someone that I knew well.

I offered to drive Dixon home, as he was still looking a bit under the weather. Ignoring his protests, I dragged him to the car as the girls and I left. We all tossed our gear into the back. The girls got into the rear seats, and Dix sat in the front passenger side.

We drove along in silence for a time, then I had to stop for a red light. Without warning, Dixon undid his seat belt, opened the door, and dashed out into the night. I yelled at him to come back, and almost ran out after him. Unfortunately, the light turned green and the car behind me began honking his horn. I leaned over to shut the door, and drove the car down the street and around the corner where Dixon had run. There was a subway entrance there, and I thought that I saw the top of Dixon's head go down the stairs. I drove just past the stairs, pulled over, and stopped. I went to undo my seat belt, when Lee put her hand on my shoulder and said in a quiet tone, "Let him go, Felix."

"Dammit, Lee, he's ill."

"He's well enough to run, Felix," said Gail calmly. "And he knew what he was doing. You know how stubborn he can be about doing stuff for himself."

She paused for a moment before adding, "Remind you of

anyone?"

I could hear her smile even without turning around. Ah, shit.

"Yeah, I guess you're right," I growled.

"You worry too much, old man," Lee said with friendly laughter in her voice.

"I worry about all of you, Lee. I worry about all of you."

With that, I checked for traffic, put the car in gear, and headed back to the apartment. It had been a long and productive day, and it didn't look like things were going to get any easier. To my amusement and disgust, I realized that it felt damned invigorating to be working on something with my friends. Like old times. Too bad it had to be about dealing with those fucking werewolves.

CHAPTER SIX
Something Old, Something New

The next day was a busy one for the three of us. We arrived at the ROM earlier than normal to get a head start on the day. Lee was able to spend a half-hour in Gail's lab helping us get the samples ready for shipping to Clio. She got the packaging assembled and labelled while Gail and I got the samples. Even arranged the necessary descriptive paperwork, laying it out for us to complete and affix to each sample. Even though she had to leave before we were done, it saved us a lot of time and hassle.

In the end, Gail decided to send along the organs she had extracted as well as the tissue samples meant for DNA analysis. I labelled the containers with the organs while Gail started on the paperwork, with explanations of why she was including them. She had to type those up an actual typewriter of all things. It seemed that's just the way those multi-part forms had to be filled out. I sneered at that until she pointed out that doing it this way avoided leaving an electronic trail. As penance for not figuring that out on my own, she had me make the coffee. Fair enough, I suppose.

After packing the samples, and adding some dry ice for cooling, Gail left to carry the package to Shipping. I would have done it, but that was the normal procedure and so less likely to raise unwanted questions. While she was doing that, I emailed Clio to let her know that the package was on its way, and that there were some extra organs in there for analysis. I wasn't specific, of course. Clio was smart enough to figure things out on her own.

Gail was gone somewhat longer than I expected, and I was beginning to get a bit worried. Finally I heard her voice in the hallway, followed by her laugh. The door opened and she came in smiling. A positive sign, I assumed.

She waved away my questioning look and headed straight for the coffee pot. After filling a mug she dropped into a chair with a sigh. Closing her eyes, she concentrated on the aroma of the coffee while taking appreciative sips. This went on for a minute before she opened her eyes, sat up, and returned to the here-and-now.

"Sorry, Felix—I needed that. I ran to the shipping room and caught the courier just before they left. Unfortunately my rushing had caught the attention of a couple of security guards, and they followed me out of curiosity. After I came out of the shipping office all out of breath, they insisted that I have a rest in their office which was just down the next corridor. They're good guys, and do like to make sure that everyone is taken care of. So there was nothing for it but to let them fuss over me. That led to a chat over a cup of coffee, and then they insisted on escorting me back here. There have been a few instances over the years of people needing assistance but being too proud to ask for it. It's a slow day for them, and they do mean well despite being a bit over-protective at times.

She chuckled with amusement for a moment, then she raised a finger as if remembering something. "Ah. Yes. Uhm, Felix, would you mind too much if I gave the guys some of your coffee? I know you don't have a lot left, but theirs is vile. Worse than anyone else's, actually. That's why I had to have some of yours to wash the taste of theirs out of my mouth."

I shrugged and said, "What's mine is yours, kiddo. You can give them the rest of it, if you like—there's only a couple more pot's worth. We have a bit more back at the apartment. Not much, though."

Gail pondered that for a moment. "OK, we'll give them the rest of what we have here. What's at the apartment we'll save for the weekend when we get together at Stan's. The others will enjoy it a lot, I think. You're still fine with tea, yes?"

I nodded. "Yeppers. At home I usually only drink coffee on the weekends, and tea the rest of the time." The mention of home gave me momentary pause and a sense of loss. My throat was in dire need of clearing, so to cover that up I got myself a cup of coffee. No sense in letting it go to waste.

Gail—bless her—chose to overlook my momentary weakness and said, "OK, that's settled. We'll ..."

The opening of the door interrupted her, as the head of Security—I couldn't remember his name—strode in.

"Oh, hello, Mr. Thansworth," said Gail in a friendly tone. "My friend Felix and I were just talking about your staff. We've got some extra coffee that Felix brought with him, and I was about to take it down to the Security Office."

Thansworth seemed taken aback. "I just came down to see if you were all right. A couple of the lads mentioned finding you on the run and out of breath. Thought I'd check on you myself to make sure everything was good."

Gail smiled and shook her head. "It was nothing, Mr. Thansworth. I was just rushing to get a box of samples out to the courier before he left. The samples I sent out the other day seem to have gotten misplaced or something, so I wanted to get the replacement samples out without delay. As for the breathlessness ..." She paused to make a wry face before replying, "I'm afraid that I'm getting a bit out of shape. Too much sitting around in the lab, I'm afraid."

She became a bit more serious. "Your men very kindly made sure that I was OK before letting me on my way. A professional way of ensuring that I really was OK and not trying to cover up something serious. And I appreciate that."

Thansworth harrumphed and muttered something about his men just doing their job.

Gail smiled at his mild embarrassment and added, "I couldn't help but notice that the coffee in your office is quite awful. Can't you get the cafeteria to give you anything better?"

Thansworth shrugged and turned up his hands, signalling that such things were out of his control.

Gail turned and filled a cup with coffee. She handed it to

Thansworth, saying only, "Try this."

He made a weak protest until the aroma hit him, and he stopped to take a careful sip. Followed by a larger swallow. An appreciative smile came to his lips, and he made a happy sigh. Frowning, he said, "Here, you can't have too much left of this excellent coffee. I really hate to take it from you. It is lovely stuff, I must say." He took another appreciative sip.

Gail just laughed, "Mr. Thansworth, please. You know that I'm always happy to share with you and your men. Look, there's enough here for a couple of pots. Please take it."

Thansworth looked first at her, then at me. I smiled and nodded. In truth I didn't mind. A policeman's lot was not a happy one, and a security guard's lot was usually even harder. The good ones were gold and made the world a better place, with little in way of thanks coming their way. This wasn't about that horrible tipping custom I'd seen since coming here—this was just one friend helping out another.

"Well, that is most generous of you, Dr. Andershank. And you too, Mr. Kurtsius."

Well how about that—he remembered my name. And pronounced it correctly, too.

I handed Thansworth the container with the coffee. "Keep the container. It has a proper seal on it and built-in moisture absorber. Should help keep your coffee fresh longer. Just air it out for an hour or so once a month, and that'll re-active the absorber. And don't keep your coffee in the fridge."

Gail had to laugh at that. "I'd listen to him, Mr. Thansworth. He gets deadly serious about his coffee. And his tea."

That got an honest smile out of Thansworth, and he gave a respectful nod of his head.

"Thank you both once again. I'll take this back to the office right away. The staff will appreciate this. It has been a while since I've been able to obtain decent coffee for them."

With that, he drained his cup and handed it to Gail. With a nod to both of us, he turned and left the office. We could hear the sound of his footsteps fading as he walked down the hall.

"What was that about not being able to get decent coffee?" I asked. "The cafeteria coffee isn't that bad."

Gail grimaced as she turned to wash out the mug in the sink. "Idiotic office politics, I'm afraid. A couple of years ago, some high-level manager got her nose out of joint for some reason, and decided that only the professional staff deserved decent coffee. Anyone else would just have to make do with something lesser. As a necessary cost-cutting measure, you understand. Petty and stupid. And embarrassing as hell. People started going out of their way to slip better coffee from the cafeteria to the non-professional staff. Management put the word out that anyone caught would be punished. For his part, Mr. Thansworth put the word out thanking people for their support, but not to take any more risks. And that was that, I'm afraid."

It was a refusal to put up with any more of that sort of crap that convinced me to take early retirement some years ago.

She finished washing the cup and hung it on the cup-tree to dry. Turning to face me, she asked, "You in the middle of anything?"

"Not so much," I replied. "Been busy helping you this morning. Was thinking of maybe looking at pictures of the other Priests and Drones at the farm, or maybe looking at the images of those artifacts again. Hadn't started anything, though. You need help with something?"

Gail nodded. "I do, indeed. There's more photographs to take, and you're a better photographer than I am. Not to mention that it would go better having another pair of hands to help. You OK with that?"

I sighed. Fascinating cadavers were one thing, but ooky bits and pieces were quite another. And heads on their own were just damned creepy.

"Sure. No problem. Let's finish our coffees and get started."

★ ★ ★

The photography session actually wasn't too bad. We had to pause a few times when I started gagging. Gail didn't mock me at all about it, which was kind of her. In the end, though, I was glad that I had toughed it out. After washing all the fragments, it became evident that there were a lot of those strange symbols for us to study. Gail had already tagged each fragment, so we could associate the DNA or symbol analysis with a specific fragment.

The symbols on each of the Priest heads were unique, and different from anything we had seen. In addition, a couple of the hands had new symbols on them. Those looked to be grown rather than carved, so we hypothesized that the hands were from Priests. Maybe the symbols indicated a different rank or sect. Impossible to tell for sure. So many questions and almost no answers.

Completing all that didn't take too long. It wasn't quite time to break for lunch, so Gail decided to stuff all the remains into proper body bags. I raised my eyebrows at that. She assured me that body bags got used for all sorts of creatures, not just humans. So we put the corpses each into their own bag, and the fragments into a third. All the bags went into the cooler. Such a lovely chore to do before lunch.

Gail suggested that we clean up, as by now it wasn't too far from lunch.

"What about the mess?" I asked, pointing around at the various puddles of ook and blah on the tables and floor.

She just shrugged like the hardened professional that she was, and suggested that we leave that until after lunch. That was fine with me, so we got cleaned up and went out to the office area. Gail called Lee using the internal telephone system. There was no answer, so I texted her. We sat in companionable silence for a couple of minutes, before being interrupted by the ringing of the phone.

It was Lee wondering if we were ready for lunch. We assured her that we were, and headed off to meet her at the cafeteria. We got there ahead of her, so we grabbed a table and waited. A waiter pounced on us almost as soon as we sat down, so we tried to put him off until Lee arrived. He suggested ordering now for all three of us, as they were running a bit low on the one decent sandwich available.

That was nice of him, so we ordered for ourselves and Lee. The busboy showed up with the buns. Lee showed up just after we'd finished ours, and were debating about splitting hers. We explained about ordering for her, and she agreed that we'd done the right thing.

She was a bit miffed that we'd almost grabbed her bun. And was not mollified when we pointed out that we'd only been debating about stealing it. "Only lusted after it in our minds," was how I put it. The waiter arrived with our sandwiches before a serious argument could erupt. With a final glare, Lee ate her bun before turning her attention to the sandwich.

The waiter hadn't steered us wrong at all. It turned out to be a nice smoked meat sandwich. A bit light on the meat, but there was almost enough for a decent meal. The coffee was more watered-down than usual. They had overcooked it to add extra flavour, so it all balanced out. More or less, I suppose. Anyway, it was all tasty enough to demand our complete attention. Aside from the occasional positive comment, we focused on the food until it was gone. There weren't any deserts available, which was a shame, though better for our waistlines.

With the meal completed, we settled back to sip on our coffee. The place hadn't filled up yet, so we didn't feel guilty about lounging there for a while. Keeping our voices low so as not to be overheard, we summarized our morning's work for Lee's benefit.

Lee replied, "I've been makin' printouts of the reconstructed fresco, as well as the individual fragments. It's really impressive to look at in full scale—was thinkin' that'd be a good project for us tonight. I'm going to be busy for the rest of the day finishin' off the image processin' work, and writin' it up for Manderpootz. On the plus side, there's a good chance that I could knock off work a bit early. How 'bout you guys?" Gail and I looked at each other and shrugged. In truth, aside from cleaning up the mess left by the autopsy, we had nothing planned.

I said, "I figured to work on building up an image database of the symbols we found on the specimens. Shouldn't take too long." Gail added, "My quick-and-dirty DNA analysis should be about done, and I want to take a look at that." By her attitude, however, she wasn't holding out much hope for getting any useful results out of that crude equipment.

Our musings were interrupted by the sound of Gail's phone buzzing away. She frowned, looked at it, then answered the call. Her initial surprise changed to delight, and she said something about taking it straight to the lab and that she'd be there right away. She ended the call and turned to us with a grin. "Got a priority courier shipment addressed to me. Looks like it might be from Clio."

Well, that was hopeful news, or at least had the potential for being interesting. We drained our coffee cups and headed out to our respective work areas, with a promise to text Lee with details of the shipment. When Gail and I arrived at her lab, there was a box sitting on one of the desks. It was roughly the size of laptop, and about a hand-width high. It was, indeed, from Clio. Gail opened it up with practised ease, and cooed at the sight of the contents.

I'd never seen her coo with delight before, and was curious to find out what had pleased her so much. It turned out to be a set of spares, plus a service manual, for her fancy DNA sequencer thingie. There was also a note from Clio saying that she hoped that these were the correct parts, and if not to let her know. Clio also added that she had enormous faith in my ability to swap out electronic modules designed to be easily replaced. And to do so without causing irreparable harm to a delicate and expensive scientific instrument. It sounded like Clio was feeling better.

With a smile, Gail handed me the box of parts and asked, "You up for this, Felix?" I grunted an affirmative before asking a question of my own. "You got any tools?" With a laugh she opened up a drawer in her desk and hauled out a small toolbox and handed it to me. I recognized it as one that I'd given her a few years back. It would have everything I would need. When I make a toolkit for a friend, I do it up right.

"OK, so where is the ..." I began. Gail pointed to a large cube over against the wall covered with an opaque plastic dust cover. I'd been wondering what it was—sometimes it never pays to ask questions.

"Let me know when you get to the calibration stage. There

are some standard solutions that I'll have to make up for you. Nothing fancy, though best to make them up fresh each time. I'll go do the cleanup of the autopsy area." With a wave she was gone.

I turned and walked up to my new adversary. My eyes narrowed into a steely glare. My expression was one of firmness and unwillingness to take any backtalk from anyone. When dealing with machinery of any kind, it was important that they realize that you were not to be trifled with. Never show fear. They could sense fear.

The first thing to do was to remove the dust cover, and to do it with care. It attracted dust, and would release it into the face of anyone foolish enough to touch it. It was one of their primary defence mechanisms. Once safely past that danger, I pulled the machine about a metre away from the wall so as to have easy access. Someone had left the power cord plugged into the wall socket.

Brilliant. Keep a broken machine plugged into the mains power so that all the power wobbles and spikes could keep hammering at the electronics inside and maybe cause some serious problems. Or a fire. I unplugged the cord and shook it at the machine. "Don't go messing with me, you no-good hunk of crap. I know Ohm's Law and I have a service manual. You will bend to my will." Like I said, you have to show them who's boss.

Which reminded me—I checked that the service manual was actually for this particular model, and was delighted to find that it was. It made things harder, and sometimes impossible, when the manual didn't match the machine being repaired. Clio, bless her, was no fool. Neither was I, which was why I flipped through the manual to get a feel for what sort of creature I was facing, comparing the pictures and descriptions with the machine in front of me.

That done, I began a visual inspection to make sure there was nothing obvious that needed attention, looking for signs of charring or damage. There were no obvious signs of trouble, so I opened up all outside flaps and began exposing all the innards. It was always a delight to see complex equipment unfold out of itself, like a hypercube expanding into normal space. Also an encouraging sign that it was designed for ease of service. I began going through the extensive checklist with high hopes that I might actually be able to do something useful here.

Time passed, and I guessed it to be about an hour judging from the stiffness in my back when I tried to sit upright. Attempting, and not quite succeeding, in keeping my groans of pain to a minimum, I got to my feet and walked around to get the kinks out. I turned around to find Gail standing there, holding out a cup of coffee.

"It's cafeteria coffee, I'm afraid," she said with a grimace.

"Most welcome, nonetheless. Thanks, Gail."

"So, any news about the patient?" she enquired.

"No obvious problems. Some spider webs and dust bunnies needed cleaning out. The next step is to plug it back it, run the internal diagnostics, then replace any fried components."

"Finish your coffee first. Need any help?"

"Nah. You might want to start making up those test solutions, though. Just in case I do get the sucker to work. That'll save some time."

"Smart idea. Anything else?"

"Hmm, come to think of it there is. How 'bout mailing those pictures of the extra symbols we found on the fragments to the rest of The Group? May as well keep them up to date."

"On it. You done with the coffee?"

I drained the cup and handed it back to her. Yeah, it was coffee. Of a sort. Guess I was going to have to get used to it. Or drink more tea—assuming I could find decent tea in this wretched city, hive of scum and villainy that it was. With a sigh I bent back to work. With any luck at all, this thing would be up and running inside of an hour.

To my surprise, it only took forty minutes to get the device running again. As Clio had suspected, her replacement boards and lamps were exactly what were required. Gail was delighted to find it working, and handed me the vials of the various test solutions. We decided to combine a few of the tests—the manual said it was OK to do that except when diagnosing specific issues. We loaded the required solutions into the machine, and started the test. The results came back in just a few minutes, and showed that the calibration was just a shade off on a couple of them.

Gail declared that her test solutions were sufficient for calibration purposes, so we told the machine to run its self-adjustment protocols. We ran the same samples again, this time with perfect results. We loaded in a different set of samples, and after a couple minutes the results came back indicating the machine was now completely functional.

Gail was almost giddy with excitement. She removed the calibration samples, and set the machine to do a flush cycle. "That takes about ten minutes," she explained. "Just enough time for me to get the sequencing samples ready."

As she worked she explained what she was doing. "The calibration solutions just test the basic operation. These samples are from known sources of DNA. That way we can compare the output of the machine to what we expect to see. In this case I'm going to jump the gun a bit and add some extra samples in addition to the test samples."

I interrupted with a grin. "You're adding samples from our specimens, aren't you?"

"Indeed I am," she answered with a broad smile. "It'll take hours to analyze just the verification samples. Which means letting it work overnight. So we might as well throw in some of our unknowns, too. It'll all be done by the time we get in tomorrow morning. By filling up the input tray, I can process about a third of our specimens. We can finish processing the rest of them tomorrow."

The machine let out a brief trilling sound to let us know that it was flushed and clean and ready for use. Gail picked up the tray with the samples, inserted it into the machine, then set the machine to work. After a brief self-check, it emitted a satisfied chime, and began chugging away doing its DNA analysis thing. I had glossed over that part of the manual—I'm a "stuff goes in, results come out" kinda guy.

Glancing up at the clock we could see that it was not quite an hour to go before quitting time. "To heck with it," said Gail. "We've done more than enough for one day. Lemme call Lee."

While she did that, I cleaned up the bits and pieces that I'd left lying about, and put the tools back into the case.

It turned out that Lee was ready to leave in five minutes or so, and would meet us here at the lab in ten. It actually took her less than that to get down. She barged through the door carrying an armful of cardboard tubes and binders. Those turned out to be three sets of the printouts she had mentioned at lunch. We decided to leave one set in the lab, and take two sets home with us—one for us, and one for The Group.

For ease of transportation we put the smaller printouts into our knapsacks, dividing the larger items between us. After wrapping them in plastic for protection, we headed out.

Just as we were about to turn off the lights and leave, Gail hurried back to her desk. Ignoring our enquiries, she grabbed a piece of paper and affixed it to the DNA sequencer. "Do Not Disturb—Working On Samples" it read. As we left, Gail explained. "It's been so long since that thing has worked, that Security or the cleaners will assume there's a problem if they see it on. This way they'll know that I left it on for a reason."

With that, we headed home for supper and an evening of looking at ancient symbols.

★ ★ ★

After a quick supper, we settled down to take a closer look at all Lee's images. As promised, it was incredible to see the life-sized pictures. The fresco alone was about two and half metres by one and a half metres in size. Lee had done an impressive job in stitching all the different images together to make a seamless whole. We rolled it out in the middle of the living room, and anchored the corners with books to keep it flat. Next, we placed photos of the various pieces around it, near where they were located in the fresco.

"I enlarged the pics of the pieces by about twenty percent," said Lee. "Thought about makin' 'em bigger, but that's the best I could do and carry everythin'." Gail and I agreed that she had made the correct decision. Spread out like this, it was manageable so long as we were careful where we stepped.

"Look, there," Gail pointed, "that's the symbol we found on

the Priest corpse. And located just next to it are the symbols we found on the hands and heads." I nodded absently, as my eyes were caught by a set of markings on the other side of the fresco. It looked familiar, but I just couldn't place it. Then it hit me.

"Oh, shit. No fucking way."

That got the attention of both girls.

"Dammit, Felix, what have I told you about your damn swearing?" Lee hissed. Gail nodded in agreement while frowning at me.

"Sorry, kids. I just figured out this set of markings over here, on the other side of the Priest symbols." I pointed to the area in question, and waggled my finger to show the specific area and draw their attention to it.

Their angry looks were replaced with puzzled ones.

"Not seeing it, Felix," murmured Gail.

I got down on my knees and traced it out, line by line.

"OK. Here's the part that looks like the letter 'J', it jogs a bit there, then swings up to make a funky 'U'. There's the line, more or less straight with a few bends, that crosses that horizontal one. Right?"

Their faces showed a vague possible recognition, though they still didn't quite see it.

"It's a map of the Toronto subway system."

Their faces cycled through "ah ha", disbelief, and finally dismissal.

"Oh, don't be silly, Felix," snorted Lee.

"Can't be," said Gail, shaking her head.

"Yeppers. It is. I've been studying the map in the subway car every trip we make these past few days, just to reacquaint myself with it. This is that map."

"Doesn't look like the map, Felix. It's too distorted," Lee said with a disapproving tone. "Obvious, even to you."

"That's 'cuz the fresco shows it at its true scale. The maps in the subway are representative only."

Gail interrupted us. "He may have a point."

We looked towards her. She had been tapping away at her laptop, and now swung it around to show us. It was an aerial view of Toronto, with the subway superimposed on it. It was a perfect match to the fresco. We proved it by measuring various points against each other, and all the ratios matched.

Lee was shaking her head, "What about all those extra lines coming off of the subway markings?" "Roads," said Gail pointing between the laptop and the fresco. "Thick lines for the subway. You can see thinner lines for Queen Street, King, and there's Dundas. There's a thin, vague line running close to the subway, and that's got to be Yonge. Holy, shit. Felix is on to something. Don't know what, exactly, but something."

I'd been studying the map on the laptop and the fresco, when something leapt out at me. "Hey, there seems to be a line from the Priest symbols over to the map section. There seems to be a line from each of those different symbols to different spots on the map." I pointed out what I was referring to, and the ladies began nodding.

"OK," said Lee, "What does that part of the map refer to?" "Green Belt," I replied with assurance. "See, each of the Priest symbols is linked to different spots in a rough line moving northward on the map? That's the Green Belt. And there's some faint other lines that seem to terminate within the City—bet those are ravines."

Both of the ladies studied for a minute, until Gail muttered, "I think he's right. We know that the werewolves control the ravine system that runs through Toronto, and that they use the Green Belt for movement throughout the GTA and beyond. Which begs the question, how does this old fresco thingie, or whatever it is, know that? Know about Toronto?"

Lee pointed at other features of the map part of the fresco. "And what about these extra bits? Oh wait, that part could be the Gardiner Expressway—yeah, leading off to Highway 404 and off the map. Hmm, OK, what about these lines here at the bottom? If those other lines represent the subway and major roads, what do these represent?"

I looked at the laptop again, then back at the map. No, that couldn't be right. Except that's what the map indicated. "Uhm, ladies, those few extra lines that extend south and into another complex network? That complex network is under Lake Ontario, and those few lines link the tunnels under Toronto to something under the lake."

We must have stood there, frozen in our varying poses for almost minute. With a whoosh of exhaled air, Gail straightened up and said in a brisk tone, "Right. Time for a drink." She walked to the kitchen, got three glasses, poured out a healthy measure of whiskey into each one, and passed them around. No-one said anything for several minutes. No-one chugged their drink—aside from the first large swallow.

"This is gettin' strange," murmured Lee. "This is gone *way* past strange, dearie," replied Gail.

"We're missing something. Something important," I said with a growl. Both ladies gave me puzzled looks. "Look, this fresco seems to tie all the different things together. We've found a link between the Priest symbols and what seems to be a map of Toronto." "And beyond, it would seem," interjected Lee.

"Ignore that for the moment," I entreated, "and focus on the big picture that the fresco seems to represent. Look up at the top of it. Are those the symbols that you were talking about a while ago during Net Night, Lee? See, up there." Lee took a couple steps, then squatted down to get a better look at the pics of the individual artifacts. After a minute she gave a satisfied nod, turned to me, and said, "Yah. I think you're right. Then if that's the case ..."

"If that's the case," interrupted Gail, "it's all tied together. The Change Plague, the different types of Change Plague, the Control Plagues, the werewolves and Priests, Toronto. Why Toronto? And how does Lake Ontario factor into all this? I mean, assuming we trust the fresco, then there's gotta be a reason for that. Something in the water? Nah—it gets tested several times each day. So what could be the reason?"

By this time her free hand was grabbing at her hair and starting to pull. She hadn't done that for many years, not since she was much younger and we had first met. "Gail?" I said in a gentle voice. "You gotta focus on your breathing, kiddo. Focus, please." "Huh? What?" She realized what she was doing, and dropped her hand from her hair with an embarrassed sigh.

"Sorry," she said. "This is all just so overwhelming, you know? I mean, sure, ancient horrors are rising up. So why is everything in the city so dirty and run down? The Control Plagues just make people accept things as they are, do the same old routines. Well, in Toronto that means keeping things clean. So why are things so dirty?"

A damn good question, and I was annoyed with myself for not thinking of it. We all looked at each other in silence for a space of a few heartbeats. In a flash it hit me. "Hey, could it be as simple as lack of money?" Both of them looked at me. Lee shook her head and said, "Don't think so, Felix. This is Toronto. Canada's biggest city. Financial centre of the country."

"Sure, but what about all those empty buildings?" interjected Gail. "And the reports of people leaving for parts of the country with less of a werewolf problem?"

"Why would they leave if the Control Plague keeps them in the same mental rut?" I asked. "Every disease has its natural immunes," said Gail. "Maybe those are the ones who left. Though would enough leave to make a difference?"

Lee had been following along with an intense look on her face. Wearing a frown of concentration, she added her own thoughts. "Depends on who left. If all the top talent leaves, that means that the second- and third-raters are left to take care of things."

That got me thinking. "What about the equipment required to maintain all those services? If things start to break down, there's a limited cadre of people who can fix things. Throw in problems with even getting spare parts, and the problem gets compounded. For manufacturers of any sort, for office buildings, as well as civic staff. What if all the services people are doing the best they can, but their equipment is failing faster than it can be fixed or replaced?"

"Oh, shit."

Gail and I turned to look at Lee. She was sitting bolt upright. "Uhm, guys, don't forget that all those civic services depend on City Council to decide on a budget. And what is it that Toronto City Council does better than anyone else in the country? Sitting on their asses and arguing without getting anything done."

We all looked at each other with shock. Was that all it took to reduce Canada's biggest city to ruin? Create an economic dislocation and program the most dysfunctional city council in the country for endless dithering and bickering?

"No, no," said Gail. "Toronto is too big to fail like that. So is Canada. Too big, too robust."

I shook my head as I answered, "No, it's not. We're seeing it happen. Everything is rusting out and beginning to fall apart. Even big, robust societies can decay from within if the correct pieces are attacked in the correct order. And that's what we're seeing now, I'm afraid. At some point we'll reach the point of no return, and it'll all fall apart beyond our ability to maintain or restore it."

That observation cast a definite pall over our little group.

Lee took the opportunity to change the subject. "OK, fine. So what do we do with this? I mean, this is all wild speculation, you realize." I took a slow sip of my drink before answering. "We write it up. We write up our observations and speculations and email it out to The Group. We're meeting in a couple of days, and we can hash it out more then. Someone will come up with a piece of information, or know someone. Whatever. We write it up and trust that we'll figure it out."

"Will we be able to figure it out in time?" asked Gail. Damn. I was hoping the girls wouldn't think about that part. No, not girls—grown women. Bright, courageous, and strong.

"Lee, how 'bout you write this up in summary form? Gail, you help her with that. Send it out as an email blast. I'll clean this up—we're done for the night. Get some rest, and we'll go at it fresh in the morning. OK?"

Reluctant as we were to stop at this point, this was a marathon, not a sprint. The ladies were experienced enough to know that, so they swallowed their disappointment—washed down with the last of their drinks—and went about their assigned tasks.

Less than a half hour later we were in our beds trying to get some sleep. I don't know about the others, but my own dreams were filled with visions of ancient artifacts and memories of snarling visages. Not the most restful sleep I've ever had.

CHAPTER SEVEN
Tumbling Into the Double Helix

We all woke up at the crack of dawn, which was a bit unusual. Everyone was a bit groggy from the lack of restful sleep, so we decided to make a large breakfast. I was about to make a pot of tea, when Lee suggested that we use some of our diminishing supply of good coffee. No-one argued, so I started that brewing. "Only another couple pot's worth of decent coffee left," I noted, yawning. "More if we cut it with that crappy stuff you've been using."

That got a grumpy mumble from both of the ladies. Their early rising to the contrary, neither of them were morning people. I sympathized with them, but had more practise at waking up early. The past few years had drilled that into me. Being the most awake one, I made breakfast. It was a scrambled-together whatnot of meat and potatoes, with a little onion tossed in for taste. Hearty fare that would be good for what ailed us.

Neither of the ladies grumbled about excess calories as I heaped their plates. That would come later when they they were awake enough to feel guilty about eating so much. I'd always had problems convincing them that breakfast was the most important meal of the day.

My own share was somewhat smaller than theirs—hey, I'm an old man and don't eat as much as I used to. After gobbling it down, I took first crack at the bathroom. A shower and a shave left me feeling a lot less dreary and draggy, and quite looking forward to a cup of coffee. When I got to the kitchen, the ladies got up and hustled out to the bedroom to begin their own cleansing rituals.

It turned out that the somewhat guilty look on their faces wasn't due to the volume of food they'd eaten—they'd drained most of the coffee. Wretched creatures. At least they'd left me an almost-full mug of it. About all I'd wanted, to tell the truth, though I'd never tell them that. Some things were better left unsaid.

To save some time, and to give myself something to do, I wandered about sipping coffee and getting my own gear together for the trip to work. Well, their work. I chided myself for slipping into old habits like a silly old man.

That task didn't take too long. So while the ladies were still getting themselves ready, I amused myself by leafing through the sheaf of pictures of the individual artifacts. Some of them were tickling a remembrance that I couldn't quite dig out. They had evoked the same feeling from me last night, but had gotten lost in the excitement of the new discoveries.

A sudden realization caused me to slap my forehead. Stupid old man—these were the plague cycles that Lee had mentioned to me, ages ago before I had to leave the farm. Well, days actually. It just seemed like ages.

I put those to one side and shuffled through until I found the small picture of the entire fresco. Yep, there everything was—Priest symbols on the bottom left, map on the bottom right, and these plague cycle curves on the top left. There was a bunch of stuff filling up the rest of the fresco—maybe words? Worth asking Lee about, anyway.

At that point the ladies emerged ready to do battle with the working world, and began putting together their own knapsacks of stuff. I interrupted them to point out what I'd found. Both of them were aghast at failing to notice those curves themselves.

"Don't beat yourselves up too much," I pointed out. "We've been hit with a lot of information in a short time. And been recovering from that damned Control Plague or whatever it was. This still needs to be looked at. Maybe Gail and I could take a detailed look at it after we get to work. Lee, maybe you could see if you can find out more about that writing, or whatever it is."

Gail was chewing the inside of her lip as she studied the photos, and gave a sharp nod. Lee grunted assent, then mentioned that she was seeing Manderpootz that morning. Perhaps he could shed some light on that stuff.

Looking up from the pictures, Gail said, "As we travel to work today, it might be best not to discuss any of this, hmm? Too many ears around, and we don't want to make waves and call attention to ourselves."

That made a lot of sense, and we made the trip to the ROM in relative silence. I was beginning to feel like a conspirator of some sort. I bided my time by looking around at everyone in the subway car, trying hard to be casual about it—and felt like a total fool. After a little of that, I sighed, closed my eyes, and sat in a meditative state until our stop came up. Just like a regular city dweller.

We made a somber little group as we walked to the ROM and through the various security checkpoints. Even the security guards noted that the ladies were less than their usual cheerful self. No-one remarked about me. I guess that a grumpy old man isn't that unusual in these parts. Or was it just me? Now that was something to ponder.

After getting through all the checkpoints we went our separate ways, agreeing to meet for lunch. Gail and I headed down to her lab. The sight of her DNA machine thingie signalling that it had completed its run cheered her up quite a bit. It turned out that we'd forgotten to hook the machine into the network and get it synced to her computer. She downloaded the results onto a data key, loaded that onto her computer, and immediately became absorbed in the results.

So much for her help in examining the photographs of the artifacts. Oh, well. With a shrug and a smile I set myself up to work at another desk. Before starting, I made a pot of tea. There was no way I was going to work without caffeine, and was adamant about not drinking the dreck that passed for coffee around here. Not after consuming the real stuff for breakfast.

When it was ready, I poured a cup for each of us. Gail uttered a soft grunt that I took for gratitude when I gave her the cup. She was well into whatever it was the data was telling her. It looked like gibberish to me. But then, specialist data often looked like gibberish to anyone not versed in the arcane lore of that field of study.

My phone buzzed for attention—a message of some sort had arrived. Fishing the phone out of my pocket, I discovered that it was from Lee. It seemed that Manderpootz was giving an impromptu lecture on the artifacts and fresco, and I should attend. She gave me the room number, and said to get there on the double.

I told Gail about it. She refused to leave her analysis. When I asked her where the room was, she made vague motions with her hand before returning to her work. I would have to find it on my own, so off I went. I almost took along the photos before remembering that I wasn't supposed to have them. Instead, I took a laptop and a paper notepad. Gotta look the part if you're going to be wandering around.

I wandered down the hall towards the elevators. I knew where those were, and knew that I had to go up a couple of floors. Along the way I ran into Mr. Thansworth, and before he could ask me what I was doing, I asked how to get to the meeting room. I explained that Lee had summoned me to a conference, but forgot to explain exactly where the room was.

It was a darned good thing that I had asked for directions. The room was located in one of those out-of-the-way sections that only staff go to. After thanking him, I hurried off heading deeper into the maze of corridors. Soon I came to yet another set of elevators. These were an older set, left over from a time when the building was new. They were now used only by staff who had been around long enough to learn the secret ways—sort of like The Knowledge of London's cabbies.

I got to the meeting room with no trouble. There was a small crowd gathered around a stocky older gentleman. He stood before a large whiteboard, gesturing and talking at moderate volume. I saw Lee standing at the rear of the room, befitting her lack of advanced degrees, and casually walked in to stand beside her. She turned to give me a nod of greeting. Motioning with her chin towards the front of the room she whispered, "Professor Manderpootz." I noticed the careful use of his honorific.

Even though her voice was almost inaudible, a couple of heads turned to see who was being so crass as to speak. Then Manderpootz himself pointed at me and demanded to know who I was.

Sigh. Lovely.

"Felix Kurtsius, Professor."

He frowned and said with some irritation, "No, no. I want to know *who* you are. What you are doing here."

There was something in the tone of his voice that raised my hackles and set my teeth on edge. A voice thick with privilege and self-importance, or so it seemed to me. Though it had some years since I had dealt with his noxious kind, I remembered the drill. I arranged my face into the proper aspect of hopeful gratitude.

"My apologies, Professor. I'm a field investigator. I brought in some samples for Dr. Andershank to study. She suggested that you were the best man to talk to about some of the things I've seen. When she heard about this discussion group, she insisted that I shouldn't pass up this opportunity."

A few heads nodded at the mention of Gail's name. She had an excellent reputation, and specialist degrees up the yingyang. Manderpootz gave a disparaging "humph" and stared at me for a few seconds. When I failed to wilt under his gaze, he dismissed me from his attention and continued speaking.

Just as well, since I wouldn't want to explain exactly what those samples, nor what those things I'd seen, were. When all eyes were pointed away from me, Lee gave me a small smile and a nod.

Lee had been correct the other day in her assessment of him. Pompous prick though he was, he did seem to know his stuff and had everyone's rapt attention. Shortly after I arrived, he rather imperiously called upon Lee to set up his laptop to project pictures onto the whiteboard. After she finished, her only thanks was a dismissive wave, and she returned to the rear of the room. Just for a moment she laid a restraining hand on my arm. Hell, I wasn't going to say or do anything. Even managed to keep my face from showing what I was thinking.

Tamping down my anger at his treatment of my friend caused me to miss the first few explanations of some of the fragments. My focus snapped back when he brought up an image of the fresco. He dismissed the lower half of the fresco as being a mere backdrop for the important story told by the upper part. The only other scholar who had examined the fragments, some decades ago, suggested that they were probably invocations to deities. Although Manderpootz had some doubts about that interpretation, he was inclined to agree that that they were of little consequence.

After that brief interlude, he got down to discussing the upper part in detail. What I knew to be plague cycle curves, he described as "cycles of life" related to the deterioration and downfall of the civilization. The other markings he explained as descriptive text that he had only begun decoding. Because this civilization was so ancient and little-studied, little was known of their writing system.

Still, after many years of study Manderpootz had managed to understand much of it. This latest fresco was the most complete artifact ever found of that civilization. As such, it afforded a unique opportunity for their department. Under his direction, of course. Oh, this was all presented in a proper academic manner, but there was a certain amount of self-promoting "blah blah" in his explanation. Even so, it was interesting all the same.

The fresco, he claimed, was a description of how Armageddon had been visited upon a once-mighty civilization. Several waves of evil had been visited upon the inhabitants, and had almost destroyed it. One final wave had been yet to arrive, and the ruler decreed that a record be made before the final doom came upon them. There was something about blood and plagues yet to come, a future time when something would arise or come about, and a final doom visited upon Mankind.

Manderpootz pointed out that plagues were a fact of life back then, and isolated societies often considered themselves to be the centre of humanity. His interpretation of the text was, of necessity, rough and incomplete, however the sense of it was clear. He pointed to a section at the top, which he said had been added by a later civilization. Although the writing was in a well-known form of Sumerian, there was no way to identify which civilization had added it. The text spoke of a great doom that fell upon those who failed to placate the gods.

What was curious, however, was the mention of "gods" in the Sumerian script. It was a form of the word that didn't relate to any of the Sumerian deities, so it was unclear what was being referred to. There were some glyphs linking down to the original text, towards the "something that would arise" text. One possible interpretation of that text might be "God above gods" or "True God". Manderpootz took pains to point out that all this was somewhat preliminary, and again emphasized what a unique opportunity this presented to their department.

With that, the lecture appeared to be over, and the crowd gave the professor an enthusiastic round of applause. Both Lee and I joined in. For myself, I was somewhat overwhelmed by the data dump I'd just experienced. What worried me were the similarities between the ancient dooms and the Change Plagues. And that mention of "final doom" was a touch frightening.

"What did you think, Felix?" asked Lee, keeping her voice down. "Fascinatin' stuff for sure."

"We're going to have to give this a good, hard think," I replied, taking equal care to keep my voice low. Not, it would seem, careful enough.

A loud, cultured voice intruded upon us. "I am delighted that you were so enraptured by the tale I told. Please tell me, Mr. Kurtsius, what were these strange things that young Dr. Andershank felt you would need my help with?"

Ah, shit shit shit. He had got a room full of sycophants, and he focused on me and my dodgy story. My old disciplines kept my face from reflecting my inner turmoil.

"Thank you for the opportunity to hear this lecture, Professor Manderpootz," I said, without having to lie or exaggerate. "I am curious, though, about why you were so dismissive of the lower portion of the fresco. You suggested that it was an invocation of their deities, and I couldn't help wondering if it was somehow related to that True God that you mentioned."

Manderpootz puffed out his cheeks before replying. He seemed torn between a chance to show off his expertise and curiosity about me. Vanity won, of course.

"Well, yes, of course I gave the abridged version of my studies," he said, puffing out his chest a bit. "There are indications—only the merest hints, you understand—of a connection of the sort that you refer to. Miss Neilan, here, is assisting me in the painstaking and exacting process of image enhancement of the artifacts. Under my guidance, of course. This here ..." he gestured towards the image on the whiteboard, "is just a preliminary workup. I feel that it is of the utmost importance to share information at every stage of an investigation. Advancement of our knowledge is a team effort these days."

He paused, gave me an appraising look, and enquired in a silky voice, "Which brings us to yourself, Mr. Kurtsius. What information do you have for me today?"

Crap. On a stick. Sideways.

"Well, Professor, I hate to bring what might be speculation to you. I've heard reports of symbols being associated with the Changed. Symbols that sound somewhat like those in the bottom part of your fresco." I didn't have to feign reluctance in speaking about this—I'd have to tread with care.

The professor leaned in towards me, his eyes boring into mine. I could smell his breakfast on his breath—top-quality sausage and eggs. "What sorts of reports, exactly, have you heard?" he asked with an edge to his voice.

He was getting rather more into my personal space than I was comfortable with, forcing me to lean back a bit before replying. "Uhm, nothing definitive, sir. No photographs. Just verbal descriptions of transitory encounters. Some of the described symbols sounded similar to those in the lower left quadrant of your fresco. Sir."

Manderpootz leaned back, and regarded me with a neutral

gaze. "These ... descriptions, as you call them. From where do they come?"

"Up north. Algonquin Park area. Most of the reports seem to come from campers who were canoeing. A couple reports from trappers in the Chochrane area."

"Were there any other observations associated with these reports? Strange lights or smells or anything of that sort?"

"No, Professor, just the visual sightings."

He seemed to relax at that, which was interesting. I'd taken care to mention areas far away from, and having no connection with, the Great Lakes, much less Lake Ontario. The bastard knew more than he was telling. And why had he asked about lights and smells?

"Interesting, but I'm sure that it is all coincidence. Many cultures, including Native American aboriginals, have symbologies that to a lay-person could be mistaken for such as these." He pointed at the image of the fresco.

"I'm sure that you are correct, Professor. Still, it always pays to consult with the experts about such things. For confirmation." I applied the very best butter.

"Yes, yes. Well, you have your answer," he said in an absent-minded tone as he dismissed me with a wave of his hand. With that, he turned on his heels and walked out of the room without saying a word to anyone. His adoring fans, realizing that the show was over, went back to their sad little lives. Some even favoured us with nasty looks. Cool.

After everyone had left, I helped Lee pack up the equipment. There wasn't all that to do, mind you. I just needed something mindless to occupy myself while I calmed down. Lee's eyes were twinkling as she worked. She knew all too well what sort of reaction I had to that sort of high-handed treatment.

"Pretty good, even if you are out of practice," she murmured, trying hard not to laugh.

"Damn good," I growled. "You shouldn't let that asshole treat you that way, Lee."

She paused and sighed. "Yeah. But he has important friends. Friends who would be happy to see to the dismissal of anyone who annoyed their pet." Then she slapped my arm hard enough to sting.

"And don't you go callin' him names, Felix Kurtsius. He's a damn fine researcher—they all are. As individuals, each and every one of them is good people." Then she signed again, this time more deeply. "But get them together in a group and...well, you saw it for yourself. They puff themselves up tryin' to outdo each other, and barely tolerate any not of the tribe. Worse, they sometimes come up with some silly scheme or other that grabs the attention of the group. When that happens, they develop a bad case of group-think and a laser-like focus on the goal. On the other hand, they've done a lot of good work, so management tolerates their occasional bouts of foolishness. Support staff like myself learn to put our heads down and get on with the job. Not much else we can do."

I sighed. I did, indeed, know all too well what it was like to have to suck it up to keep a job. Developed the ulcers and twitches to prove it, too, until living at the farm cured those. Thinking about the farm gave me something of a sad chill in my bones. Guess it must have shown on my face, because Lee asked what was the matter.

"Ah, nothing. Just got thinking about how lucky I was to escape garbage like that by moving to the farm. Now the farm's gone, and I'm back putting up with crap again. I'll be fine."

Lee gave my arm a squeeze. "We'll get your farm back, Felix. Though in the meantime, I love havin' you around again. Like old times. Good times." "Good times," I agreed, clearing my throat. "Hey, I need to get back to Gail and see how she's doing. Meet at the cafeteria just as it opens for lunch?" "Sounds like a plan, old man. See you guys later."

With that, we went our separate ways.

★ ★ ★

I arrived at Gail's lab to find her pacing to and fro. As I walked through the door, her head jerked up and she rushed over to intercept me. Grabbing me by the arm, she dragged me over to her computer. "Damn, am I glad to see you, Felix. I was about ready to explode. How did the lecture go? Wonderful. Now take a look at what I found."

Gail twisted my shoulders, forcing me to face her monitor. She stepped to one side with her arms wrapped around herself. I peered at a screen showing a bunch of dabs of varying shades of gray. It looked like the sort of DNA chart seen in crime shows. Off to the right of it was a bunch of characters separated by dashes—I figured it was the DNA genome analysis. Impressive enough, but meaningless.

"Well, Gail, it looks ... uhm ... interesting," I managed to get out after staring politely at the screen for a few seconds. "Oh for fuck's sake, old man, it's fucking obvious," she spat out. After a moment she gave a deep sigh, lowered her head in embarrassment, and gave it a shake. "I'm sorry, Felix. You wouldn't understand this stuff, of course. Sorry for snapping at you like that."

Taken aback by her cursing, I smiled and patted her shoulder. "S'ok, kiddo. I gather this is important stuff or you wouldn't be excited about it. Let's grab a cup of tea, sit down, and you can give me the executive overview of it. Preferably in words of one syllable or less."

She snorted with amusement and nodded. We grabbed mugs of tea and sat down in front of her computer. We sat for a bit in companionable silence, while Gail mellowed out her calm and arranged her thoughts.

"OK, Felix, you know what DNA is, right?"

I gave her a dirty look.

She had the grace to blush. "Sorry, too basic. Alright, a basic DNA analysis allows us to see if, for example, a specific suspect left a trace sample at crime scene, or to test paternity, that sort of thing. That's the set of blobs on the left-hand side of the screen." She pointed at the monitor.

"The stuff on the right-hand side is the analysis of the entire genome. The detailed coding of the DNA."

I nodded. That much I knew from newspaper and magazine articles.

She pointed to the bottom of the screen. "That down there is a summary of all the samples that we analyzed overnight. Notice anything?" They all looked about the same, and I said as much.

"Exactly. Those are the results from each of the different Priest samples we have. They are all close—almost identical. Not quite, though, and in a strange way. Each has a different mother, but an identical father. Given that, we should be seeing a lot more variation between them. For these Priests, though, it's like the mother's contribution was minimized."

That startled me. "That can't happen. Can it?"

Gail replied in a sharp tone, "No, it can't. And yet it has. They're not clones, just the next best thing to it."

"How would that even be done?" I asked.

She puffed out her cheeks and made a sound of annoyance. "Damned if I know. What it looks like, is that they took eggs from different women, sperm from a single donor, and somehow used the eggs as an all-but-blank canvas upon which to express the sperm donor's DNA. Beyond that, I can't even hazard a guess. This isn't something that I've ever heard about, even in whispers."

I pondered that for a moment. "That all kinda fits, in a weird sort of way. The Change Plague, or rather the series of them, indicates a scary-advanced knowledge of genetic tinkering. One that has been getting more refined over the last few years. On top of that, there's the Control Plagues, which also point to advanced biotech knowledge. This near-clone stuff just sort of fits in with that, don't you think?"

Gail nodded, wrapping her arms around herself before speaking. "That's what has me worried. This level of genetic knowledge and manipulation is way beyond what we have—movies and paranoid fiction to the contrary. Orders of magnitude beyond. This isn't some biohacker geek, or even group of geeks, tinkering in a basement lab. This isn't university lab stuff. This would involve a major—a *huge*—research effort over many, many years. This is large industrial nation stuff, and the willingness to use up people like we use lab rats. It means several human generations worth of effort, at a minimum. Efforts of that magnitude, over that length of time, leave traces. Or at the very least, whispers. Like the Manhattan Project had, and this sort of effort is way beyond that in scope and time-scale."

106

I nodded at her reference to the Manhattan Project. It was something that I actually knew something about. Not first hand, of course—I wasn't that old. The Manhattan Project was the effort of the United States to produce their first atomic weapon—which meant producing fissionable material and researching how best to utilize it. A huge project eating up tremendous amounts of physical space, resources, and trained people. There were lots of leaks, but those were tamped down to mere whispers and vague rumours. Today, what with the Internet and even modestly open government data, that sort of effort would stand out like a sore thumb. If only as a black hole where resources were consumed.

"Hmm, hidden over generations you say. Uhm, how about, say, North Korea? They've been isolated for generations and have no problems using people like expendable lab animals." Gail shook her head. "No. They haven't had the tech to do this sort of thing over a multi-generation time period. No-one has, Felix. And that has me scared."

She was shivering by this point, so I put my arm around her shoulder. She turned and embraced me, squeezing hard, as if to somehow block out the fear she was feeling. Her breathing was rapid and ragged. After a bit her breathing evened out and she stopped holding on to me like a drowning person. She stepped back to wipe at her eyes before turning away to blow her nose. Damn—I'd never seen her rattled like this before.

In an attempt to bring the moment back to something approaching normal, I asked, "What about the other samples? You said there were still more to run." After giving her nose a final wipe, Gail turned to face me. "Already percolating in the machine. Should have them before quitting time."

I nodded and gave a soft, approving grunt. "Do we still need Clio's labs to do this analysis?" "Oh, yes," she said, with an enthusiastic nod. "That'll give me an independent check on my results. And their equipment will give more accurate results. Our calibration is still a bit off."

I made a dismayed sound, and apologized. "No, no," Gail was quick to interject, "you did everything right. These fine-tuning calibrations are done in several passes over several days to dial everything in. No, you did a great job for the amount of time you had to work on it. And it is more than accurate enough for the quick-look I wanted. Clio's labs, though, are certified for medical and forensic analysis, which means that their equipment is as close to perfect as it is possible to get."

At that moment, my phone buzzed an alert. Oh, yeah—I'd set the timer to go off just before lunch so we wouldn't forget. "Oh, hey. Lee and I arranged to meet for lunch just as the cafeteria opened. Should get a better choice of food by being first in line. Shall we boogie?"

Gail laughed and agreed that lunch sounded like a fine idea, so off we went.

★ ★ ★

We got to the cafeteria about a minute after it opened. Lee was waiting at the entrance, allowing us to go in as a group. The place was about one third filled, giving us our pick of tables. In a repeat of the previous lunch, the waiter told us which sandwich choice was the best, and without hesitation we agreed with him.

While waiting for our order, we munched our dinner rolls in silence. It was all quite lovely until we were told that there was no coffee, only tea. That wasn't a hardship for us at all, though some of the other diners weren't so understanding. I saw it as yet another indicator of a crumbling social infrastructure having problems delivering foodstuffs. Not that I mentioned this at the table—that was a topic to be discussed in private.

While waiting for our food, Lee filled us in on what she'd been doing since the lecture earlier this morning. Turns out that the great and wonderful Professor Manderpootz was in a bit of a humour afterwards, growling and barking orders to everyone in his vicinity. He wanted special attention paid to the individual artifacts, in hopes that image enhancement would reveal more details.

"Enhancin' noise just leaves noise," explained Lee. "Or worse, the illusion of new information. Manderpootz, for all his bluster, is quite aware of that. Oscillated between hope and despair for over an hour before he threw up his hands and stomped off in a huff. It turns out that the pictures we've been looking at are about the best we're goin' to see. Those artifacts are just too old for anythin' better."

"Did you try ..." I began. "Yep, yep, yep, and that other one too," Lee said with a smile. "I do this for a livin', old man. And you're the one who got me started in this stuff. I've gone back to basics, done the fancy stuff, and even tried the wacky far-out stuff. It is what it is. The latest enhancements are a bit better for a few of the artifacts, but nothin' to write home about."

After our sandwiches and tea arrived, we focused on slaking our appetites. I waited until Lee was taking a sip of tea before casually asking, "Ah, well, I assume you've done the standard x-ray fluoroscopic images of the artifacts. You know—the basic stuff."

It warmed my heart to know that I could still make her snort tea out of her nose. Gail must have seen the look in my eyes, because she made sure that she finished swallowing before I spoke. The two of us sat in amused silence as Lee used her napkin to clean herself and blow her nose. The waiter hurried over to make sure everything was all right. I assured him that it was, before adding, "You can dress her up, but you can't take her anywhere." He left, smiling.

"You are an evil old man," Lee hissed, trying hard not to smile. "That I am, and don't you forget it. I gather that it was a good question?" "A most excellent question, actually," Lee said in a far-away voice as she drummed her fingers on the tabletop. "Asked it m'self, too. Manderpootz hummed and hawed, and implied without actually sayin', that it had been done or was waitin' to be done. 'Sides, I was pulled into his project at the last minute and he rushed me along with the standard camera-image analysis and I plain forgot about the x-ray analysis. Hmm ..."

Gail and I exchanged an amused glance as our friend became lost in her internal world. "Earth to Lee," whispered Gail, leaning in to wave her hand in front of Lee's face. Lee batted her hand as if brushing away an annoying insect. "That x-ray analysis. It should have been done already. Manderpootz always does it first thing. Always. Except this time. Very strange."

The cafeteria was filling up faster than normal. I guess people had figured out that the early bird got the tastier worm. The waiter caught my eye and glanced at his watch. I smiled and nodded. It was time to go, so we got up and headed back to our respective duties.

As we walked out Gail turned to Lee, "Oh, we never did tell you about the data I've uncovered." Lee just muttered, "Later. Tell me later." Her mind was focused on a puzzle, and nothing was important enough to impinge on that. Gail sighed and shrugged. She didn't take any offence, since that would be like the pot calling the kettle black. We went our separate ways in silence.

Back at the lab, Gail checked her DNA analyzer. It still had a couple of hours left to go. With a sigh she headed back to her computer and called me over when she saw that she had a couple of emails. One was from Clio, and the other was from Grant. Both were encrypted with keys that the Group used, which was interesting.

Gail had problems recalling the different encryption keys. Good thing I knew them off by heart. Both emails used our second level of encryption—just above basic, but not too secret. Clio wanted to know if Gail mixed up or contaminated the samples—they were almost identical and there was something strange about them. Gail uttered a short, sharp laugh before sending off a reply stating that there was no contamination.

"That seems a bit terse," I said after reading it. She replied with a smile, "The puzzlement will do Clio's soul good." I declined to enquire further. Some things were best not poked into by mortal man.

As for Grant, he said that he and Dix and been working on the fresco images. They'd have some neat stuff to show us all at the next meeting, and that we should all prepare to be amazed.

Well, with any luck Gail and I would be able to trump that. For some reason she seemed rather pleased about the prospect. I tried to tell her that pride goes before a fall. Her sharp response was, "Don't harsh my vibe, Felix. We rule, they drool." I had forgotten how competitive Gail could get, and wasn't sure whether to be pleased or concerned. Decided to opt for the former.

To divert her, I asked why the Change Plague, and its variants, only seemed to affect such a small percentage of the population. Was there some genetic component to the infection? That put her into full-on researcher mode.

Turned out there had been some discussion amongst local researchers about that very topic, and opinion was divided. The problem was that the Change Plague seemed to modify itself as soon as it infected a host, so no treatment or vaccine could be developed. What we needed, Gail surmised, was access to the base virus used to create all the different plagues.

"Hold on," I said. "Are you saying that there is a single source for all these different plagues?"

"Has to be," she replied. "The odds of a brand new virus being developed each year are so low as to be impossible. No, in all probability it is the same base virus being modified. In fact, I suspect that the overall infection rates are constant."

I pulled up the infection-rate data that Dix had supplied me. Sure enough, I had missed that little detail. Although the infection rate in any given week or month had considerable variation, the overall yearly numbers were about the same. Score one for Gail and her expert intuition.

"Oh, well done, Mistress of Biology," I intoned. "How does that help us?" She just grinned and said, "What that means, Mister Nerd-boy, is that only specific people are at risk from the various plagues. And that there is in all likelihood a genetic component to the probability of becoming infected."

I grinned back for a moment before becoming serious again. "So how does an eons old fresco predict multiple Change Plagues, not to mention a very accurate representation of the rate of infection for each variant?"

Gail just blinked at me for the space of several heartbeats. Her vacant look indicated that she was focused on the problem. After a minute her gaze shifted back to me. "For that to happen, the specific genetic component limiting the spread of the various Plagues here and now must have been affecting the spread of it back then—whenever 'then' was."

Oh. My.

"Uhm, Gail, does this mean that what determines who gets infected here and now depends on if their ancestors came from that ancient civilization?" She nodded, although she seemed a bit stunned by the realization.

"And—oh, let's just blue sky this—after all this time that particular genome is going to have spread thither and yon, not just Europe and North America, right?" She nodded.

"Which means that a wider range of infection is just a matter of time, right?" Again, she nodded.

"Which means that unless we can find a cure, this latest variant of the Change Plague is going to spread world-wide, right?" She nodded, but her expression was glum. That changed as something occurred to her. "Maybe we can find the cure by finding out the genetic markers targeted by the Change Plagues. So how do we go about doing that?"

She began musing to herself. After a few seconds she turned to me, and with an evil grin said, "Give me your blood, Felix."

"EXCUSE ME?"

She replied in an annoyed tone, "Just a sample, you idiot. You've been swimming in werewolves since the beginning. If there was any chance of getting infected, you would have by now."

"Hey, maybe it's because the plague is fragile. I've got UV lights all over, and have always been careful about disinfecting after coming into contact with the wolves. And I eat a lot of garlic and onions."

"Just roll up your sleeve. I need a sample for analysis. No, just hold still, damn it. Maybe by comparing the DNA of the infected with someone who can't get infected, I can figure out what the target group is. Gimme the sample and I can have it analyzed in a few hours."

I rolled up my sleeve, none too happy about this. "What about getting other exemplars?" I asked.

Gail just grabbed my arm and inserted a small hypodermic into it. Blood oozed out and she drew back the plunger to get more. Removing the hypodermic, she squirted the sample into several vials and added a solution of something or other to all except one. After finishing with me, she extracted a sample from herself and processed it in a similar fashion. "OK, this should be done before we leave today."

I was about to complain about the trauma inflicted upon my poor body, when the door burst open and Lee ran in.

"That worthless little shit was holdin' out on me, but I found it," she exclaimed in triumph.

Gail and I looked at each other. This was unlikely to end well.

"Lee, honey, what did you find. And how?" I enquired, although I was beginning to get a bad feeling about this.

"Manderpootz. He always does the x-ray analysis of his samples, Always. Except this time he didn't tell me about it. Didn't mention it at all. So I looked, and found the images, and have been enhancin' them. That stupid putz was trying to do it on his own and gettin' nowhere. So I did it. Analyzed the images, I mean. You'll wanna see this."

With that, she went to Gail's computer, plugged in a data key, and began typing.

Gail glanced at me in surprise. Turning back to Lee, in a calm, quiet voice she asked, "Hey, Lee. Did you just break in to a senior researcher's computer and take his research without authorization?"

Lee just nodded. "Yeah, yeah. Just wait till you see what I've found."

Enough was enough, and I had to say something. "Lee, if you get found out, you'll get fired."

Lee kept typing away, and images began appearing on the screen.

"Lee. Stop."

She stopped typing and turned to me. "Dammit, Felix, I know what I'm doin'. I know what I did." She turned to Gail. "Yes, I'm going to get fired over this. The world is going to end, and real damned soon, and I want to know why."

She turned to the screen and pointed at it. "Take a look."

It looked like the fresco, except with lines of various colours threaded through it. "Very pretty, Lee. What are we looking at?" asked Gail.

"It's all in different colours," said Lee. "That means different material densities. Whoever made the fresco went to the trouble to make the different features out of different materials. Look." We looked again—this time with an eye to the details. The map section was multi-coloured with a purpose. The subway system was one colour, the major roadways a different colour, and the highways yet another colour. There were tendrils of a unique colour extending out to a complex network of yet another colour.

"Remember those?" asked Lee. "That complex network on the bottom is under Lake Ontario. A lot of those other lines correspond to known roads or subway lines. What do those other lines mean, and where do they go? What do they correspond to?"

The three of us peered at the diagrams before us, trying to make sense of them. There was a lot of information, and we'd need time to figure it out. We started to talk about ways to overlay current maps and maybe turn off specific items, when the PA system began spluttering. After a few honks and burps it cleared up and demanded that Lee report to her supervisor's office. The voice sounded like that of Professor Manderpootz.

"Uhm, Lee, sweetie," I asked, "please tell me you properly exited the computer you hacked into?"

"Ahh, I'd like to, but ..."

"Screw this shit, kids, we gotta boogie," said Gail with an edge to her voice.

Lee and I could only stand there big-eyed, as Gail shoved us aside and began shutting down her computer. "Well don't just stand there, you idiots, pack up your stuff and get ready to bug out."

This was not researcher-Gail speaking—this was take-charge-Gail, and she was deadly serious. I grabbed what little I had and put it into my pack. Lee had recovered enough to dash around and grab our coats. I was about to ask her about her own stuff, when the door banged open to reveal Mr. Thansworth.

"Oh, there you are, Ms. Neilan. You need to get out of here right now. You other two should leave as well. I brought your things from your office, Ms. Neilan. I hope I retrieved everything. If not, don't worry about it for now. You all need to leave. Follow me and I'll sneak you out the back."

The ladies hesitated for only a moment before moving. Thansworth helped Lee and Gail on with their coats. With a jerk of his head, he turned and walked out, leaving us to follow. I shrugged on my own coat, grabbed my pack, and followed.

We hurried down a set of seldom-used corridors. I knew they weren't used much because the lighting was so poor in them. Sudden travel down dingy corridors? This was getting more than a bit outside my comfort zone, and I began to wish that I'd brought my pistol. The ladies, though, seemed quite content to follow the Security Chief. Moreover they were comfortable with the area we were moving through. That calmed me down somewhat, though not by much. With a final turn, we came to a door. From the looks of it, a fire door for emergency use only.

"Alright, go through here. You know the way up to the street from here?"

"Yes we do, Mr. Thansworth, and thank you so much. We don't want you to get in trouble over this," said Gail, a bit out of breath.

He offered a wan smile. "By the time I got to your lab, everyone was gone. And somehow the security circuits in this part of the building were off. I've been warning them about the poor maintenance of these things. Damn budget cuts. Step lively, now—the security cameras will come back on in a minute." With that he opened the door and motioned us out.

As we went out, Lee paused to give him a brief hug. Within seconds we were out and trotting up the inclined walkway towards the street. We got to the street level and maintained a brisk walk towards the subway entrance. Once there, we trotted down the steps. Although we were quite safe at this point, we maintained a brisk pace until we were standing on the subway platform waiting for the train.

We stood there huffing and puffing and grinning like fools. It wasn't long before Lee stopped puffing enough to ask Gail if she had the data key. Gail paused her own puffing long enough to grunt an irate affirmative. I was glad to see that the ladies were puffing at least as much as I was. Still, I suspected that they'd recover a lot faster than I would. Getting old sucks, sometimes.

When the train arrived, we clambered in and headed back to the apartment.

CHAPTER EIGHT
Countdown

We spent the time on the subway lost in our own thoughts.
This was getting serious. At best, Lee would be up for some
sort of discipline. At worst she could lose her job—or even face
criminal charges. Though you wouldn't know it from the look
on her face. A slight, self-satisfied smile that didn't leave for the
entire trip. Gail tried to glare at her, but that turned into an
amused smirk.

There was more going on here that I was aware of. I
suspected that if I knew the full story, I'd be heading back to
kick someone's ass for real. So took my cue from them, and just
sat in quiet contemplation while the train rattled on.

We finally arrived at our stop, and we marched back to the
apartment. No-one was saying anything, and I was damned if I
was going to start. For one thing it wasn't my place. For
another, I'd start tearing a strip off that idiot woman for doing
something so foolish. Imagine not properly closing out after
breaking into a system—I had taught her better than that.

No-one said a word until we got back to the apartment. As
the door closed, Gail grabbed Lee by the collar of her coat and
hissed, "What were you thinking?"

The two stood there glaring at each other for the space of a
few heartbeats when my phone warbled for attention, followed
by Gail's and Lee's. Without a word the two women decided to
postpone their glaring contest, and we each examined our
phones. It was a text from Stan urging us all to assemble at his

place as soon as possible and no fooling this was serious.

"Think we should bother going?" enquired Lee. "Oh, I suppose," replied Gail in a languid tone. Then she continued in a tone that got increasingly caustic, "It isn't like we have anything else to do. BECAUSE SOMEONE GOT CAUGHT DOING SOMETHING ILLEGAL AND WE HAD TO RUN FOR OUR LIVES."

Before things got too serious I interjected, "Uhm, maybe we should take the photos along with us. Oh, and don't forget the coffee we were going to take. That would be good to take with us, don't you think?"

The ladies stopped glaring at each other long enough to glare at me. I gave them my wide-eyed look of innocence—it never failed. "Don't give me that crap, old man. It hasn't worked on me for years," said Lee with a sniff as she began collecting the photos to take with us. Gail snorted her agreement, and went to the kitchen to collect the coffee.

An emergency meeting likely meant that no-one had remembered to get food. When the ladies weren't looking, I decided to grab some snack bars to take with us. After a moment's thought, I also grabbed a roast from the fridge and tossed it into my pack. There was more meat back in Gail's lab. We hadn't brought it all back because the lab's cooler was better than the fridge. Although maybe after today the lab would be off limits. Never mind. The Group needed food this evening, and I'd get the rest of the stuff from the lab somehow.

After a quick bio-break, we headed back out. On the ride down the elevator I informed the ladies of my executive decision to take the pickup to Stan's. It was early enough to avoid rush hour, it was safer than public transport, and I wasn't going to accept any arguments from them over this. They looked at each other and shrugged. It was obvious that they had assumed we'd be taking the pickup. Sigh. So much for the wisdom of executive decisions.

As we were pulling out of the apartment parking lot, Lee said, "I saw you take that roast, you know. You could have asked." "And the snack bars," Gail added. "We saw that, too." Sigh. They'd known me too long—and I was out of practise at being sneaky.

It was a quiet trip, which suited me just fine. All that running around and being sociable was hard on a man.

We soon arrived at Stan's house, and for once found a parking spot close by. I wasn't sure if that augured well or not. Decided that any good news should be accepted at face value at this point. When we got to the door, Clio greeted everyone with hugs.

The three ladies babbled on, as was their wont. I kind of tuned them out while I got my coat off. After hearing hearing my name being mentioned in their conversation, I re-focused on what was being said. I missed the words, but saw Lee pass the roast to Clio, to the latter's obvious delight. What I did pick up was that Lee and Gail were taking full credit for bringing it and strong-arming me into bringing along some of my snack bars for dessert. Clio just sighed at me, more in sorrow than in anger. The ladies took the roast off to the kitchen, continuing their conversation.

"I gather it was your idea to bring the food," said a quiet voice at my side. I spun around to see Jack standing there with a wry smile. "C'mon in to the living room," he said. "I've got some cold beer. It'll help to dull the pain of being blamed for the sin of being male. Here, let me toss your coat into the closet."

We went into the living room, sat down, and Stan handed me a glass of beer. None of that silly nonsense of drinking beer out of the bottle, no sir. These lads treated beer with the respect it deserved. We sat and drank in silence. They both looked so guilty that I had to ask if anything was the matter.

They exchanged looks, and finally Jack spoke up. "Clio's been feeling antsy the past couple of days. Says she's tired of tripping over idiot males all the time. We're damned glad that Lee and Gail are here to give Clio some female company. She was getting ready for a right good snarl when you lot showed up. Sorry that you got blamed for doing the right thing. Better you than us, friend."

Both of them raised their glasses in a silent salute, which I returned, and we all took a healthy gulp. I grunted in amusement and responded, "We live to serve."

That called for another sip, and none of us particularly minded that necessity. Stan's homebrew was reaching professional quality, and I told him so. We spent a few minutes discussing the finer points of brewing beer, waiting for the ladies. Clio had been making some homemade potato chips and had decided to serve those as pre-dinner snacks. The roast would be the main course and it was going to take a couple of hours to cook, even with the oven in convection mode.

Stan made sure that everyone had a full glass of beer as we sampled Clio's chips. They were damned tasty, too. Baking instead of deep frying made for the best chips, we all agreed. Helped to have fresh potatoes, too. Stan had duplicated my tub idea, and had several expandable tubs for his potatoes. Gave him enough to trade with the neighbours.

Jack's cell phone buzzed and he bent down to look at it. I was about to ask about Dixon and Grant, when Jack raised his head and said that the two in question were coming together and would be arriving in a few minutes. They'd gotten delayed by a traffic accident, but were now clear of it.

So we chatted about inconsequential things as we waited for the final two members to show up. Impatient as I was to find out the reason for the emergency meeting, it would have been rude to get into serious discussions without everyone present. Finally the tardy duo showed up, and after greetings had been exchanged and glasses poured, we got down to business.

As per custom, Stan stood up and faced The Group.

"Thank you all for coming. So much has come up that I decided that we needed to get together sooner than later. We need to pool our information, and the best way to do that is face to face."

Everyone nodded at that.

"OK. First of all, thanks to Lee and Gail and Felix for getting that data on the artifacts to us. Shall we start with that, or deal with other issues first?"

Gail put up her hand. Stan nodded at her to take over, then sat down. Gail stood up and began, "The discussion of the artifacts is going to be a long one, judging from what the three of us have found out about it so far. We've also got some new

120

information about those that we haven't had a chance to pass along, so we need to tell you about that. First, though, I need to tell you about my autopsy results, since that's a good segue into the artifacts."

Everyone nodded in acceptance, although I could see that Grant and Dix were itching to talk about something else. Gail summarized the results of the autopsies, including the different symbols found on the bodies and fragments. After pausing for a few seconds to let that information sink in, it was time for the real bombshell. She summarized the results of her DNA analysis, and how the Priests were near-clones and what that meant in terms of the biological capabilities of the unknown enemy.

No-one disputed the use of the word "enemy". It was all too evident that an attack was taking place. The likes of which the world had never seen before and was ill-equipped to recognize, much less fight.

Clio listened with intense concentration as Gail spoke, and at the end she verified Gail's results as matching those of her own labs. The two agreed that further analysis was necessary, but out of Gail's league. Clio said that she had contacts with the local research community, not just analysis labs. In fact, some of those researchers were already analysing the data and the organs.

She went on to say, "I'm sorry that I did that without checking with the three of you first, since it is your asses on the line here. The opportunity to talk to these researchers came up, and it seems that they are already working on the Change Plague. You are so far ahead of them, and they are going to need time to look at all this, and time is getting short, I think. These are the sorts of people who can develop a cure, if one is to be found. They'd already figured out the trick with the anti-virals to treat the Control Plagues, by the way, and gave me a small supply to treat whomever I want. There seems to be pockets of research going on, and it is time to get all those resources working together. Sorry to take over here, Gail."

"You made the right call, Clio," said Gail, "although I'll admit to being a bit concerned about it being traced back to me. That could raise some uncomfortable questions."

"No, no," responded Clio, "That's a valid concern, for sure. I ran it all by Stan and Jack to make sure that any identifying information was wiped before passing it on. They've got some experience with that sort of thing."

That reassured Gail, and the rest of us gave murmurs of agreement. This was so much bigger than us, that I was beginning to despair that the efforts of our small group would not be enough. Trust the others to have wider personal networks than I, and be plugged into professional networks.

Once we'd all settled down from that small shock, Gail went on to explain that we had new information about the artifacts, then nodded at Lee to take up the tale. Lee stood up and said, "P'raps Felix is the best one to give an overview suitable for a lay audience. He's better at doin' that sort of summarizin' than I am." With that she nodded at me and sat down.

After taking a small sip of my beer to clear my throat, I stood up. I gave them an overview of what Manderpootz had said about the artifacts and the reconstructed fresco. I also described how he had dismissed the bottom half. How he got very interested at the possibility of finding new symbols that matched those on the fresco. For sure he knew a lot more than what he was telling.

From what we knew about the workings of the various Plagues, it was obvious that there was a large and widespread scheme being carried out. What Manderpootz had divulged about the fresco showed that the plan had been going on for thousands of years. And that plan was somehow reflected in the design of Toronto. I went on to give an overview of how we had figured out that one part of the fresco was a map of Toronto's subway and downtown roads, with extensions into Lake Ontario.

The resolution of the symbols on the artifacts wasn't all that great, so details were hard to pin down. However, Lee had recently done an analysis of x-ray imagery of the artifacts. That gave a lot more detail to the symbols than were visible. Unfortunately, we only had time for a cursory look at the new data before arriving. With that, I turned it back to Lee. Grant and Dix had been on the edge of their seats as I talked, and looked as if they were ready to explode. Until, that is, I mentioned that Lee had uncovered a finer level of detail. That got their undivided attention.

Lee stood up, and gave a brief summary of the x-ray images. She passed out copies of the results to everyone, and several minutes passed as people studied the images and compared them to the originals.

Finally Stan stood up and took the floor once again. "Uhm, that was just a bit more than I was expecting, to tell the truth. Uhm, I know that Dixon and Grant have been working with the map portion of the fresco, and have some discoveries that they would like to share."

The two young men, previously so eager to show off their work, became shy. This was not unexpected, to be honest, and we all waited for one of them to start. Finally, at the gentle urging of Clio, Grant stood up. After an initial stumble, he recovered and began to describe his work. Both he and Dix had a lot of experience with geographic information systems, so had spent their time comparing the map on the fresco with current maps of various sorts.

There were a number of features that appeared suggestive, although the resolution was lacking. Rather than discussing their theories, might it not be better to incorporate the x-ray images into their maps? Lee gave enthusiastic agreement, and got together with the two young men. The three of them hunched over a pair of laptops, muttering amongst each other. Clio and Gail moved together to start discussing DNA analysis results, and what sorts of things the other researchers should be looking for.

I sipped on my beer and munched a couple potato chips as I tried to think of the implications of all this. Stan and Jack moved to sit beside me, and I looked up at them with a smile. The smile wasn't returned.

"Uhm, Felix ..." began Stan, before he came to an embarrassed halt. "What Stan is trying to say is ..." said Jack, before he, too, came to a halt. I looked back and forth between the two of them, and grunted in amusement. They were acting like kids who were afraid to admit to something. I was pretty sure about what.

"Look, Felix," Stan said, "we were worried that you'd be upset about Clio passing the data on to other researchers. I know that we've always kept our data amongst ourselves. But like Clio said, the opportunity came up and it seemed like the right thing to do."

I nodded and replied, "You made the right call. It's as simple as that. Just one question—did you include all my data in what you passed on to the other researchers?"

They nodded, adding that they'd sanitized any identifying metadata so that it couldn't be traced to me. "That's not what's worrying me. Passing on that stuff was the right call, too. No, it's just that some of that data wasn't mine. Was given to me in confidence, just before I had to leave my farm."

Stan brightened at that. "Oh, you mean Dixon's data? He already told us that he was the one that supplied it to you. He's fine with passing it on, so long as it was to a small group of trusted researchers. Which these are. They'd heard rumours of its existence, and were thrilled to actually get their hands on it. And those pictures of the Changed at your farm blew them away. None of them had seen that quantity or quality of information. Your analysis reports were well received, too. That, on top of the specimens you retrieved and Gail autopsied, had them giddy with excitement, according to Clio."

For a moment I was too stunned to speak. "You mean to say that these researchers haven't been getting the most recent information about the Changed? Seriously?"

Both of them shook their heads. Jack added, "All such studies were completed years ago, when the Change Plague first came out. No-one thought that there was any reason to duplicate those studies year after year—not after the first few years showed no real changes. Then the budget cutbacks came, and the economy tanked, and it was a struggle just to keep the basics of health-care going. And it's becoming more of a struggle just to keep body and soul together, much less do new research. That's why the data from Gail and yourself is getting treated like gold. They've got the people and facilities. Just not much in the way of recent hard information to work with. From what Clio tells me, you and Gail have earned serious cred with some top-end science teams."

Before I could respond to that, a loud buzzing began sounding from the kitchen. Turned out to be the stove's timer, indicating that the roast was done. Clio and Gail headed off to the kitchen, and a minute later came out to announce that dinner was ready as soon as the roast was carved. Stan headed out to the kitchen to do the honours, while Clio asked everyone to decide whether to carry on or have some food first. After a quick discussion, food won out. However, the compromise was to have hot beef sandwiches instead of something fancier.

After everyone made themselves a sandwich, piled more of the chips on a plate, and topped up their beer, we all stood around in the kitchen and ate. This was just like old times, I thought to myself. A too-warm kitchen, everyone standing around eating and laughing without a care in the world. Finally the last bite was eaten and the last bit of beer drunk. Clio set the coffee on to brew (after thanking me for bringing the beans), and we all headed out to the living room once more. She also announced, to the approval of all, that coffee was to be accompanied by my snack bars.

A few minutes later we were all drinking coffee and nibbling at chunks of snack bars. It was a quite wonderful way to spend an evening. The coffee was even almost the equal of my own—although she'd had to stretch it a bit with some of their stash of mediocre coffee.

With our physical selves now fuelled and ready to go, the discussions recommenced. Once again, Grant stood to describe the work he and Dix had done. This time, though, he included the new images from Lee. Dix unrolled a large printout of their original GIS handiwork, and Grant and Lee held it up for everyone to see. It was along the lines of what the ladies and I had figured out. Using their expertise, they had pushed the original images to the limits of accuracy and superimposed it with real maps. The lines on the original images showed up as thick lines when superimposed onto a map, too wide to be of any serious use. As Grant pointed out, the accuracy was on the order of a city block, more or less. Enough to be indicative, just not of any practical use if we wanted to verify it.

The three of them grinned, and both Lee and Dix held up the laptops so that everyone could see the new results. Grant approximated the new data by hand-drawing it on the printout.

"OK, everybody, there's more new information than I've drawn—as you can see on the laptop screens. You can see that the lines indicating the subway are bang-on to the reality. There are a few minor variances, but the bulk of it is right on. Lee figured it to be better than ninety-five percent alignment. That's not the best part, though. See where I've marked dots on the printout? Those correspond to dots in the x-ray images. Notice how they correspond to specific spots. It looks like that auxiliary tunnel system that the map indicates has doorways at a few specific locations in the city. Like you noted, Felix, there's a few scattered throughout the Green Belt. Those seem to be correlated with large drainage outlets. Same thing for the ravine system that runs through Toronto. You'll notice that there's a couple of dots located right downtown. Under specific buildings in fact."

The three of them paused to grin at each other before continuing.

Dixon took up the story as he blurted out, "One of them is located in the ROM, and the other is under City Hall." The stunned expression on everyone's faces seemed to be all the payment that the three of them would ever need. It was quite a bombshell, that's for sure.

"OK," I said, since no-one else seemed to want to say anything, "so we've got an ancient map that indicates major Toronto infrastructure almost exactly. Right?"

The three nodded.

"Fine. And we've got that auxiliary network that creates a separate series of tunnels or something that goes under Lake Ontario and has outlets—doors or portals or whatever you want to call them—at specific locations that correspond to specific infrastructure. Right?"

Again they nodded.

"And, finally, we have a couple of these doors that seem to be aligned with two major buildings in Toronto."

All three of them were nodding their heads.

I looked around the room at everyone before asking the obvious question, "Assuming that these doorways turn out to be real—and I'm sure they will be, since that seems to be how the werewolves get around the city and GTA—now what? Do we go to the authorities and tell them we have ancient artifacts that are thousands of years old that describe secret tunnels under Lake Ontario? And that's where the werewolves are coming from? Is that what we should do? Oh, and which authorities do we tell about this?"

That wiped the smiles off of everyone's faces right quick. They began talking amongst themselves, their voices intent but quiet. I just stood back and watched. There didn't seem to be much agreement going on, though things didn't get heated. Just a lot of head-shaking and sighing.

For myself, I just stood back and thought about things. The question I had raised was beyond my level of expertise to answer. I didn't know anyone in authority, for one thing. For another, I had spent a large part of my life distrustful of authority and finding ways around it to do what I thought was the right and proper thing. I'd let the socially-oriented people deal with the question.

I decided to spend some time looking at the processed x-ray images that Lee had produced. I shuffled through them, frowned, and unrolled one of the full-sized printouts of the fresco. Taking the x-ray images, I tried to arrange them on the fresco. Something wasn't right. I called to Lee. She broke off her conversation with Stan and wandered over with a frown.

"Lee, what are those spots that occur in that set of x-ray images?" I asked. "Oh, just artifacts of the image processing," she replied.

"Not those little speckles. I mean these larger ones. They may vary in size, but seem to be real, not artifacts." She peered, and again insisted that they were artifacts.

"OK," I acknowledged, "how come these larger spots only

occur on this set of images? All the others just have the small speckles. And, yes, I agree with you that the small speckles are artifacts. Those larger ones, though, are something different." Lee frowned as she took the photos and compared them against the others that I'd placed on the fresco.

"That's not the most interesting thing," I added. "Where on the fresco do those photos that you are holding go, exactly?" By this time the others had ceased their conversations and were watching us. Lee was frowning with concentration by this time, as she struggled to place the photos in the appropriate spots on the fresco. "The x-ray image isn't quite a one-to-one match with the visual, ya know," she muttered with some irritation.

Grant came up to help her, and the two of them puzzled at it for a couple of minutes before I interjected, "You're going about it all wrong, you know." All eyes turned to me. "They don't match up with any pieces on the fresco. That's the trick. They fit into some of the places where we didn't have any artifacts to take photos of."

The realization of what that meant finally sunk into Lee's awareness, and she blurted out with vehemence, "That fucker Manderpootz. He was holdin' out on us. I *knew* it."

With that, she was off on heated rant filled with invective and promises of dark revenge. It was actually quite impressive, since she didn't seem to be repeating herself. Still, there was work to do. I waited until she paused for breath, caught her attention, and said, "The important thing is to find out what he was trying to hide. Nail his balls to the wall later. Right now, we need to figure out what these new images mean."

I took the images from her to prevent any further crumpling. Bending over the fresco I placed the photos into the blank areas, using as markers the supportive elements seen in both sets of images. After finishing, I stood up and stepped back. Lee reached down and switched the location of two images, then stepped back.

Dixon stepped up and switched another couple of images. Then took one of his original pair and swapped it with another. Everyone stepped up to take a careful look. After a few minutes of study, we all agreed with that final placement.

The new images appeared to form yet another self-contained section, like the map part. There were a few lines going off to other sections, to link that information with other sets of information. The problem was we didn't know what this new information was trying to tell us.

"Alright," said Gail pointing as she talked, "that section is the map of Toronto—I think we can all agree with that. And that section there has the symbols that we found on the Priests. Hmm, the x-ray photos have some extra detail that we'll need to look at, though let's leave that for now. Over there are the plague growth curves. Over there is the text portion that prophesies a final doom of some sort. Then there's this new section. A bunch of dots, some squiggles, and some curves. Everything else is straightforward enough, except for this new section. Why is that?" The last was muttered to herself.

"Whatever it is, it's important enough to be linked to the plague curves," said Clio pointing. "Not just any plague curve," I said. "The final one." Oh, shit. The Final Doom. Coming out of Lake Ontario. I could see everyone was thinking much the same thing.

"Stars."

Everyone looked around to see who was talking. "Stars," Jack repeated. "Look—there's the Big Dipper and Orion." Holy shit, he was right. With that hint, I figured out what those other weird squiggles and curves were.

"Phases of the moon," I blurted out. There were sounds of muttered disagreement. "No, look," I insisted. "That's a star chart. With a line heading down to the map of Toronto. There's these symbols at the bottom, occurring in clumps. One clump for each of the plague curves. It's a timetable, using stellar cartography to show the date. All the plague curves just have a phase of the moon to indicate their date of occurrence. However, the final plague has a star chart *and* a phase of the moon. To give an exact date."

There was no disagreement with this assessment, and no-one spoke for a handful of heartbeats. Finally, Stan blurted out, "OK, wait just a sec. Just because it gives a date—whatever that date might be—doesn't mean that it is correct."

I spoke up. "True. Yet everything else on this fresco is bang-on. The symbols found on the Priests. The accurate map of Toronto. The plague curves that match what actually happened. We need to figure out what that final date is. Dix, you're closest to my duffel bag. Could you reach in there and grab my laptop for me, please? I've got some astronomy software on there that might help."

After setting up on the floor, I started up the planetarium program. "OK," I mumbled, "using downtown Toronto as the reference location, and setting the display to show in rectangular format 'cuz that's what the fresco has, and setting the time to vary as I move the mouse and ..."

Well, that was a waste of time. There was just too much being shown to make any sense of.

"Limit the magnitude to, say, three or four," said Grant. "Look at the constellations shown on the photos—those are the major stars. So filter out the dimmer ones." I did that, and soon only the constellations were showing. Nodding, I said, "Smart idea. Though still a lot of time-scale to scroll through. Wait a minute—look at the constellations showing in the fresco. Those are late spring constellations, plus or minus. So, let's start in, say, February and speed up the time like so, and watch."

We watched as the stars raced across the sky, looping around and features marched across in their slow progress as the weeks went by.

"Stop," commanded Lee. "Back up a week or so. Stop. Go forward, but slow it down a bit. Yeah, that's it. Stop." We looked from the screen to the fresco and back again. It was damned close. Real damned close.

"What's the date, Felix?" asked Gail. I looked at the display before replying, "This month."

"What about the lunar cycle? Would that allow us to fine-tune the date?" asked Clio. It took some figuring, and more than one blind alley—none of us were astronomers, after all. After a while we finally got something that we all agreed on.

"It's tomorrow," I said. "The Final Doom, whatever that might be, is scheduled for late tomorrow."

CHAPTER NINE

Boiled Frogs Strike Back

To no-one's surprise, that discovery generated no small amount of discussion. The obvious course of action was to re-check the astronomical calculations. Grant and Jack were assigned to check the timing using a different program. Within ten minutes they had come up with the same answer.

Clio made the suggestion to check alternate years, on the assumption that just because we had the season right didn't mean that we had the month or day correct. She and Lee checked the odd-numbered years into the future, and Grant and Jack checked the even-numbered years. Dix and I checked previous years. Gail kept tabs on what everyone was doing, and kept us all on the right track.

After working for almost an hour it became evident that there was one, and only one, date that worked.

Finally, after nearly an hour of hard work by the group Dixon said, "It's tomorrow night. No matter how we slice and dice the data, that's the the one and only date that works."

We were all silent for a minute, then Grant spoke up, "OK, but that leads to the obvious question of what are were we going to do with the information?"

I suggested, "We might consider going to the authorities. Anyone got contacts with the police or military, or know of anyone who might? I don't."

Alas, no-one else did, either.

"We could just go the police, I suppose," said Clio, after some hesitation.

"And say what, exactly?" asked her husband. "Anyone that we approach cold with this is going to want solid proof that there is something. We can't go to them with a story about ancient artifacts. There's been enough bullshit about the Change Plague bandied about over the years."

Lee muttered something that no-one caught, so we all turned to her. She blushed, as she had been talking to herself. With some prodding she said, "What about the Control Plagues? I mean, you all remember how they affected us. How do we know who's infected and who isn't?"

With a slow nod, Gail said, "That's a good point. On top of that, there's the problem of chain of command. Think about it. Talking to, say, the police cold means that we walk into a police station and talk to a constable. If we're lucky, he'll pass us on to a sergeant. Who then passes us, or maybe just the information, up through the chain of command. Someone, somewhere along the way, is going to have to make a decision to investigate to determine what, if anything, there is to our crazy-sounding story. And that's if we are very lucky. I suspect that the odds are pretty high that we'll be ignored or arrested for creating a disturbance. Or even for just causing brain cramps amoung the police—that's classified as interfering with a police officer, these days."

Everyone sat digesting those thoughts for a minute. Finally I spoke up, "OK, given that your logic is sound, Gail—and it seems solid—what is it that we can do? It seems to me that we need to short-circuit the process and bring solid proof. Which means that we need to do a preliminary investigation ourselves, and present the findings to the police or whomever. Can't say that I'm thrilled with this idea, but we're up against a tight timeline."

They all stared at me, aghast at my suggestion.

Stan began drumming his fingers on his legs, a sure sign of his intense concentration. Finally, he looked around at each of us and said, "Felix has a point. And all we'd need to do is a quick in and out, enough to grab some photos and videos of these tunnels."

"And if we come across some werewolves?" said Clio with ice in her voice.

"Pictures of those in the tunnels will just clinch our story," insisted Stan, unmoved by her tone.

Jack piped up, "And it's not as if we're planning on a firefight or anything. It's like Stan says—we go in, take some pictures for proof, then out."

I shook my head. "Nope. Pictures of tunnels won't cut it as proof."

Everyone turned to stare at me, some with raised eyebrows. "Sorry, folks. Pictures of tunnels won't cut it," I insisted. "We need to prove that there are werewolves as well as an extensive tunnel network. Even better would be proof of a facility. Something capable of staging the attack that we're trying to convince them is imminent. Something that will convince them to take quick and decisive action."

That got a heated discussion going, with some angry words from Clio thrown in for good measure. She was furious that some of our group, especially her husband, were looking on this as some sort of grand adventure. Lee and Gail managed to calm her down before she got too wound up.

After that, we started over and came to a consensus that although we had to inform the authorities, before we could do that we needed proof. As for that proof, only something substantial would do it, something more than pictures of a single tunnel. What that "something" might be was a question we couldn't answer, since we didn't know what we'd find down there.

"Uhm, folks, I hate to be a wet blanket," interjected Grant at this point, "but we haven't even proved that these tunnels exist. Or that there are entrances into them."

The kid was right. Our first task was to confirm the existence of the entrances. It boiled down to a single choice—the theoretical doorway located in the ROM. It was close by, close to the rest of the underground network of tunnels, and we stood a chance of gaining surreptitious access to it. Why surreptitious? For the same reasons we couldn't approach anyone in authority.

Our overall plan was to get inside the tunnels, then do an armed reconnaissance. That is, take weapons to defend ourselves in case we encountered werewolves, but not to initiate combat. The primary purpose was to get photographic proof of some sort. Proof that would convince the authorities to take quick and effective action. None of us were soldiers, after all.

That left the question of where in the ROM was this secret doorway? After some discussion, we decided that it would most likely be in the deepest part of the building. Both Lee and Gail recalled that there was a special storage room in the basement that never seemed to be used. Off limits, in fact, since the creation of the ROM over a century earlier. Access was apparently restricted and required special permission and a key from the most senior management. They knew that much only because an elderly researcher told them about a time, when he was very young, of a co-worker trying to gain entrance to it. The co-worker was dismissed, as was anyone who asked too many questions about his leaving. It became something never to be spoken of, and then eventually all but forgotten.

"Uhm, Gail, so why would no-one but senior management know about this room?" asked Grant. "I mean, if it's a door to these tunnels, and the room's been there for over a century..." He shook his head and sat back.

"For that matter, how can that ancient fresco reflect the layout of Toronto?" interjected Stan. "Whatever it was that caused Toronto to be built the way it is could certainly affect the layout of the ROM."

Dixon piped up, "Don't forget those various control plagues. Just because we're only seeing them now doesn't mean they couldn't have been around for a long time. Toronto's been around, as a city at least, for a couple hundred years. Someone's been controlling how the city has developed for at least that long."

We were all silent for a time, trying to understand the implications. Finally, Jack summed it up as only he could, "Enough with the history and the how. We need to break into the ROM, find and break into a special locked room that we've only heard rumours of, find and open an ancient doorway that may or may not exist, explore tunnels that may or may not exist, find proof of imminent doom that may or may not exist, and take that proof to the police so that they can stop said hypothetical doom. Oh, and maybe fight off some monsters. Those, at least, do exist."

No-one appeared to want to say anything, so I spoke up. "Jack's right. The plan assumes that we can break into the ROM, evade Security, find and break into that storage room, all without getting caught. If we fail at any part of that, we're looking at arrest and prison. And that's the easy part. Think about that long and hard before you make your decision."

"What are you going to do, Felix?" asked Dixon. Several others nodded.

Before I could do more than open my mouth, Lee spoke up, "We're goin' in. Just me and Felix."

"The *three* of us," Gail added with some emphasis, glaring at both Lee and myself.

In the end everyone decided to join this quixotic quest, and it didn't take much time at all for that decision to be made. It came down to everyone wanting to do something—to stand up and fight back. The boiled frogs wanted a kick at the bastard controlling the heat—even Clio, despite her earlier objections. After that it was a matter of discussing logistics.

The first issue was when to stage the break-in. That part was easy—it had to be in the wee hours of the morning. We figured that a quick reconnaissance shouldn't take any more than two hours—three at the most. We'd be out before the city woke up. That left us a few hours to prepare and get some rest.

The next task was to assemble our various kits. It turned out that we had everything at hand for a straightforward op like this. That was fortunate, as it saved us from having to waste time getting people to and from their homes.

I put on my work vest, since it was capable of holding a lot of equipment and ammo. For weapons, I had my 12-gauge pump-action shotgun and a revolver, with enough ammo for a couple of reloads. That would be more than sufficient, since we weren't planning on fighting. The larger miscellaneous gear would fit into my backpack.

Stan and Jack had rifles, ammo, and backpacks of their own. Clio had the shotgun I'd given her. She also decided to take along equipment suitable for taking biological samples, something both she and Gail could do. Fortunately, she had those supplies at hand, left over from a field exercise a few years ago.

Grant and Dixon each had a Glock and one spare clip. Stan had a couple of spare backpacks and canteens for them.

Both Lee and Gail declined to carry a weapon, insisting that without proper training they would be more danger than help. There was some truth to that, so they were the designated record-keepers and videographers. Gail would also carry our first-aid supplies, since she had medical training.

We needed to travel light, so we limited our consumables to a supply of water and high-calorie food suitable for a day of hiking around. Though we expected to be gone no more than a couple of hours, better to have a bit more than we expected to need. On the other hand, water was heavy, so we discussed how much of that to carry. We finally decided to take as much as we could and hydrate before we entered the tunnels (assuming the damned things even existed). At that point we'd decide how much to carry with us.

Practicality would limit us to a maximum of two water bottles each. Both Felix and Stan each had one of those jogging belts that held a couple of small water bottles. They suggested that they could take those along with the two larger bottles. I wasn't too happy about that extra load. When hiking, every gram counts after a while. Still, they insisted, and the decision was made to let them make a final decision just before entering the tunnels.

With preparations completed, we decided that we could afford two hours of rest. That'd give us time to have a hearty breakfast, and time to drive to the ROM, arriving there well before dawn.

We all lay down to rest, but I'm not sure if anyone got any real sleep.

★ ★ ★

We travelled to the ROM in a pair of vehicles, and parked just out of sight of the security cameras. Dixon had travelled with Lee, Gail, and I so we could discuss how best to deal with the security system. I argued for a minimal approach—disabling the fewest number of cameras and other sensors. The problem with that, unfortunately, was that it would draw attention to that specific area. Worse, disabling a small series of sensors pretty much just draws a map of where you have been, and indicates where you were going.

My solution to this was to make the cameras in a wide area appear to be operating in an intermittent manner by making a short video loop of static and a breaking-up image. Easy enough to do after we hacked into the system and could grab a current snippet from the video feed.

Lee said, "That's a smart idea, old man. Very sneaky, even for you." She paused for a brief moment before speaking again. "Wait a minute. You got that idea from somewhere else, didn't you? Was it one of those dumb detective books you read? Those silly 'Yancey Franklin' books?"

"Hey, don't be dissing my taste in books—you're a fine one to talk. Besides, I like those detective novels. Not great literature, perhaps, but fun to read. And with some neat ideas in them," I replied in a mock-haughty tone.

After we parked, Lee was able to get Dixon into the security system via a WiFi connection. From there, Dix broke through the security protocols, and within a minute had full access. After isolating the selected external cameras, he spent a minute recording the video from them. From that he created a loop video, and added the appropriate noise to it. Within five minutes we were ready to move. Without a doubt, the lad had talent.

We drove both cars to the parking area outside of the loading bays, we re-enabled all the cameras except the one looking at the spot where we parked. The vehicles were off to the side and wouldn't interfere with normal operations, and so shouldn't attract any attention. Both had the appropriate ROM parking stickers so they'd look OK from that point of view, too.

Getting the door open was easy, since the locks were controlled by the security system. We rushed through so it would show up as open for the minimum amount of time on the security control board. With any luck, that would be chalked up to just another transient glitch.

Once inside, we told the security software to temporarily disable sensors along the path we needed to take. I made sure they had the faked breakdowns appear at random throughout the building so there wouldn't be anything to indicate a specific path. Another idea I got from my detective novels. Having to pause once in a while to allow for the appropriate randomness slowed us down a bit, though not too much.

What did add almost twenty minutes to our time was Gail's insistence on going to her lab. She had the idea of grabbing the scent glands she had extracted from the Priest bodies and rubbing them on our boots to mask our scent. A damn smart idea, and we decided that the time penalty was worth it.

We got to the lab and ducked inside while Gail went into the storage lockers to recover the container with the glands. Looking around, we could see the room had been searched and left in a messy state. Disconcerting, though not unexpected. Gail hurried out of the examination room and crouched down beside us.

"Sorry for the delay," she whispered. "Whoever searched here left things in something of a mess. Took me some time to find the container."

I waggled my finger indicating the state of the office area, and Gail let out a short growl. She hated it when someone tampered with her work space.

We all turned and prepared to exit, when Dix hissed, "Drop. Freeze."

The faint sound of footsteps was evident in the silent gloom. They became louder and closer, then fainter as they moved away. Dix stared at his laptop screen, nodding only when it was safe to go. We left the lab to continue our quest, making sure to lock the door behind us.

Lee and Gail led the way. Dix continued to monitor the security feed for indications of anyone coming near to us. We only had one other close call as we continued down to the lowest basement level, but managed to evade detection.

We finally reached the bottom level, where we had hoped to find the mysterious secret room. Judging by the thick layer of dust on the floor, this dimly-lit area was not only unused, but unvisited by even the cleaning staff. There were two corridors to choose from, and we paused to figure out which to take.

"Over thataway," suggested Stan, pointing down a corridor to our left.

"No, I think it's over this way," insisted Gail.

"No, that way," replied Stan in a voice tinged with amusement. He aimed his flashlight at the floor to highlight footprints in the dust. There were no footprints in the corridor Gail had selected.

Muttering quiet congratulations to Stan, we followed the footsteps, turned a corner, and stopped before a closed door. The footprints stopped at the door, so this had to be it.

We discussed how to get it open. Grant reached into his pack and pulled out a lockpick kit. Clever lad. He knelt down before the door, and began probing inside the lock with his tools, one hand on the doorknob. After a few seconds he got a strange look on his face. With a small shake of his head, he turned the knob and pushed the door open.

"It wasn't locked," Grant said in a quiet voice.

This was not what we had expected. Then again, we hadn't expected footprints in the dust to lead us to the room, either.

Speaking of dust, the floor was thick with it. There were a few boxes piled off to the sides, but what drew our attention were the tracks in the dust. The tracks led to the far wall, up to a large, oval-shaped carved fresco.

"What the hell is this?" asked Clio, speaking for us all. "A seal of some type," answered Lee. "It looks...Aztec-ish. Hard to say for sure." Gail stared at her. "Ish? What the hell sort of identification is that?" Lee snapped back, "Hey, I'm not an expert, OK? This thing has Aztec elements that I recognize. Yet there's elements that seem out of place. Different symbology. So, yeah, Aztec-*ish*. Deal with it."

"Doesn't matter," I said. "The footprints go there and

nowhere else. If that's a door, then we have to figure out how to open it." Easier said than done, as it turned out. Though we pushed and pulled, the damned thing wouldn't move. Bugger. We didn't have time for this nonsense.

A sudden inspiration hit me, and I dug in my pack for the can of talcum powder I had brought. Hey, don't judge me—I was prone to sweat rashes, and it didn't weigh much.

I had everyone stand in an arc around it, shining their flashlights along the perimeter. I poured a small amount of powder into my hand, and blew it towards the seal. First along one half, then the other.

"Watch how the dust moves," I instructed.

As expected, there were several spots where the dust seemed to be blowing away from the seal. That proved there was something behind it, perhaps another room. Whatever was there, the air pressure was higher there than in this room.

"What are you doing here," said a loud, demanding voice from behind us, as the room was flooded with light.

We all spun around and saw Thansworth, the head of Security. His hand was resting on the handle of a holstered pistol. He had flicked on a light switch we hadn't seen, forcing us to shield our dark-adapted eyes from the glare.

"Ms. Neilan. Dr. Andershank. Mr. Kurtsius. What are you doing here? Who are these others?"

Gail began to move forward, stopping only when Thansworth warned her with a shake of his head.

"We were studying some of Professor Manderpootz's artifacts, noticed some strange anomalies, and decided it was important enough that we check them out as quickly as possible."

"Are you with Professor Manderpootz and his group?" enquired Thansworth.

"Excuse me?" Gail replied in a puzzled tone.

"Professor Manderpootz and his group were here just over two hours ago. He had the key to unlock the key-cabinet for this room plus written authorization to look inside. He insisted that I should leave once I'd given him the key to this room. Quite insistent, he was. All his group wore clothes suitable for working in the field, plus backpacks. Much like you and your group."

He paused as if to allow Gail a chance to explain. When she stayed silent, he continued. "None of them have checked out through security. When the security system began its random breakdowns, I ordered my staff to begin a physical search of the building. I decided to start from the bottom and work my way up. To my surprise I've found you."

Lee spoke up. "Mr. Thansworth, we'll tell you everythin'. First, though, could you tell me if Professor Manderpootz was in Gail's—I mean, Dr. Andershank's—lab earlier today?"

Thansworth cleared his throat and looked embarrassed. He moved the hand from the butt of his gun and used it to scrub at his hair.

"I'm sorry to say that he was, Ms. Neilan. He came storming down and insisted on searching your lab, Dr. Andershank. Claimed to have the full backing of the Board. Insisted it was part of his investigation into possible criminal activity. I hadn't been informed of anything of the sort, and tried to object. He called the Director, who ordered me to give my full and complete cooperation. It was most irregular, and sounded...not quite right. But I couldn't think of any way to refuse."

He paused and looked at the floor, shame written on his face for all to see.

Gail and Lee looked at each other, then both stepped forward to pat Thansworth on the arm and assure him that he had done nothing wrong. Lee apologized for putting him in such an impossible position. It was all quite touching—however, time was a-wasting. I cleared my throat to give everyone a bit of a nudge. Gail turned and gave me a dirty look.

"Mr. Thansworth," she said in a soft voice, "what happened after the Professor entered my lab?"

"Well, Dr. Andershank, he spent some time examining your computers, and seemed to find some data of interest to him. Images of some sort, I believe. He copied those to a data key, over my objections."

Crap, crap, crap. We'd forgotten to wipe Gail's computers before we left. Not that there had been time for that, of course.

Thansworth looked at Gail, who once again assured him that he'd done nothing improper. Now, however, she needed to know what Manderpootz had done.

"Well, after that he went into your examination area, and looked around at some specimens in your cold room. Insisted he be left alone for that. After several minutes, he came out and demanded we all leave the lab immediately and lock it behind us."

Both Lee and Gail looked like they wanted to explain things, without knowing how to start. They looked at me in a pleading way.

I stepped forward and gave Thansworth a thumbnail sketch of the artifacts, the fresco, and what it all seemed to imply. Told him we were here only because of the uncanny accuracy of the ancient artifacts. We needed to prove or disprove what they were telling us before going to the authorities. I showed him why there appeared to be something behind the seal, and how we were about to attempt to open it and see what was behind it when he walked in on us. I also emphasized that time was of the essence.

"One of the Professor's group had a crowbar, I'm sure of it," said Thansworth scanning the area.

He spotted it off to one side, but was hesitant to give it to us. This wasn't surprising, as his job was to protect artifacts from the sort of thing we were about to do. Lee put her hand on his arm and assured him it was necessary. With a heavy sigh, he gave her the crowbar, and she passed it to me.

While this had been going on, the others had been examining the seal at the areas we had noted. They discovered signs of scratches on both the seal and the wall behind it. I took the crowbar, put the claw behind the seal at the bottommost mark, and applied careful pressure. It actually didn't take much before I heard a click.

Repeating the process at the other points, the seal was now no longer flush with the wall. Some careful experimentation showed it could now move forward several centimetres. After that it easily slid to one side, revealing a dark passageway. The tunnel was roughly twice as wide as a regular door, quite smooth in appearance, with a gentle downward slope. The effect on us was electric. There were huge grins and high fives all around, but we sobered up as we realized this was just the beginning of our journey.

"You are quite sure that you want to go through with this?" asked Thansworth. He had recovered his normal demeanour.

"Yes," I insisted. "We've discussed this at length amongst ourselves. That's why we're here. We need to come up with some real proof that will convince the authorities to move quickly and decisively. Just telling them about a secret tunnel won't do that."

He gave a grudging nod. After a brief hesitation he asked, "Are you armed?"

We showed him the armaments we had brought, and he nodded in approval. He frowned as he realized Gail and Lee weren't armed. He insisted on giving his pistol—a Glock plus two magazines—to Gail. To Lee, he gave his protective vest, and insisted that he see her put it on.

"Mr. Thansworth," said Gail, "do you have any contacts with the police or military or someone who could do something useful on short notice?"

"Yes. I've got contacts that I'll get in touch with right away. I'll also call call in all my security people. They're steady and well-trained. We've got a limited stock of small arms, and I'll arm them. We'll have your back, whatever happens."

We started to get ready for entry into the unknown. As we'd planned, we hydrated ourselves then disposed of any empty or near-empty water containers. Gail retrieved the container of Priest glands. After smearing those on our boots, we tossed the container to one side. Weapons got checked one last time. Thansworth showed Gail the basics of how to use the pistol.

Preparations completed, it was time to go.

"Oh, Mr. Thansworth." I turned towards him as a thought occurred to me. "Just to be on the safe side, it might be best to create a barricade near the room's entrance with those boxes after we leave. Keep this doorway clear in case you and your men have to retreat. We don't know what we'll find, but if there are werewolves in the tunnel, you *will* need to retreat if they attack. Keep in mind that they attack in waves. I suggest using the corpses of one wave as impediments to the next. Raid the kitchen for onions and garlic—whole or powder. Spread it around the room and doorways, and as far down this tunnel as you can throw it. Many of them are very allergic to it. It should slow them down and buy you some time."

Thansworth nodded—he recognized the voice of experience when he heard it. As an afterthought, he offered me his tactical radio. I declined, since its range underground was going to be minimal and it was weight I'd rather not carry. Still, he insisted. So I took it, but turned it off to conserve the battery.

Flashlights and cameras were checked and turned on. Without a backward glance we headed into the tunnel.

CHAPTER TEN
Beneath Still Waters

We were quiet as we walked down the tunnel. The floor was smooth, yet rough enough to make walking easy. The passageway appeared to be carved out of bedrock, and gave the impression of having been there for a long time. After a few metres, we noticed it was widening and curving. After another few metres we passed through a doorway into a much larger tunnel. This larger tunnel was sloped, with the upslope section ending about a half-dozen metres up from us. The downslope vanished into a darkness beyond what our lights could illuminate.

I insisted we turn off our lights for a few seconds, and after a few grumbles everyone obeyed. As our eyes adjusted to the darkness, we realized that there actually was some light. There was a soft glow emanating from strips along the length of the tunnel, as far as we could see.

"You expected this, Felix, didn't you?" asked Clio.

"Kinda," I admitted. "If we assume the tunnel system is used by werewolves, it doesn't make sense for them—or whoever—to carry around lights all the time. And even dark-adapted animals need some light to see by. The Drones have human-level visual acuity, so they'd need lights bright enough for regular humans. The Priests can see in much less light, so be on the lookout for dark areas. With luck, the cameras and video gear won't have a problem with the lighting."

Interesting as this was, it wasn't what we had come down here to find. It was time to push on. The tunnel was about five or six metres wide and maybe three high. It seemed reasonable to split into two groups and keep to either side of the tunnel. We moved with care, picking up the pace as we got used to the footing and lighting.

A low rumbling brought us to a sudden halt. It built in volume, then subsided. Puzzled, we continued on, hearing it again some minutes later. With a laugh, Jack explained that it was just a subway train. The rock acted like a low-pass filter, accentuating the lower frequencies. Neat, but kind of spooky.

We had pedometers to get a rough idea of the distance travelled, and so far we'd done just over four kilometres. Based on maps and the fresco, we calculated that we were at the harbour. There was no water leaking in that we could see, which was heartening. The light, steady breeze meant air must be coming in at some point, and circulation was somehow taking place. The breeze had a slight moist organic tang to it, in contrast to the arid air of the tunnel. Interesting as this was, it was time for a brief break.

We all needed a breather and some water. Dix was in the worst state, which wasn't surprising given his exercise-free lifestyle. Even so, he was game to keep going after a rest. The others were less tired, although Grant wasn't much better off than Dixon. I was pleased to be able to keep up the others. While they might be younger, I had a reasonably active lifestyle. Of course, their comparative youth would allow them to bounce back more quickly.

I had to wonder how Manderpootz and his team had managed this. He didn't strike me as being too fit. Maybe being a field researcher helped keep him in shape. We were all careful to take a single sip of water only after we'd cooled off for a minute. Despite having Lake Ontario overhead, there was no water anywhere that I could see. Best to ration what we had.

After a ten minute break we all felt a lot better, even Dix. I suggested that everyone eat a small snack, and wash it down with another small swallow of water. We needed to keep our energy levels up.

Afterwards, we stood up and got ready to go. Stan held up his hand for silence. He, and a couple of the others, could hear something up ahead. Not voices, as such, but something. We proceeded, taking care to make no noise. Again, with one group to either side of the tunnel.

We arrived at a sharp bend. This time I held up my hand to stop everyone, then crept up and peered around the side. It was a sharp turn followed by another sharp turn. A defensive layout of some sort, I suspected. The noises—they sounded like growls—came from up ahead, beyond the other bend. I went back to the group, who by this time had bunched up together, and told them what I'd seen and heard.

This was the only way forward, and so needed to be scouted. I told them to stay put while I scouted ahead. After all, I had the most experience in sneaking around. They began to argue, but stopped when I held a finger to my lips to emphasize the need for silence. I motioned downward with my hand to indicate that they should stay put while I went ahead.

I peeked around the corner again to make sure the coast was clear before dashing over to the far wall. From there, I inched my way towards the next bend. Just as I got to the bend, I turned around to check on my friends. Well, shit on a stick. They had followed me, and were about ten metres behind me, crouched down beside the wall. Shaking my head, I turned back to the bend and looked around it, exposing only enough of myself to be able to see.

There was a group of werewolves about fifteen or twenty metres down the tunnel feeding on something. Something that had once worn clothes. It looked as if we had found Manderpootz's group.

I snapped my head back and stood there with my eyes closed trying to control my breathing. It didn't take too long, as I'd witnessed this sort of thing far too often. A slight sound to my right caught my attention—it was the rest of The Group moving up to stealthily join me. I waved at them to stop, and was thankful when they did.

At that moment, the growling diminished, though it didn't stop. It went on like that for a few seconds, then increased with a different sort of tone to it. It was the sort of sound used when they investigated something that had caught their attention. The sounds seemed to be getting closer. Oh, this was not good.

I dashed back to my friends. They realized from my expression that something was wrong and about to get worse real fast. We turned around and hurried back the way we'd come. Unfortunately, there was no way we were going to be able to cross the bend in the tunnel to reach the other side before the werewolves spotted us.

The shit was about to hit the fan, and not in a good way. We all crouched down, then released the safeties on our rifles while trying to make as little sound as possible. This was going to get ugly. With luck we'd be able to make it back to the ROM.

Without warning, a faint light appeared on the side of the tunnel about three metres behind us. A face poked out and a hand waved. It was Manderpootz. He motioned for us to move towards him. The sounds of the werewolves were getting closer, so it seemed to be a Hobson's Choice for us. Better to escape the obvious death and hope for the best, so we turned and scuttled towards Manderpootz. He was standing in what appeared to be an alcove, holding a chemlight stick. How had we missed that?

The alcove turned out to be another, smaller tunnel which we lost no time entering. When I looked back, there was no sign of the tunnel, only darkness. Ah, a door. Useful to know about, and even better to know the trick to making it work. Might come in handy.

We kept quiet as we walked, and the sounds of the werewolves became inaudible after we had travelled a few paces. After a minute we arrived at a low-lit room. Manderpootz told us to stop here. He took a couple of small chemlights out of a pocket and activated them. They gave a welcome glow.

"You can speak here," Manderpootz told us. "Normal conversation is safe. Do not raise your voices too much, of course."

Each of us spent a few moments checking that the others were OK. We were all breathing a bit hard from fear and exertion, although Dix was having an especially bad time of it. He knelt on the floor, unable to catch his breath. This was beginning to worry me. I walked over to him and put my hand on his shoulder.

"Asthma," Dix got out before I could say anything. "I started developing it last year, and it got worse over the winter. It cleared up for the past few months and I kinda hoped it was gone." He hung his head, ashamed that he had become a burden to us.

Gail knelt beside him and made gentle enquiries for details. He allowed her to take his pulse, examine his eyes, and peer down his throat. After the brief exam, she settled back on her heels and asked, "Did you bring your inhaler, Dixon?"

He nodded before adding, "Almost empty, though. When I got better, I didn't bother to refill the prescription. It's been sitting in my pack for months. Something in these tunnels seems to be setting me off."

Gail nodded and replied in a gentle voice, "That would seem to be the case. Now get out the inhaler and take a dose. No, don't argue with me. We need to control this before it gets any worse."

Dix did as commanded, and took a puff from his inhaler. Gail took it from his hands to check it, and sighed. "Only a couple more doses left, I'm afraid." Dix nodded in agreement, still radiating shame. Gail patted him on the shoulder, gave him a friendly smile, and told him not to get upset about it.

I broke in. "I suspect it's the werewolves causing an allergic reaction. Sometimes, though not always, being downwind of them would get me a bit stuffed up. A useful way to detect 'em even if I couldn't see 'em. Don't know why it only happened sometimes. Different breed, maybe?"

Gail and Clio looked at each other for a moment, then both nodded. "We know whoever is behind this tinkers with their genetic makeup on a regular basis. Maybe one of the variants causes that sort of reaction. Or maybe it is as simple as some people are allergic to cats while others aren't. Can't say for sure," opined Clio.

"Which leads us to here and now, and why Professor

Manderpootz is standing here," growled Lee. That angry tone focused us on the next immediate issue.

Manderpootz made a soft harrumph, but otherwise stayed silent. I asked, "Were those your people the werewolves were chowing down on in the corridor?" Everyone looked at me in horror. I explained what I had seen, taking care to keep the details to a minimum. A little of that sort of thing went a long way.

As for Manderpootz, his face seemed to grow pale, although it was impossible to tell for sure in the dim light. His mouth worked without making a sound. He made a curt nod.

Lee and Gail started towards him, forcing me to interpose myself between him and them, and take control of the interrogation.

"Tell us why you're here, Professor," I enquired in a firm voice. "Any other artifacts you haven't bothered to share with us?"

He drew himself up, beginning to regain his composure and usual arrogance. "I have been studying such artifacts for decades. I share what I learn with my colleagues, or sometimes with people with specialist talents that might be of use in the study."

I could hear a low growl coming from Lee—or it might have been Gail.

"Lee's image analysis skills, you mean," I said. Manderpootz nodded his agreement.

"Yet there's something more about those symbols you haven't bothered to share. When I mentioned seeing some symbols during your lecture, you leapt down my throat demanding more details. Lee's reconstruction of the star map gave you the date and time, just like we managed to figure out. There's more to all this, and those symbols are the key. Aren't they?"

Manderpootz just stood there, with his head held high and the arrogance of the self-important on his face.

"Your arrogance and failure to share information caused the death of your colleagues, Manderpootz," I spat out. "Whatever this Final Doom thing is, I've been through a living hell because of the damned werewolves. And I suspect what is coming will make that seem like a gentle rain, in comparison. Whatever is coming, has to be stopped. And we're the only ones with a hope in hell of doing that. Speak up, *right now*, or your friends will have died for nothing."

He may have been an asshole and a fool, but he wasn't a monster. The repeated references to the deaths of his colleagues were like body blows to him, and had much the same effect. Within seconds he had collapsed to his knees and began sobbing. What I had mistaken for arrogance turned out to be an attempt at self-control.

With a bit of gentle prodding from Clio, the story came out between sobs and gulps for air. It turned out that there were, indeed, more artifacts, including another, smaller, fresco. The symbols we had found on the Priests were the key he and his colleagues needed to link the fresco we knew about to this new fresco. This new fresco described in detail a deity calling itself "the True God" that the first fresco had only alluded to.

Apparently the True God came from beyond the furthest stars. It could control and remake men with a touch. The self-proclaimed deity was of immense age, and had lain sleeping deep within the earth until awoken by that ancient civilization. After that awakening came the creation of monsters that did its bidding. Then, for some unknown reason, it was again buried deep in the earth. Some time after that—several generations at least—the first of the plagues came. Then another, and another, each changing people in new and more terrible ways. Somehow the men of that time communicated with the entity. They were told that although they were not yet worthy, their ancestors would be. The True God, in his infinite wisdom, would create a "palace of creation" in a far land scoured and cleansed by ice. When that land had been blessed, and the stars aligned, the True God would arise from its resting place and create a perfect kingdom that would last for eternity. Until then, the True God would have eyes and ears in all corners of creation.

Lovely.

"OK," I said. "something calling itself the True God has come to this planet, has been experimenting on humans for millennia, and now the time has come to unleash a final transformative bio-plague upon the planet. With Toronto as ground zero. We sorry lot are trapped inside a labyrinth of caverns it has spent who-knows-how-long creating, with no idea of what exactly is going to happen or how it is going to happen. Oh, and no fucking clue of how to stop it, or any means of contacting anyone with enough firepower to kill it. Does that about sum it up?"

Manderpootz, who by this time had stopped sobbing, raised his head and said, "That is not entirely true, you know."

We all turned to stare at him.

He looked up at us, wiping his eyes and nose. In a soft, clear voice his said, "There is a map. That is how I knew of this room and how to get to it. The map is accurate. It shows where the New Breed are grown, and where the plagues are created. The map shows many things."

For someone who hated guns and had never been trained in their use, Gail had her pistol out before anyone else could react and held it to Manderpootz's head. He froze at the touch of the barrel.

"Who were the men you brought with you? Gerraldson? Franklish? Smythe?" she asked with a hiss.

Manderpootz nodded, "Yes, yes. And others. Good men, I assure you."

Gail's face became a study in hatred as she said with ice in her voice, "Yes, I thought so. I knew them. Some of them had families. I knew them, too. What were you planning to tell them? Were you going to explain how you led their husbands and lovers into a deathtrap? And for what? Prestige? Honours?"

Lee was beginning to get a feral look as well, and was advancing with slow steps.

"No, no, you do not understand. It was for science. For knowledge. We had all studied this for so long. We had to know. We had to be certain," Manderpootz moaned. It sounded like he was trying to convince himself.

Clio spoke in a calm tone, "Gail. Lee. Please. This isn't the way ..."

"Shut up, Clio," said Lee, with a dangerous edge to her voice.

"This isn't your fight. Those were *our* colleagues he led to their deaths, on another one of their stupid schemes. For nothing. *Nothing.*"

I had to intercede here—Lee and Gail weren't vicious by nature, just shocked into a temporary rage. "Not for nothing, Lee. We have a chance to make their deaths count for something. You owe them that. You owe their families that."

That got their attention, and they turned to face me.

"If what shit-for-brains tells us is true, we have a chance to stop whatever is going on. To make their deaths count for something. To save their families. Stan, go check his knapsack. See if there is a map."

Stan hastened towards the pack, opened it up, and looked inside. After a brief search he held up a folded sheaf of papers.

"Great," I said. "Spread it out here so we can all take a look."

Stan spread out the papers, with Jack and Clio helping. There was a large map, about a metre square, plus a dozen photographs of various artifacts. Despite themselves, Lee and Gail began to get interested. To my great relief, they were also losing the rage that had threatened to consume them.

While everyone else was focused on this new information, I moved over to Manderpootz. I bound his hands with a rope from an outside pocket on my knapsack. His protests stopped when I whispered, "Stay still, you fool. I'm trying to save your life."

After finishing laying out the papers, Stan and Jack and Clio stood up and stepped back. Lee and Gail swung back to face Manderpootz, so I held up the rope to show he was secured. Gail put the pistol back into its holster, her hand shaking a bit. That was OK—I had noticed earlier the safety was still set, so the gun couldn't be fired. Don't think anyone else noticed, though.

"OK, asswipe, what's this map showing us?" Grant asked with a snarl.

Manderpootz was having problems pointing with his hands tied, but no-one gave a damn. Finally he sighed and did the best he could. He pointed out what he referred to as birthing chambers for the New Breed. From his explanation, those seemed to be what we had been calling Priests. He hadn't seen them, so couldn't give us any details of their appearance. However, they were described in the new fresco as ascended beings who served the True God.

When pressed for details about the plagues, he said with some reluctance that there was a facility for creating them. When pressed for details as to how it was done, Manderpootz stopped talking. No amount of prodding could get him to say anything more, and he had the look of a man trying hard not to remember something horrible.

Realization struck me, and my spine felt like ice. "It's women. All those women I saw being herded by the Priests when I escaped from the farm. They're being used as incubators to grow the Priests—the New Breed—and as bioreactors to grow the plagues."

From the look on Manderpootz's face I could see I was right. No-one said anything.

"We have to stop this," said Dix into the silence.

We all looked at him.

"That's our future, don't you see? The Final Doom. Humans are going to be reduced to ... to ... mechanisms for growing these New Breed types. All to serve this alien thing's idea of a perfect world. It's going to alter everything on the planet to suit its needs. Whatever that fucking alien thing is, wherever it comes from, it means to use us. Replace us. Destroy us."

None of us disagreed with his assessment.

"OK," said Stan bending down to look at the map, "how do we get from here to those other places? How do we stop it when we get there?"

Manderpootz just stared at him. "You cannot stop a *god*. What is it that you expect to do?"

I tugged on his leash and said, "We fight. We do whatever we have to do. This isn't a fucking god, you idiot, it's just an alien with delusions of grandeur and too self-centred to worry about anyone else. A boss. Remind you of anyone, Manderpootz? Hmm? OK, time to check our resources. Stan, check out shit-head's pack."

What we had was little enough. We had come equipped for a

fast in-and-out reconnoitre, and none of us were soldiers. On the plus side, we were techies and scientists in an alien facility. We had a few pistols and rifles with enough ammunition to do some real damage for a time, some flares, a few knives, a tomahawk, some rope, some twine, matches, flashlights, miscellaneous items of electronics, and some food and water.

Alas, there was nothing that would go boom or could be combined to go boom. Could have been worse, I suppose.

Without any warning the room seemed to wobble a bit, just for a second. Or maybe it was just me. The backpacks hadn't moved, so it wasn't the earth moving. Glancing around, I noticed the others seemed to have wobbled a bit, too. That made me feel better. Still, what the hell had happened? I wiped at the sweat on my forehead, and figured the heat and stress were starting to get to us.

First things first. "OK, everyone, eat something and take a sip of water." They all looked at me as if I had gone mad. "No, I'm serious. We need to make some plans here, and that can't be done right if our bodies are out of whack. The elevated heat and humidity are starting to get to us."

Clio and Gail backed me up on this, and so we took a couple of minutes to take care of our physical needs. Even Manderpootz got some food and water—I didn't want him slowing us down. As we ate, we discussed the details of what was on the new map.

The room we were in, and its associated tunnel, seemed to be part of an auxiliary tunnel complex. This auxiliary set of tunnels had a special notation on the map—although to what purpose we couldn't tell. Fortunately for us it appeared to be seldom used. There were a number doorways in the main tunnel system marked with a unique symbol. According to Manderpootz, those were all in major corridors and had especially large and sturdy doors.

The tunnels systems, both main and auxiliary, looked like a maze. After a bit of study, though, there appeared to be a system to it. There were a number of hubs, at least a couple dozen, each interconnecting with the others via the tunnels. There were major transport routes, and smaller ones. It almost had the look of a flow chart for a gigantic factory.

Actually, that wasn't quite correct. There were a few hubs with a very limited set of connections, and those were always smaller routes, which made them look like dead ends compared to the others. The lesser hubs were all concentrated in a section of the complex some distance away from our current location.

There were a few symbols on the map that Manderpootz claimed not to understand. One set just before each of the dead ends, and a couple more scattered around.

From what we could tell, the main complex was roughly teardrop-shaped, perhaps a half a kilometre in diameter and maybe a hundred metres thick at the thickest. We were currently well into the extended portion, just inside the main ovoid. There was too much to explore without a plan.

There was a heated discussion about where we should be going. About the only thing we all agreed on was that going back to the ROM for help was out of the question. We'd be spotted for sure, and a running firefight was not something we were equipped or trained for. On the other hand, the auxiliary tunnel system seemed to offer us both safety and a way to travel around within the complex. Well, relative safety.

The plan we came up with seemed reasonable. Our first objective had to be to get more information about the plagues and bioengineering systems. There were several locations marked by unknown symbols which could be worth checking out just in case they might be of interest. Gathering information was our first priority, matched only by getting that information out.

The next priority was to figure out a way to destroy this facility, if at all possible. Manderpootz grumbled when we discussed that option, then shut up damn quick when everyone glared at him. We used the cameras in our phones to take photos of the new map and the other artifacts, and added the new information to our paper maps. It was vital everyone had a copy of the updated map and was clear on how to get back to the ROM if we got separated.

Manderpootz described how to locate the doorways to the auxiliary tunnel system, as well as how to operate them. Finally we were ready to go. The plan was to stay together, if at all possible. If things went bad, we would head back to the ROM any way possible.

It was time to go. We all took another careful sip of water before heading out to our first destination. The map matched the reality of the tunnels, which was a pleasant surprise.

We got to our first doorway into the main tunnels, and Manderpootz showed us how to operate the one-way window mechanism built into the doors. It wasn't obvious how it worked. Both Grant and Dixon wanted to take a closer look at it, but a glare from Gail returned their focus to the task at hand.

The coast was clear, so we opened the door and entered the main corridor. Just ahead was a location marked by one of the symbols Manderpootz couldn't translate. It was just a few metres from us and upon inspection it appeared to be a large maintenance closet. There were tubular objects that looked like pipes. We could feel a slight vibration when we touched them, and it sounded as if something was being pumped through them.

"It's a pump control station, I think. Or, rather, a sub-station," whispered Grant. He pointed to some half-moon shaped levers. "Those seem to be controls—possibly valves. The question is, what is being pumped?"

"Better question is, what would happen if we closed or opened up all the valves throughout this facility," whispered Jack. "What we need to find is some sort of master control room. Gotta be something of that sort, somewhere."

Stan and I stood guard while the others examined the small room. There were symbols marked on the pipes and controls that matched some on the map. After a bit of discussion it was decided that the pipes, or maybe the controls, were connected to one of the areas in the dead-end area. Other sub-stations like this one also seemed to have connections to it. Perhaps it was the control room. Maybe. If we were lucky.

A brief discussion confirmed that our next destination was the plague complex. It was not too far away, so we popped back into the auxiliary tunnel. The low hum of the pumping station faded behind us as we travelled onward to the next door along our route. So far we hadn't met up with any more werewolves, and that was beginning to concern us. Were they out hunting us or waiting for us? Pondering on the question as we trudged along, I had a thought.

"What if there just aren't that many werewolves?" I suggested. "I mean, yeah, there are a lot of them. They've got to be spread real thin right now, though. They're cleaning humans out of areas outside of the city, infiltrating the ravine system of Toronto, and preparing for this Final Doom event. It's presumably another bioweapon of some sort, so great masses of soldiers aren't required in this facility at this stage of the True God's plans. There doesn't seem to be too many guards, at any rate. Did you see many, Manderpootz?"

He shook his head. "No. We thought this facility to be deserted as we wandered through it. Then that single band of werewolves found us and attacked us. Those are the only ones any of us saw."

"OK," I said, "that seems to be one thing in our favour. So long as they don't know we're using these auxiliary tunnels we should be safe."

"Wait a minute, Felix," said Gail. "Are you sure about that? This facility is huge—there's room for one hellofa lot of werewolves."

"Exactly," I replied. "This facility was designed with expansion in mind. Maybe they need a redoubt while the Final Doom does its work. Or maybe the alien just likes lots of room. Whatever the reason, it works to our advantage so long as we're careful."

Lee spoke up, "Didn't one your reports talk about the werewolves somehow survivin' the winter? And you couldn't figure out where they might have hidden? Well, p'rhaps this is that place."

Everyone looked around, uneasiness writ large on their faces.

"They aren't here right now."

We all looked around, and to our surprise it was Grant who had spoken up. He usually lurked in the background of events. Though rarely offering an opinion, he was quick to lend a hand when needed. "Felix is right," Grant continued. "They pretty much seem to be all gone topside, to wage their battle against humans. So this facility is all but deserted. More or less."

Everyone agreed with the assessment, so we kept moving with a bit more confidence. We arrived at the door outside of the plague complex, then activated the window. I peered out and saw a large room. It was better lit than the main corridors, though still not bright by our standards. There were numerous pits in the floor, with something floating inside each of them. They were too far away to make out, so I used my monocular to get a better look. I soon wished that I hadn't.

As I had suspected earlier, the floating objects were women. There were pipes embedded in their bloated bellies, connected to mechanisms built into the walls.

At first I thought—I hoped—they were dead. Then I noticed their slow, steady breathing. The others made whispered demands to know what I saw. With a sigh, I turned around. Hands reached for my monocular to see for themselves. I held it out of reach, and with a few words described what I had seen. The hands withdrew, and everyone grew silent.

"We have to check this out," said Clio.

"Agreed," said Gail. "This seems to be where the plagues and other bioweapons are being manufactured, using those poor women as bioreactors, as Felix suggested. We need samples. And to see if we can save any of them."

Their faces were set in stone, so that meant talking sense into them was not going to happen. I designated Stan, Jack, and Grant to stay behind with Manderpootz to guard our exit. Clio and Gail were to take samples and check out those poor women. Lee and Dix were to assist them as required. I was point guard. Everyone nodded to show their acceptance, and we were all set to go when Manderpootz cleared his throat.

"I may be of some assistance," he said. "If there is writing, I may be able to decipher it."

Lee growled, "Bring him." The tone of her voice allowed for no discussion. The look on her face made it clear she'd be only too willing to help the Professor join his dead colleagues.

We entered the plague room, alert for any danger. All we heard were the gentle gurgles of moving fluids and the intermittent gasps of pressurized air. We got to the first woman, and it was about as bad as we had feared.

She floated naked in what looked like a sunken bathtub. Her belly was distended, and her skin was wrinkled from exposure to the fluid. Tubes entered every possible orifice, plus a couple of extra ones to either side of her belly. She appeared to be completely hairless. Gail and Clio knelt to examine her, and Lee spoke soft comforting words into the woman's ears.

Gail stood up, put a hand on Lee's shoulder and said in a calm voice, "She can't hear you." We all looked at her, and Gail pointed to scars around the eyes and the base of the skull. "Lobotomized and paralysed." Left unsaid was that, with any luck, there was no functioning mind trapped inside the body.

We began to take a look at some of the women in the other pools. Their condition was identical to the first. Manderpootz had been examining some of the symbols around each pool. He brought my attention to the symbols around the latest victim being examined.

"There—those symbols match the symbols used to describe each of the plagues." He gestured around the room. "Each of these poor women is being used to generate one of those plagues. Note also they appear to be grouped in small clusters. It would appear each cluster is dedicated to one plague."

Gail and Clio decided to split up and work their way around the room to take samples of each plague. Lee and Dix went with them to give whatever assistance they could to speed things along.

I took Manderpootz with me to examine the general setup. It may have been based on alien thinking, and even alien technology, but plumbing was plumbing. There were pipes, valves, containers, and indicators. Everything was as done as simply as possible, which made a lot of sense. Simple was more reliable, easier to build, and easier to maintain.

Along the wall I could see the symbols for each of the different plagues, and I nodded to myself as I encountered each one. Then I came to several I didn't recognize. Looking towards the centre, I could see a smaller group of pools that fed each one of those.

"What are these for?" I asked Manderpootz.

He bent forward to examine the inscriptions. "The meaning is not clear. Unless ..."

The silence grew and I gave him a nudge. "Unless, what?"

"What? Oh. Oh, yes. The artifacts ... the, ah, shall we say the exclusive artifacts ... make mention of minor plagues. In the context of controlling herds of animals."

"The Control Plagues," I whispered to myself, then repeated it to the Professor.

He nodded as he replied. "That could be the case, yes."

I walked towards Clio, dragging Manderpootz with me.

"Clio."

"I'm busy."

"Yes, I know," I said, keeping my voice gentle. "Sorry. The ones over there are being used for the Control Plagues. Might be worth taking samples of those, as well."

Clio took a deep breath, held it, and let it out. She was working as fast as she could under these horrid conditions, and was showing signs of strain. Understandable, of course. But there was more to do.

"Yes, of course," she said. "Let me finish this one and the next, then I'll take samples of those."

She turned back to her work, and I left her to it.

I walked away, taking care to scan the area and to listen for any strange sounds. The room was actually almost peaceful in there, if one ignored what was going on in it. There was the faint tang of antiseptic making it smell like a hospital. Finishing my survey, I turned to where Stan and Jack waited, and waved to signal that all was well. They waved back, then continued their own sentinel duties.

Ten minutes later it was all done, and we were packing up the samples. Without any warning, I heard a splashing sound, followed shortly by another. Two of the victims appeared to be having convulsions. Both Clio and Gail began to move towards the women. I grabbed them both by their arms, and pulled them back.

"They're as good as dead. There's nothing you can do. We have to leave. Right now."

161

They both looked at me with defiance. With angry snorts they pulled their arms out of my grasp, and continued with the packing up. I was urging them to hurry when a series of sounds began. There was a loud "clack" followed by the chime of a bell and a brief pause. The pattern repeated itself over and over.

Positive it was an alarm, I urged everyone to grab their stuff, packed or not, and run back to the tunnel. We all ran, carrying whatever items had not yet been packed. Even Manderpootz carried his share, and the old fart could move when he had to.

We reached the tunnel and closed the door with perhaps a second to spare before the first of the werewolves arrived. I kept the window activated so I could see what was happening. Within the space of a few seconds, half a dozen Priests—judging by the symbols on their bodies—arrived and surrounded one of the two convulsing women.

They stood there watching for a moment before one reached down. There was the glint of polished metal next to the woman's throat, and the convulsions ceased. The process was repeated on the other woman. One of the Priests barked out a loud command and several Drones appeared. Tubes were removed without gentleness from the bodies. The corpses were lifted out of the water and carried away.

The Priests went around to each of the other pools, checking on the condition of the women. Then one stopped, bent down, and picked a piece of plastic wrapping we had left behind.

Ah, crap on stick. This would not end well.

With a complex series of growls and barks he got the attention of the others, and they began a quick search of the area, coming up with another wrapper. After a series of barked commands a dozen Drones appeared. Those were dispatched to the various hallways, while the Priests held a brief conference. They began to search along the walls, a search pattern that would lead them to our tunnel. I blanked the window and turned to face the others.

"Shit has hit the fan. They know someone's in the area, and they're coming this way. We gotta get the hell out of Dodge," I said, heading back the way we had come.

"No," said Manderpootz grabbing my arm. "We must go

162

down the other corridor, deeper into the complex. If they enter into here, they can trap us in that first room. Our only hope is to go forward, where we will have more paths open to us."

Damn. The asshole was right. I looked at the others, and nodded to show I agreed. After a brief pause, they each gave their own nods. Our course decided, we moved further into the complex, taking care not to make any noise.

CHAPTER ELEVEN
Out of the Frying Pan

We had trotted down the corridor for about five minutes before coming to a fork. It was time to make a plan, before this "tactical withdrawal" turned into a panic.

"OK, we need to take a minute here to look at the map and decide where we need to go," I insisted. Despite a bit of grumbling about wasting time, they halted. Maps were dug out of packs and everyone studied them with care. A muted, but heated, discussion began about where to go from here. It lasted longer than it should have, given the circumstances, so I said, "Enough."

No-one paid any attention.

"Enough," I hissed and gave pokes to everyone within reach. That got their attention, even if it was at the cost of their angry glares.

"Anyone hear anything?" I asked, holding my finger up to my lips to signal for quiet. We listened for handful of heartbeats without hearing any sounds of pursuit.

"I've never known werewolves to be quiet, especially on a hunt, so I think we're safe for the moment. OK, people with maps—we're looking for someplace where we can regroup. Look for a room with two or three tunnel entrances. No more, no less. Something that looks like it's in a quiet neighbourhood—away from the main routes, I mean."

Everyone's breathing began to get a bit less strained, which was a positive sign. It was important to get them focused on something they could do. My own map skills and spatial sense were modest at best, so I left the map-reading to those who could do it well. To my surprise, within a minute my companions found two possible locations. Both had lots of forks and intersections between us and them, so any pursuit would have trouble finding us. I hoped.

They expected me to make the final choice. I looked at the selections, thought for a moment, then pointed at one.

"That's the furthest away, Felix, and puts us deep into the heart of this hell-hole," noted Lee.

"Also makes pursuit trickier," I pointed out, "and won't be expected. We have maps that seem accurate, so that helps. We need to find a place to hole up, rest, and do proper planning. That room looks to be about, what, fifteen or twenty minutes away? Not too far. Agreed?"

Everyone agreed, so off we went. It actually took us closer to forty minutes to reach the room, and we were all damned tired by the time we got there. While waiting to catch our breaths, we began to properly stow the precious samples we had taken. Clio gathered up the strays that people had tucked into pockets and packs when we had to bug out.

It turned out that we'd managed to collect a complete set of all the different plagues, plus some spares. After some discussion, Clio decided to take the Change Plague samples, and Gail the Control Plagues. The spares were divided amoung the rest of us—just in case.

"So who dropped those damned wrappers?" snarled Grant. Finger pointing was not helpful right now.

Lee opened her mouth to say something when Clio beat her to the punch. "Not important. Could have been any of us. Could even have been me."

That earned her some glares, and not just from Grant. Things were getting heated, so I felt the need to intercede. "Those were Priests, and they've got one hell of a good sense of smell. That's probably what tipped them off first, you know, and got them looking around in the first place."

"Can they track us, do you think?" asked Lee.

"Dunno. Maybe. There's air circulating throughout these

tunnels—can't you feel it? Won't take long for it to dissipate our scent. The Priests' sense of smell isn't super good, in my experience. Better than ours, yes, though not bloodhound good. On top of that, we smeared our shoes with those scent glands. That's got to be confusing for them, too."

Tempers seemed to be abating as our breathing returned to normal. Because of the heat, I suggested a small sip of water was in order, and everyone agreed. It tasted damn good, if a bit warm and flat.

"Alright," said Stan. "We seem to be safe here, for the time being. We've got samples of the plagues and we've all sorts of photographic evidence. All that should be enough to convince the authorities to take action, yah?"

"If we could get this stuff out, sure," said Grant, with a hint of stress in his voice. "How are we going to do that?"

"Let's all take a look at the map, OK?" I suggested.

We spread out the largest of the maps, and gathered around it. "We are right ... here," I pointed, and Lee put a water bottle on the map to act as a marker. "And we came from ... there," I continued, and Lee put another bottle at the indicated location.

"That's our way back to the ROM, and those other spur lines appear to lead outside of the city. The spurs are out, 'cuz the werewolves use 'em to move troops. That leaves the other entrance inside old city hall. Not sure I'd trust any exit that I hadn't seen open."

They all nodded as I talked. Basic info, but it never hurt for everyone to be on the same page.

"Alright," said Jack, "so our only safe—and I use the term loosely—route out of here is the way we came. Right? We know there's at least one group of werewolves guarding the route, and if the alarm is out there's going to be more. That means we have to draw them away somehow, and hope that clears the route home. The trick being, I should think, to generate some catastrophic situation to which they must respond."

He paused to take a deep breath before continuing. "Right now we've got nothin' to do that with. Which means we need to find something. And that means exploring some more. The only places we know about for sure seem to be the dead-end area, and what looks to be the breeding area. Dunno 'bout you, but the latter scares the living shit out of me. That leaves just the one place, far as I can see. Thoughts?"

Though none of us liked the idea of moving from our safe hidey-hole, Jack was right. We had to find some way to clear our only route home. To our surprise, Manderpootz spoke up. "Where is the True God? If we created a threat to him, would not his creatures flock to protect him?" An excellent point, and we were all a bit ashamed for not thinking of that ourselves. Where was the worthless shithead-from-space hiding?

"Any indications on the map, Professor?" asked Clio. He just shook his head.

"Well, we'll just have keep our eyes open for signs of it as we go along," I said. "OK, so we need to head towards the dead-end area. Keep in mind that we need multiple escape routes from it, if we can manage it."

It was vital to keep our mental gears moving. Mental paralysis could be a real danger when faced with an overwhelming situation—as I had learned all too well these past few years. Slow at first to get into the spirit of things, in short order the Group had mapped out primary and alternative routes there and back. We could keep to the safety of the auxiliary tunnel system, and pop into the main corridors as required. The chosen routes got copied onto everyone's map, so that no matter what each person would be able to find their way.

Clio suggested that before we headed out, we should have a snack and some water. I objected on the basis that we had limited amounts of either, being mostly concerned about the water. Gail pointed out that since we were about to make a major physical push, it would be best to start as refreshed as possible. I deferred to their expertise, and we took a few minutes to refuel.

At the end of it there was enough food for one more snack each. Everyone's water supply was down to about the half-way point. I insisted we balance out the water so that everyone had the same amount—to redistribute the weight, if nothing else.

Dixon's water supply was way down, so I topped his up with some of mine. He objected until I pointed out I had more experience with this sort of thing than he did.

I was getting concerned for him. Between the exertion and the heat and humidity, he looked to be in rough shape. Grant seemed a bit better off in terms of water, though not much better off physically. He was beginning to show similar problems with his breathing as Dixon. Gail decided to give them both an antihistamine and decongestant to ease their breathing. That helped them only a bit. After a moment's hesitation, she suggested each of them take a hit from Dixon's inhaler. That seemed to do the trick for both of them, but depleted the inhaler.

Finally, it was time to go. We headed off at a modest pace towards the dead-end area. The tunnels appeared well maintained, and wide enough that we could walk two abreast. Every minute or so we paused to listen for signs of pursuit, but none was detected.

Instead we heard, or rather felt, a low-pitched throbbing that seemed to come from all around us. It was almost a rhythmic drumming. The consensus was that it was probably a result of something being transported in the pipes we had seen earlier. The dead-end area seemed to be associated with them, so perhaps it was a main collection or circulation point. Our hope was it would be a control station, or at least something we could use to our own advantage.

All in all it took us nearly an hour to get to the dead-end area, about twice what it should have. However, the closer we got the more often we stopped to rest and listen for sounds of pursuit. The low-pitched throbbing had increased in intensity, becoming an unpleasant physical sensation that felt like a weight. The oppressive heat and humidity added to our discomfort.

We finally arrived at the first of the doors located just outside of the target area. It seemed like a reasonable place for a quick look around. I took the lead, activated the window, and peered into the corridor. A quick scan of the area showed no activity.

The entranceway into the target area appeared to be roughly

circular. Or perhaps better described as rectangular with rounded corners. Unlike the entrances in the plague-breeding area, these seemed have an organic look to them. In fact, this entire area seemed to be a blend of organic and stone, with more organic features the further into the dead-end area I looked.

I gave a whispered commentary to the others as I made my examination. There were no obvious threats, so I asked if we should exit here or try one of the other doorways further in. While the others debated, I kept a careful watch. The short debate came to an end and someone asked me my opinion.

"Both have advantages and disadvantages. Overall, I'd say we should go out from here. The first thing we do when we enter, though, is figure out where the inside doorway to these tunnels is. That can be our emergency exit. Always useful to have one of those, especially in a dead-end area."

There was no disagreement with that, so I lead the way, followed by Dix and Grant, with the others staying in the tunnel. The three of us scampered across the corridor, to stand before the doorways leading into the target area.

Taking a quick peek around the doorways, we saw nothing except more corridors that all looked the same. I motioned at Dixon to stay put and examine the doorways in more detail, while Grant and I went inside. He nodded and began his examination while the two of us continued on.

The two of us followed our original corridor for about ten metres until we hit a branch-off point. I motioned Grant to stay put and keep watch while I went on for a bit. He nodded and I continued down the left-hand corridor. I had spotted a patch of darkness that might have been another doorway, and turned out to be correct.

Pausing for a moment, I signalled to Grant that everything was OK and that I was going to take a quick look inside. After nodding a confirmation to me, he caught Dixon's eye and held up his index finger to indicate that Dix should stay alert. I peered around the corner of the doorway, saw nothing, so took a couple of steps inside, making sure to hug the walls.

Jackpot.

Unlike anywhere else we'd seen, the walls and floor were covered in a faintly luminescent material that had a detailed pattern in it. The colours were difficult to differentiate in the dim light, but appeared to be dark greens and blues. I touched a wall, and it felt warm, somewhat soft, and smooth. The ceiling was lost in darkness, making it impossible to judge its height. The room itself was roughly circular, and perhaps twenty metres across. The sounds of my footsteps seemed to be absorbed by every surface.

There were a number of...desks, for want of a better word. They were large lumps extruded from the floor that had what looked to be controls and indicators on their tops. The walls had some sections that were dark, and some that had patterns and symbols on them. With a start, I recognized some of those patterns as being sections of the map of the facility, but with much more detail.

It wasn't immediately obvious what this place might be used for. There were levers and knobs, glowing lighted things, and what might have been dials or something serving the same function. It looked like the inside of a large industrial control room, and the layout had a similar feel to it. Form followed function, I devoutly hoped.

I stood there for at least a minute, lost in the wonder of it all. Could have stayed gazing at everything for a whole lot longer. Then I remembered there were friends waiting for me, and the urgency of our mission. Retracing my footsteps, I collected Grant and Dix. The three of us hurried back to the others in the tunnel. I stood to one side and waved the other two in, closed the door, and opaqued the window.

I held up my finger to my lips to signal for silence, then made "shoo shoo" motions with my hands to get everyone back into the tunnel for a dozen metres or so. I think the big grin on my face telegraphed the news I had to say, for none of them looked unhappy with my precautions.

I described the room and its resemblance to a major control centre. They all wanted to head straight for it, but I held up my hand to dissuade them. "We'll get there in a bit, but first I think we need to check out the next doorway and see where it opens into. If it's into the control room, great. If not, it might be something just as important to check out. That'll only take about five minutes to do, and could save our lives. Right?"

Everyone agreed, despite being loathe to pass up the fascination of the control room. Survival trumped curiosity. While travelling down the corridor, I tried to keep track of our location in relation to my short journey into the dead-end area. It seemed to me that we were a bit further along and a bit further away from the control room. My guess turned out to be correct.

The map was a bit vague about this entire area, which was surprising given how accurate it was for the rest of the facility. The best we could figure out was this door opened up on the other side of the control room and into an adjoining corridor.

Arriving at our destination door, a look through the window revealed no danger so we exited as a group. As expected, the control room was about ten metres down this new corridor, which had its own set of branches. Entering the control room, I had to grin at their reactions of wonder and awe. Soon they began walking around doing a first-pass look. Half the group went clockwise around the room, and the other half went counter clockwise.

We had just started our walk-around when, without warning, a series of symbols lit up on the ceiling of the chamber. Not brightly lit, but glowing with a soft light-blue glow. I heard a gasp from someone off to one side, but was too busy gaping at the symbols to see who it was. The ceiling appeared to be at least five or six metres away, but it was difficult to gauge it exactly.

"No way," I heard Grant say. "That big symbol in the centre is the fresco that led us here."

"Except this one is complete," added Dixon.

"And that one over there matches the Professor's smaller fresco," said Clio, pointing over to one side.

"There appear to be representations of several smaller frescos surrounding the main one in the centre," said Manderpootz in an soft, awed voice. His gaze swept from one figure to another, obviously trying to see it all as it unfolded.

The large main fresco lit up to a lighter, brighter shade of blue. Small blobs of green moved about, then faded away. After a minute, it all faded back to the original soft blue glow, then returned to darkness.

"What the ever-loving beejeezus was that?" asked Jack.

As the Group began discussing it, the process repeated. After a minute of darkness, it repeated again. It seemed to be a regular display of some sort, but we couldn't figure it out.

"Look, this is all terribly interesting, but we need to look at the rest of this. Please," I pleaded. With understandable reluctance, everyone returned to their walk around the perimeter of the room. All except Stan. The look on his face was that of a man trying hard to recall something he couldn't quite remember.

"Uhm, Stan, we gotta..." I began. He held up his right hand, clenched with only the index finger extended. "Wait," was all he said. The display on the ceiling cycled through its pattern once more, then became dark again. "It's a transportation display," said Stan, turning to look at me. "Like those fancy maps on the subway with the moving lights to show where the train is. It's showing the movement of something or other around Toronto and the GTA. Mostly outwards, but with a few coming in." I just gaped at him, not knowing what to say.

"No, really," he insisted. "I worked on this sort of stuff for the TTC a few years ago. This looks really similar. Could be wrong, of course." He shrugged and grinned.

"Does it help us right now," I asked. "Nah. Probably not. Just one more thing to ponder, I guess," he replied, and with that he returned to his walk around the room. I moved around to follow the group going the opposite direction. After about ten minutes we met at the starting point to compare notes. Everyone's impression matched my own that this was a control room. The question was really how much of the complex it might control.

The key to understanding it came from Clio and Gail—they recognized controls matching features in the plague room, and from that we figured out which symbols referred to pipelines, storage tanks, and valves. That still left an awful lot of unknowns. Grant pointed out that a lot of the pipes and valves related to many of those unknown features. His guess was they had something to do with cooling or an industrial process. There were lots of pipes, and some of them seemed to be large ones, judging by the relative sizes on the displays.

Manderpootz pointed out sections of the wall with symbols matching the unknown symbols on the map, and others matching symbols for those large doors we had seen earlier. Dixon pointed out that the doorways into the control room all seemed to have doors of their own, and what looked to be controls located on the wall next to each one. Which was interesting, as no-one could recall seeing anything similar in the first rooms we had seen.

"Great. All this is great. Now, how can we use this to create havoc—or better yet, destroy this place?" I asked, trying to focus myself and everyone else on the problem at hand.

Manderpootz's face fell as I said it, and he looked as if he was going to object. I quickly added, "The Final Doom—whatever it is—is going to be unleashed within hours, if it hasn't already begun. We have to either stop it, or get out and tell the authorities about this place so they can blow it back to Hell where it belongs."

He looked defiant for a moment, then sighed and nodded his head. It was the loss of all this new knowledge that disturbed him, and I could even agree with him. The looks on the faces of the others showed the same conflict. This place was the ultimate candy for nerds like us.

"The man has a point, and we can all see it," I pointed out. "But this is survival time—for us, for humanity, and for the entire planet. It's time to kick ass and save the world, and damn the consequences." That got their attention and complete agreement.

I suggested another quick sip of water to take the edge off the oppressive heat and humidity—we needed to keep on top of our physical needs. The rich, moist, organic smells held a whiff of something not quite right, and grated on my nerves. Those things, combined with the damned thrumming, had everyone on edge. I noticed Grant and Dix taking extra large swigs of water instead of sips. They both looked like they were in dire need of it, so I refrained from commenting.

While the others worked at studying the various controls, I kept a restless watch. In theory it would have been better to stay in one spot to conserve my strength, but I was too nervous. Besides, I had high-octane go-pills in my pack if a short-term boost was needed. Illegal as hell, but that was the least of my concerns right now.

Jack held up his hand and hissed for attention—we were all keeping our voices low, just in case. He pointed at the section of controls he'd been studying, then up towards the display further up the wall.

"If I'm reading this right, there are pipes going up into Lake Ontario above us. If you follow the pipes ..." he waved his hands to other sets of controls to either side, "it would appear this is how they get the water needed for the various industrial processes they have going on. That means big pipes, I would think. Again, if I'm reading these controls correctly, I can open up those valves into the lake here ..." he pointed at a set of controls, "close these big ones being used to send cooling water to various places ..." waved at a different cluster of controls, "and open up these here," a final wave at yet another set of controls, and he stepped back with a big grin.

We all stood there in silence, until Clio spoke up. "Uhm, sweetie, what will that do?"

Jack's face fell as he realized we couldn't see the punchline. "Big pipes feed water under high pressure into small pipes that can't handle the load. Small pipes burst causing flooding all over the installation. Shutting off the cooling means all their processes requiring that cooling will overheat and fail. With luck, causing even more bad things to happen. You wanted havoc? This should do it."

Stan spoke up, "We can magnify that by shutting off some of their main doors, like the big ones we passed earlier. The Professor and I have been studying the controls he saw, and it looks like we can seal off major sections of this installation. Any burst pipes in those areas will fill up those sections pretty fast and do a lot of damage to any equipment."

Gail added her own observations. "Lee and I think we've found a way to drain out the accumulation tanks used to store the various plagues. It looks as if there is a back-flow purge feature in the controls. There are also other tanks of indeterminate function. However, they're connected to the purge controls. With luck, they have a sanitation function. Worst case, we can drain their plague storage. Best case, we can destroy it with their sanitization agents."

I beamed. "We have a plan. Step one, smash and destroy everything we can. Step two, get the hell out of Dodge. Can we bypass the carnage as we escape, do you think?"

"We can shut all the doors except the final one that we need to get back to the ROM," said Stan.

"The flooding will start back here and work its way up. We should have a good chance, so long as we move fast," said Jack.

"All the biotech stuff seems to be in the levels below where we need to exit, so that shouldn't affect us," said Gail.

This was beginning to look like we had a decent chance of surviving.

All this while the representation of the large fresco had continued to pulse periodically. Suddenly, one of the smaller frescos lit up with a soft green light. Then the large centre fresco lit up in the same colour. The background throbbing sounds increased in tempo and volume. The intensity of the green light on the smaller fresco increased until it was almost too bright to look at. A line connecting the smaller fresco with the larger appeared, and the bright green light moved within it. As the light moved along the line, the light faded from the small fresco. Within seconds, the small fresco had returned to its original pale blue colour.

As the light within the line moved, it reached the main fresco. The background throbbing intensified and became like a drumming that filled our bodies. It became hard to stay upright.

Within a few seconds, the light drained from within the line and filled the large fresco with bright green light. Finally the drumming and throbbing faded, as did the light within all the symbols. Within seconds, they had all faded into darkness. The large fresco was the last to fade away, but within seconds it was once again invisible.

As I opened my mouth to say something, the room seemed to wobble. A wave of nausea ripped through me, forcing me to my knees. From the moans I could hear, it was obvious I wasn't the only one affected. Dixon and Grant looked wobbly, but were still standing. Everyone else had collapsed. I tried to stand, but the nausea was too much, and I fell back with a groan. I could feel a pressure building inside my skull. Pressure tinged with a sharpness that cut like a knife made of pure pain behind my eyes.

The pain eased up, and I vomited noisily. Retching sounds let me know I wasn't alone in my weakness. I looked up to see Dix and Grant staring across the room at a doorway that led further into the dead-end area. A noise like fingernails along a blackboard seemed to emanate from the corridor. The sound pulsed in time with the rhythmic flickering of a green phosphorescence that had appeared. There was a pulsating glow in the air that became more pronounced as the sound got closer to us. The glow made it hard to focus on what was coming. A blast of pain dropped me to the floor again.

After what seemed like an eternity of torment, it stopped. I lay there gasping for breath, feeling the warmth of my vomit against my cheek. The incessant thrumming seemed to be increasing, sounding even more like drums. The overwhelming smell of burnt matches wafted into the room.

The True God had arrived.

CHAPTER TWELVE
Homeward Bound

Of our group, only Dix and Grant were still standing. I had no idea how they were doing that. With a yell, Grant took out his pistol and dashed into the corridor. He ran around the bend and out of our sight. We could hear shots being fired in rapid succession.

The nausea and pain ceased, and I worked at levering myself up into a sitting position. The shooting stopped for a handful of seconds before it resumed. Grant must have reloaded. He needed help, but despite my best efforts I couldn't get up. My hands weren't working any too well yet, though feeling was returning to them. I hadn't noticed when they had gone numb.

The shooting stopped, and I could hear Grant yelling. First curses, then just incoherent rage. The sound of his voice got closer, and I could see him backing up, one slow step at a time. Just before he turned the corner, he grabbed the knife in his belt and threw it at something out of our sight. Yelling a scream of defiance, he paused and tore off his pack. After hurling it at something down the corridor he turned and ran towards us.

Before he could reach the doorway, something shot out and impaled him. A tendril or tentacle—it was hard to tell exactly, because the shimmering had become a painfully bright strobing that made it difficult to focus on. When the tendril touched him, Grant stopped as if frozen. He made a soft whimpering sound as his eyes locked onto mine. Then he disassembled into a pile of gore and body parts. It was as if all the different parts of his body no longer wanted to be together. A phosphorescent glow danced along the remains on the floor. An intense drumming sound filled the air and resonated within our bodies. The smell of burnt matches became stronger.

Dix stumbled towards the doorway, then pawed at the controls. A door ejected from within the wall and sealed the room off from the corridor. The whole of the door was transparent, and I could see something—a large indefinite shape—coming around the corner. Something that was impossible to focus clearly on, as if wasn't entirely solid. The nausea began to return, and I became lost in a haze of dry heaves.

Still fumbling at the controls, Dix managed to opaque the door. The nausea vanished, and he collapsed to his knees, sobbing.

Clio got to him first, and cradled him in her arms. She stroked his head until his sobbing quieted down. Jack stumbled over to the two of them, and pulled them several metres away from the now-closed and opaque door. The others regained their feet, stumbling as best they could towards each other.

I was still on the floor, unable to get into a sitting position. I waved away offers of help, ashamed of my weakness and inability to protect my friends. Stupid, worthless old man.

"What is that ... that ... *thing*?" croaked Lee.

"That is the True God," said Manderpootz. He sounded almost reverent.

The others were trying to rinse the vomit out of their mouths with what little remained of their water. I was about to warn them against wasting it, but realized they were right. Water was the least of our problems right now. I took a few sips of my own water, wasting the first few in rinsing out my mouth and throat and spitting it out. That helped a bit, although my throat still felt raw.

Little by little, strength came back to me. My breathing was no longer a series of gasps. I felt well enough to try to get up, and made it without falling over. I took it as a good sign. My legs felt wobbly, but that was just the numbness wearing off. Lee came over to help me, taking my arm to steady me as I walked.

I took a few steps, stopped, and stood erect. She looked hurt when I removed her hand. I gave a wan smile to help ease the sting of that, then turned to face the group. There was no time to waste. One of our friends had just died to protect us, but there was no time to think about that. The longer we sat, or thought about what had just happened, the harder it would be to move. That was something I'd learned the hard way.

"The shit has hit the fan. Time to unleash havoc and try to reach home." They all looked at me with numb expressions. Then they began to argue with me and each other about what to do next.

"SHUT THE FUCK UP!" I yelled, forcing anger to show on my face—we had no time for reasoned discourse. Only Lee had ever seen me rage-angry before, a long time ago. This was the first time for the rest of them. It worked well enough to get their attention.

"Dix. DIXON," I roared until he looked up at me. "Get off your ass and start shutting all the other doors. Just leave open the one I came in the first time. Lee, you and Clio go with him to find out how it's done. Start with the doorway we all just came in."

I grabbed Lee by the arm and shoved her towards Dix. "GO. RIGHT FUCKING NOW."

Maybe it was my inspiring speech, or maybe the touch of nausea that began tickling at our heads. In any case, they trotted off and Dix shut the door I'd indicated. The nausea stopped once the door became opaque. The three of them went to the remaining door, and Dix began explaining how to work the controls.

Taking a firm grip on my emotions, and willing my legs not to buckle, I turned to the others and spat out orders. "Stan, start shutting all those larger doors you mentioned. Gail, start wrecking the plague room. Jack, once Stan has shut the doors, turn off the flow of cooling water. Figure out what else you need to do make the flooding happen. Time to get those bastards distracted and too busy to worry about us."

They stood unmoving for the space of a couple of heartbeats

before heading towards their stations. Gail gave me a long, hard look. I gave my head a slight, slow shake warning her that now was not the time for discussion. She frowned at me, then went back to studying the controls in preparation for her task.

"Doors ready to deploy," said Stan. I nodded at him, and he began operating controls. The only sign something might be happening was a change in the indicator lights along his group of controls. As he threw the last switch, we could hear a faint, short thump. That gave us all a reason to smile. Not much of a smile, to be honest, but better than anger or fear. We were beginning to strike back.

"Ready with the plague room," said Gail with an angry edge to her voice. I nodded at her. She hesitated a moment, took a deep breath, and began operating controls. Her compassion and empathy were wonderful traits, and I hated like hell to force her to do this. She knew the stakes, though, and was tough enough to do what needed to be done.

"Cooling water disabled," said Jack. "Ready to start the flooding."

I looked at him and said, "Hold up on that for a sec. OK, everyone, grab your gear and get ready to head out. Chop chop, let's hustle. We'll go out that first door I came in, and into the auxiliary tunnel. If that's blocked, we'll head up the main corridor. All set? OK, everyone except Jack and myself go stand by the door."

As the others grabbed their gear and headed to the door, I grabbed Jack's knapsack and went to stand by him. Clio started to come towards us until Jack waved her away. I handed his pack to him, and he put it on. "Ready?" I asked him with a grim smile.

"Yah. Throw this bank of controls to open up all the smaller pipes. Throw this bank to isolate the inrushing water to the smaller pipes. This bank of controls way up here opens up the floodgates to the Lake itself. Easy peasy," he said with a grim smile of his own.

I turned and looked at the rest of the group standing in the doorway. While the others watched us, Stan scanned for danger. He gave me an "all-clear" wave, so I turned to Jack and said, "Let 'er rip."

He began by closing the smaller pipes. I helped with that, as there were several dozen of them. After that, we began on the dozen or so controls that isolated the flow. That left just four controls left, which we hoped would open up the floodgates and let the deluge begin. We each grasped two of the controls, then using a nod to synchronize our actions we engaged them. We heard a satisfying "thunk" as the controls were set, so we turned to head towards the door and our friends.

A loud CLACK stopped us in our tracks. We looked back and the four main floodgate controls had returned to their normal position. Jack and I rushed back and again activated the controls, but they would only stay engaged so long as we held them. Smart design. Bad for us.

I signalled the others to stay where they were while Jack and I struggled to come up with a solution. It was simple fix, actually—all we had to do was jam the controls in the active position with something.

We each dropped our packs and did a quick inventory. I had two spare knives. Jack had a small crowbar and a can of bug spray. I raised my eyebrows at that, and he shrugged with a smile. We got to our feet and began setting up. We managed to create a bridge of sorts to jam each control against the other. It was a hideous kludge, but it worked. Jack and I grinned at each other, shouldered our packs, and jogged across the room to join the others.

Dix and I hung back as the others ran towards the entrance to the auxiliary tunnels. Dix suggested shutting and locking the doors to the control room. Before we could begin, a loud CLACK echoed. We turned to see the four control switches back in their safe position and the bracing items scattered on the floor. Shit.

I felt myself spun around and a strong shove against the small of my back drove me forward and to my knees. By the time I got back up and turned around, the door was shut and locked. It was still transparent, and Dix stood there with a sad smile and tears running down his cheeks. He gave me a small wave, shrugged off his pack, and ran towards the control panel and began to re-assemble the bracing. He paused once to mouth "go away" at me, before turning back to his work.

I couldn't move. Another friend that a stupid, worthless old man had failed to save.

I felt a gentle hand on my arm, and saw Gail standing next to me.

"We have to go, Felix," she said in a soft voice, tears running down her cheeks.

I nodded, and we walked towards the tunnel and the rest of our friends.

Time to go home.

★ ★ ★

It took us over two hours to reach the main corridor that led back to home. Sometimes we were forced to catch our breaths. Sometimes we had to run as if the legions of Hell were on our heels—which they were, actually.

Each time we passed one of the hidden doors, we peeked into the main corridors to check on the progress of our sabotage. To our immense satisfaction, there was increasing chaos. Groups of werewolves could be seen rushing to and fro throughout the facility. When we opened the door into a corridor, we could hear sounds similar to the alarm in the Plague chamber, but with a different pattern. We took that as a positive sign.

Sometimes we had to loop around in the tunnels to avoid detection. It was damned discouraging to have to retrace our route, knowing that every minute counted. On one of our loop-backs we passed a birthing chamber. Like the plague rooms, we saw pools with bloated women floating in them. Some pools were filled with small pods, which Gail and Clio identified as amniotic sacs. The sacs had small, dark, writhing somethings inside. A steady stream of werewolves rushed in to take a sac and then rush out with it.

We watched in horror as Priests went from woman to woman, slicing open their bellies to remove the amniotic sac, which was then placed it a pool with the others. It was like watching ants scurrying to save their eggs from a damaged nest.

I, for one, was grateful that our pressing need to escape forced us to stop watching and hurry onward.

The previous thrumming of fluids being piped around had been replaced with random clankings and gurglings. We didn't know for sure if Dixon's sacrifice had been in vain, until we looked out into a corridor and found it filled with water. That gave us a certain amount of satisfaction until we noticed a small amount of water at the base of the door on our side of the tunnel. That was strong encouragement to hurry on.

By the time we got to the main corridor, our supply of drinking water was long gone. We stood panting in the auxiliary tunnel just outside the corridor. From there we faced a long slog uphill, so a brief rest seemed to be in order.

Well, "rest" was perhaps the wrong word—"recover" being closer to the truth. The trip here had been stressful and exhausting. We'd been lucky enough not to meet up with any werewolves. A couple of times we felt the faint hint of nausea that preceded the True God. Each passed quickly enough that I would have dismissed it, except everyone else had felt the same thing. Our nerves were on edge as we tried to recover a bit before the final push. Someone muttered the old line "water, water everywhere, but not a drop to drink." It got a weak laugh from everyone. Aside from that, no-one did any talking.

After catching our breath, I insisted we each check and minimize our packs. All empty water containers got discarded, along with the little food we had remaining. No-one was hungry and there was no water to wash it down with. Likewise, first aid kits were tossed aside, except for a few wrap-style bandages that could be used to bind up pretty much anything. Ammunition for the guns got put into pockets or belt pouches for easy access. The plague samples got re-distributed amongst all our packs—we couldn't predict which one of us was going to get through, so we prepared for the worst. I was astounded we'd made it this far, to be honest.

Peering out the window of the door I looked around as much as I could, but saw no obvious dangers. I looked behind me, and everyone nodded to show they were ready. An hour's worth of hard uphill slogging faced us, but home was at the end of it.

I cracked open the door and peered out. Seeing no threats, I motioned the others to follow me. Instead of the gentle breeze that had greeted us when we first arrived, we felt a strong wind blowing up with a roar from within the structure. The rapid changing of the pressure caused our ears to pop every so often. "Water pressure is forcing the air out," yelled Jack. "That's a good sign."

"What's that sound?" yelled Clio. Lee replied, "Sounds like the rapids before a waterfall."

We all realized what that meant, so we turned and headed up and out at a fast walk. We turned the corner to head up the main corridor and saw some flickering lights far, far ahead. "Keep walking, keep walking," I insisted. "We'll find out what those are soon enough."

Strange though they might be, they were of no immediate consequence. This was our only way out, so we had to keep going. We walked at a measured pace as the blowing wind gusted. We felt the occasional dash of moisture, as if it were beginning to rain.

Pretty soon I noticed that we had started to walk faster, perhaps in response to the wind and moisture. That would tire us out too quickly, so I had everyone slow down. Best to keep to the pace that would allow us to get home, whatever was coming.

Unfortunately, "whatever" turned out to be werewolves coming up behind us.

At first there were only a couple, which Stan took out with his rifle before they got too close. All too soon we saw a few more, and a few more after that, until soon there were at least a dozen of them. We kept to our steady pace. If one of us stumbled, the others would grab onto them and drag them along until they got their feet under them again. Walk, walk, and keep walking. March or die.

The werewolves kept up a steady pace that was only a bit faster than our own. That struck me as somewhat peculiar. Their normal hunting pace was a flat-out run. I took the monocular from its belt pouch. After checking that the floor of the corridor was clear of obstructions, I turned my head around as best I could to take a look at them while I walked.

The group consisted of Priests, for the most part, with a few Drones. There were more coming up at some distance behind them. A worrying trend. I spun to face forward once again. After focusing the monocular on the flickering lights up ahead, I almost wished I hadn't.

Gail must have seen something in my expression, because she gasped out, "What's up ahead? What's wrong?" I shook my head. It took all my breath to wheeze, "Werewolves." She closed her eyes for a moment, heaved a sigh, and nodded. Bad enough that we were not going to get a chance to rest along this final leg of our journey. Now, at the end of it, we faced a fight for our lives while exhausted.

Still, something bothered me about what I'd seen. Why were they even there? Waiting for us? That didn't seem right. And why were those lights flickering? Come to think of it, what were those lights? I'd never seen werewolves use flashlights before.

Stan and Jack had slipped back to walk with me, as my investigations had slowed me down to a few paces behind the others. Stan yelled over the roar of the wind, "How ya doin'?" In reply, I pointed ahead and panted out, "What are those lights?", before handing him the monocular.

He kept up his pace while looking through the monocular, never missing a step. After examining the scene for a moment, he passed it on to Jack who performed the same feat. Ah, to be young again.

Jack yelled, "Torches", and passed the monocular back to me. Stan nodded his agreement and shrugged as if to say "So what?"

"Werewolves don't use fire," I said, breathlessly. "That's new."

They both started cursing, mouthing the words instead of wasting precious breath speaking. Smart lads.

After exchanging a glance, they each grabbed one of my arms and power-walked me up to join up with the rest of the Group. A good idea—though they could have asked or warned me, dammit. The two of them made sure the ladies and the Professor knew about the threats ahead and behind us. Better to know than to be surprised.

So we kept walking, step after exhausting step. My legs burned, but damned if I would slow the group down. I took a perverse pleasure in seeing Manderpootz start to finally slow down a bit. This was beyond the pale for us all, not just the two oldies.

Finally, we were about the length of a football field away from the werewolves in front of us. We could now see that they were fighting someone in the tunnel that led up to the ROM—had to be Thansworth and his people.

I called the Group to a halt. They looked at me with puzzlement. We were all grateful for the rest, though cognisant of the need to keep going. I was having problems catching my breath. Finally I managed to get out, "Thansworth. Radio."

Gail understood immediately, and dug into her pack for the radio he had given us. Pressing it against one ear, she covered her other ear with a hand to muffle the roaring of the wind whipping us from behind, and the roar of the army of werewolves ahead of us. The others and I stood watch, with guns at the ready.

While Gail tried to make contact, I motioned for Stan to take a shot at some Priests coming up behind us that were too close for comfort. He nodded, aimed, and fired twice in rapid succession, working the bolt action like a pro. Two of the Priests fell, and the lead group halted their advance. With any luck, that would buy us some time. I turned to tell Stan to reload, but was pleased to see that he didn't need me to tell him that.

By this time Gail had managed to make contact with Thansworth, and was explaining that we were about a hundred metres away from the tunnel. She finally lowered the radio and waved at me to join her. I stifled a groan and hurried over as best I could—I had little in the way of reserves left.

Gail frowned as she watched me move towards her. As I leaned towards her, she yelled, "Thansworth is holding the tunnel while the werewolves attack. He says to wait five minutes to give him time to mount an offensive to clear the tunnel, then run like hell. His words."

Five minutes. He may as well have asked us to hold for five hours. None of us were in any shape to run, much less uphill. Not to mention fight a battle with werewolves while doing it. It was getting hard to think straight, and my legs felt wobbly.

This seemed like the time for a power pill—a high-dose stimulant. I fumbled at a side pocket with hands that refused to cooperate. Gail slapped my hands away and got out the vial of pills. She read the label and frowned at me. With a sigh and shake of her head, she gave me one. After a moment's consideration, she indicated that she was going to give one to everyone.

I nodded, and managed to dry-swallow the pill. While waiting for it to kick in, I took another look at what we had to face. The werewolves coming up behind us were holding position. The ones behind them were almost ready to join them. I sighed. Once they had amassed enough troops, they would charge at us. That's just what they did.

A glint way at the bottom of the tunnel caught my eye, and I took out my monocular for a closer look. It turned out to be water beginning its rise up the corridor at a slow but steady rate. It looked like Dixon's sacrifice would flood the entire facility. A good man. Him and Grant, both.

The thought of my two dead friends caused me to choke up, and I wiped the tears from my eyes. Jack came up beside me, laid a hand on my shoulder, and looked concerned. I pointed at the water and handed him the monocular. It only took him a few seconds to understand, and when he lowered the monocular his own eyes needed wiping. He clapped me on the shoulder, handed me the monocular, then went to tell the others. Dixon and Grant deserved that much recognition, even if the knowledge would likely die with us.

A roar from below brought me out of my reverie. One of the Priests stood in front of his group, gesturing as he spoke. Just like during the attacks at the farm. I slung my shotgun, then pulled out my pistol and took a measured stance. The power pill must have kicked in, because my breathing was easy and my mind clear.

I knew what to expect and what to do, and waited for just the right moment. The Priest finished his exhortations, turned to face me, and pointed. The first row of Drones began running towards us with the Priest running alongside. My first shot dropped the Priest, and the next five each dropped a Drone. As expected, the others stopped in confusion and fear. Without the Priest to drive them on, they were loathe to come forward. In fact, they backed up to join the rest of their group. The threat to my friends had been neutralized for a minute or two, I figured.

I broke open my revolver and emptied out the spent cartridges without bothering to save them. No point any more.

Reaching into my belt pouch, I pulled out a speed loader and reloaded without any wasted motions. After that, I had just enough rounds left to refill the speed loader one last time. The others stared at me with their mouths open. Oh, yeah—they'd never seen me in battle before, had they?

"When there's a group being led by a Priest," I shouted to my friends, "hit the Priest first, then as many as you can of the ones in front. Drones get scared without their Priest to lead them—for a while. The further away you are when they go down, the longer they wait before attacking again. Usually."

I motioned at Stan and Jack to keep their eyes on the group uphill of us. With luck they weren't going to notice us for a while. I waved at Gail and Lee to join me.

Lee didn't have a real weapon, just the multitool I'd given her a few days before. I pulled my tomahawk out of its sheath on the knapsack. Slipping her hand through the wrist strap, I tightened it so the 'hawk wouldn't drop off without some effort. Then I unclipped the hunting knife from my belt, and attached it to hers. Taking Lee's hands in mine, I looked her in the eyes and gave her hands a squeeze.

Letting go of her, I turned to Gail. She had a couple of extra clips for the pistol Thansworth had given her. I went through how to reload and how to set and release the gun's safety, just to reinforce the quick lesson Thansworth had given her. After setting the gun's safety, I returned it to the holster on her belt. I had her put the extra clips into her front pockets for fast access. Taking Gail's hands, I looked into her eyes and gave her hands a squeeze.

A roar from uphill followed by volleys of shots got our attention.

It was time.

I motioned everyone to huddle against the wall of the corridor the side-tunnel from the ROM opened into. That would keep us out of the line of fire as we advanced. We could see the werewolves up ahead begin to back up out of the side-tunnel, which had to mean that Thansworth was forcing them out.

Time to run like hell for home.

We didn't run, actually, though we managed to stride forward at a steady pace. When we were about fifty metres away some of the uphill werewolves noticed us and started running down towards us. Stan and Jack let loose with several volleys to clear the path. That allowed us to keep moving with little time lost.

Looking downhill, I could see those werewolves beginning to advance. Worse, they gained speed with every step. Soon they broke into a trot. I stopped, drew my revolver, and emptied it into their front line. I reloaded, pleased to note that my hands weren't shaking at all. After my second volley of six rounds slammed into them, they stumbled into a slow shuffle.

Good enough.

I reloaded with the last of my ammunition, turned, and hurried to catch up with my friends . They were now about ten metres ahead of me. I caught up with them, but the effort ate into my strength reserves. I could feel myself fading. We still had about twenty metres to go to the tunnel entrance. Not good.

The werewolves ahead of us were backing up against the far wall just past the tunnel entrance. We could only hope that the entrance to the tunnel would now be safe for us. Gail whipped out the radio and yelled that we were just a few seconds away.

Looking back, I could see the glint of rising water had risen halfway up the corridor. Damn, that was fast. The werewolves below me saw it as well, and they put on a burst of speed to catch up to us. I emptied my pistol into their ranks, then holstered it. Time for the shotgun. It held five rounds. Then it was clubbing time unless I could reload.

A quick look over my shoulder showed my friends several metres ahead of me. Time to play catch up, so I huffed and puffed and moved my legs as fast as they could go. It wasn't going to be fast enough.

The Group stood at the entrance to the side-tunnel. Stan and Jack fired into the werewolves advancing towards them from the far wall. Gail had her pistol out, holding it with two hands and pointed up, watching for anything getting in too close. Lee watched me, waving me forward, yelling something I couldn't hear. Then she stopped waving and began pointing behind me.

I stopped, whirled around and brought the shotgun up and thumbed off the safety in one smooth motion. The lead werewolf was maybe two metres away when I put him down. I pumped the shotgun and shot the next one. Pump and shoot. Pump and shoot. Pump and shoot. Pump and nothing. The next couple of werewolves went down after I hit them over the head with the barrel of the gun.

There was one more of the bastards and I was off balance from the last swing. I tried to recover, but knew I wouldn't be able to do it in time. With a shriek and splatter of blood, the werewolf fell down onto the ground. I looked around, and saw Stan standing some metres away, rifle at his shoulder. Clio, guarding his back, fired her shotgun into the pack of werewolves pressing in on them. I began slogging uphill towards them. My legs felt like lead.

For some reason, the pack attacking them decided I was a better choice of prey. Most likely because I was the solitary one cut off from the herd. My friends had their own problems, so I was on my own. Three metres away from my friends, and my legs were ready to give out.

Four Priests marched towards me, two of them with torches. For some reason I thought they should be waving pitchforks too, and the thought made me giggle. I threw my shotgun at them, overhand at a slight angle. It managed to hit the two in front, stopping them. That caused a tumble with the two behind them, which took those four out of contention for the moment.

My friends were being forced into the side-tunnel entrance by the sheer number of werewolves. I was metres away, with no weapon, and no way to help them. Stupid useless old man, up against a mob of werewolves armed with torches.

Torches. That was it.

I unslung my knapsack and opened it up to take out the can of talcum powder. I ripped off the top and tossed it to one side. With the open can in one hand, I re-slung my knapsack and stumbled uphill towards the werewolves. Several had torches.

"You've got one chance, you worthless old fuck, so don't screw up this time," I began chanting to myself.

Holding onto the can, I swung it around and forward. The contents sprayed in a large arc ahead and beside me. The cloud of talcum powder hit the torches, and the resulting exploding fireball was a thing of beauty. It knocked werewolves ass over teakettle, and set some of them on fire.

The blast forced me backwards. I hit the wall hard, then dropped like a sack of wet cement. Wet cement that felt like all the nerves on the right side of its body were screaming for attention. My vision wasn't working so well, either.

Blink.

I was lying on the ground, and all I could see were werewolves either screaming or burning. Some were doing both. Cool.

Blink.

Two streaks of flame flew out from the tunnel into the werewolves, spewing intense light and smoke. Oh. Flares. Forgot we had those. Pretty.

Blink.

I saw Lee screaming and smashing at werewolves with the tomahawk. Gail was beside her, firing a pistol. Manderpootz was swinging a geologist hammer at the skull of a Priest. The three of them were wading through a mob of werewolves that looked rather worse for wear.

Blink.

Blackness. Lights flashed all around. A large circle of light loomed ahead, coming closer. Groovy.

Blink.

Bright, bright room. Many men with guns running around. Yelling. Lots of yelling. Shooting.

Blink.

The pain started to get real bad. My throat seemed tight. It was getting difficult to breathe.

Blink.

I wafted through a doorway, a regular doorway. Oh, I guess we made it home.

Wait—someone needed to shut the door. That was important.

I tried to turn and point, but the effort made me pass out. Just before I passed out, though, I thought I saw a shimmer of water enter the room we had left.

Then blackness.

I was floating in pain. Voices faded in and out. Lights flickered and flashed.

This was getting tedious, so I decided a nap would be a fine idea.

CHAPTER THIRTEEN
Counting the Cost

When I awoke, I found myself lying on a soft surface. I tried to get upright, but stopped when the restraints and the pain made it impossible. Wasn't going to try that again anytime soon.

"Ah, you're awake. Are you thirsty?" asked a gentle female voice.

I was—very much so.

I tried to answer, but could only manage a faint grunt, so I settled for a slight nod. Just doing that seemed to exhaust me. A straw made its way into my mouth, and I was cautioned to take small sips. Stupid straw was so small a man couldn't get a proper mouthful of water. That seemed to please Gentle Female Voice, but to hell with her. I wanted big gulps of water. And a beer. Especially a beer.

And maybe an aspirin for my headache, which was now making itself known in a rather vicious manner throughout my skull. The sipping made me cough. The effort exhausted me so much I drifted back to sleep despite the pain.

★ ★ ★

After that, I started staying awake longer, and becoming a lot more aware of my surroundings. I'd always hated hospitals, and doctors poking at me, and stupid questions about how I was feeling.

Some of the machines were kind of neat, though, and the young women operating them good-looking. They seemed to appreciate a patient who spoke kindly to them, did everything they asked, and asked intelligent questions. None of them ever let on what the results of the tests were, always telling me that only "the Doctor" could discuss the results with me. I didn't recall ever seeing any damned doctor.

From what I could see on the monitors during those tests, I was fine. My internal organs all seemed to be there, and my brain and heart had enough electrical activity to produce wavy lines. So as far as I was concerned I was just fine and could leave at any time. When I tried to tell the nurses that, all they did was give a respectful nod and ask me if I'd like more jello.

I frikkin' hate jello.

Made the mistake of venting to one young nurse, and she looked so sad that I apologized and ate a double helping to make it up to her. It wasn't right of me to take my frustration out on her. I asked when I could have real food, and once again I was told to wait for "The Doctor" to approve it.

What about visitors? I was going to have to wait for "The Doctor" to approve any visits.

The one good thing about staying at the hospital, though, were the pain meds. It seems the mysterious doctor had told them to let me have as much as I wanted, whenever I wanted. I had the fluffy drug for the daytime, the smooth drug for the late afternoon, and the dreamless-sleep drug for the nights. I appreciated the latter when I began to remember why I was in the hospital.

The dressings on my right arm, both hands, and head got changed several times a day. Thanks to the drugs all I felt was a slight pressure, and any pain seemed faint and far away. All in all, a good life—except for the damned jello.

After a couple days, I asked the nurses to cut my pain meds in half. Wasn't so bad, all in all. Hurt more when they changed the bandages. On the plus side, my thinking got less fuzzy. Started dreaming again at night, though. Strange dreams I could never quite remember when I awoke. But the echos of fear and horror they left behind left me shivering and drenched in sweat. They switched me to a different drug for the nights. Didn't do more than take the edge off the pain, but I slept better.

My burns stopped feeling like raw hamburger being shaved with 20-grit sandpaper, and I began sitting up. Still hurt, though every day things hurt less. After a week they asked me if I wanted to allow visitors to see me. That seemed like a strange question, given I'd been asking about receiving visitors for days. So I politely said, "Yes, please", and waited more or less patiently.

A short time later, Gail and Lee walked in. Even though they were wearing hospital scrubs with gloves and masks, I recognized them right away. Damn, it was great to see them. They were being so quiet and polite it got to the point where I had to ask them what, exactly, the bloody hell was going on?

That bit of normality got them giggling, then outright laughing. Then I started smiling and giggling, too. The giggling kinda hurt, so I settled for smiling. I guess I didn't hide the wince of pain too well, as they stopped laughing right away and asked if I was OK. My glare got a smile out of them,. We had a nice chat for a few minutes before Nurse Fussbudget came in and chased them away. This was to be all the excitement I was going to be allowed for one day. Hell and damnation.

At least I'd managed to get some information about my condition. It was obvious the gowns and masks were to prevent infection of my burns. What about the lack of visitors and their forced politeness? Well, I'd hit my head awfully hard in the tunnels, and suffered a nasty concussion plus hairline skull fractures. The concern was there might be brain damage. Visitors had to promise to project calmness at all times for the sake of the patient.

Battered though I was, enough was enough. The next time a nurse came in, I calmly and politely insisted on seeing this mysterious doctor whom I had yet to meet. The nurse smiled and said she'd see what she could do. Later that day, I got wheeled out for more scans and testst. After returning to my room they rewarded me with jello.

Yippee.

I almost asked the nurses for an extra-large dose of feel-good juice to stave off boredom, but resisted the temptation. I had too many things to think about. I was forcing myself to remember what had happened, and the drugs interfered with that. The effort of remembering tired me out, and I spent a lot of time napping.

The next morning, I asked another nurse about seeing the doctor, and got the same non-answer. The same nurse came back in the afternoon, and we went through the routine again.

For all these days I'd been strapped into the bed—to prevent chaffing the wounds and pulling out tubes, I was told. After days of quiet acquiescence, I told the nurse that either the doctor came before supper or I'd remove the restraints and go looking for he, she, or it. The nurse just gave me a condescending smile and left the room without a word.

When she came back an hour later to check on me, I was sitting on the side of the bed rubbing my wrists and stretching out stiff shoulders. With my most innocent smile I asked her when the doctor might be free to visit me. Or would it be necessary for me to go looking?

The nurse got all huffy and insisted I get back into bed and allow myself to be strapped in, right this very instant. She moved towards me, with a stern look on her face. I stopped her with a waggle of my index finger. "Uh uh. Nope. Not going to happen. Movement helps the healing process, don't you know. Now, if you promise to go fetch the doctor, I promise not to tell everyone you unstrapped me."

Ah, you gotta love blackmail. A classic tactic, but effective. Especially when one was in the right.

I wasn't surprised when, a short time later, the door to my room opened and the doctor strode in. She was a stern-faced, no-nonsense, middle-aged woman. I recognized her at once, though we'd not spoken for a few years.

"Felix."

"Margaret."

"Feeling better, I hear. Good to see you up."

"No thanks to you."

"Your tests have all come back looking nominal."

"What are you doing looking at my tests?"

"I'm the doctor assigned to this case. No-one else wanted it.

196

Your reputation preceded you."

"You could have dropped in once in a while. How can you treat a patient you never examine?"

"Oh, I did. Every night while you slept. You're much easier to deal with when you're unconscious, you know."

"Is that what the unrestricted access to the pain meds was for?"

"Partly. And partly to determine if the blow to your head had addled you worse than normal."

"What—like a test?"

"Exactly."

"What if I got addicted?"

"Then you wouldn't be you, and we could change treatment to suit."

"A bit unorthodox, don't you think?"

She shrugged. "Perhaps. But as effective as any other test, given who you are."

"Yeah, yeah, whatever," I retorted, not wanting to concede that she had a good point. "When can I get the hell out of this place?"

"Tsk. Tired of us already? Excellent. We'll be glad to see you go. Tomorrow. Noon. One last round of tests in the morning, just to make sure."

She turned to walk out of the room.

"Hey, how about a phone to arrange for a pickup?"

"Your friends have already been contacted, and have agreed to take you after we evict you. Good day, Felix."

And with that she was gone.

I lay back down on the bed and smiled. It's always nice to visit with old friends one hasn't seen in a long while. Wondered why she, of all the doctors in all the hospitals, was assigned to my case. I did, however, make a mental note to double check, after I got out, that all my internal organs were still there.

★ ★ ★

Gail and Lee came to pick me up at the hospital the next day.

"That doctor of yours is nice," said Lee.

"Yes she is, Felix," agreed Gail. "Spent quite some time with

197

us, making sure we knew about the sort of home care regime you are going to need. Made sure we had the appropriate supplies, gave us prescriptions, enough of the drugs to tide us over until we can get the prescriptions filled, her office number, and her email. Told us to call if we had any questions whatsoever. You must have made a good impression on her."

"Uhm, yeah. Sure."

They looked unconvinced. Their mood remained irritatingly chipper all the way to the truck. My truck. They told me to sit in the back, and in the centre of the seat so as not to rub my injuries against the frame. There was an argument, which I lost. Kids just don't respect their elders, these days. So sad.

"So, Felix, tell us more about the doctor," Lee said. Damn. When would she learn to leave well enough alone? I muttered an evasive answer and closed my eyes as if napping. A minute later I opened them a slit to find both women staring at me via the rear view mirror.

"Dammit, Gail, keep your eyes on the road," I muttered, resisting the urge to add nasty comments about women drivers. They would have just laughed at me anyway. Some years ago, many of us in The Group decided to take a winter and safety driving course one weekend. All the women had started out not doing so well. After a day of professional instruction, though, they did better than any of us men. Much mocking and gloating had ensued.

We managed to get back to their apartment in one piece, with no further attempts at conversation. They had set up the couch and area around it as small, but serviceable, hospital room. Insisted I had exclusive use of the couch for as long as needed. Their offer brought a lump to my throat, especially as the apartment was small enough to begin with. I got a mild allergy attack, and had to pause to wipe my eyes. There must have been something in the air, because they both seemed to get a mild allergy attack at the same time.

Once we had all wiped our eyes and cleared our throats, Lee insisted on making some tea. Mild tea for me, because that's what Doctor Margaret had ordered for the next week or two. Though I despised tea that wouldn't dissolve the spoon, it hit the spot. We drank in silence for a while. Then Lee asked again about the Doctor.

I ignored the question. They exchanged amused glances.

This exchange repeated, back and forth, for a couple of minutes. Finally I blurted out, "We used to date, OK? Satisfied? It was a long time ago. Over and done with." The answer seemed to satisfy them—for the moment. Wretched creatures that they were.

"Kidding aside, Felix, how are you feeling?" asked Gail, allowing her concern to show.

"And we want it honest and for reals," insisted Lee.

I sighed, more from weariness than irritation. "Tired, to be honest. Bit of pain and tenderness in the burns. Burns all healed, for the most part. Bit of a headache. Surprised they discharged me so soon. I got the impression it happened a lot earlier than usual."

Gail stared at me for a moment before replying. "Yeah. About a week or two earlier. They needed the room. Lots of injuries have been occurring this past week, and hospitals are swamped."

Lee added, "Clio arranged for some new burn treatment to be allocated to you, and it helped you enough they felt it was OK to discharge you. She also knows of some walk-in clinics specializing in treatment of discharged patients, so you'll be well taken care of. There's one about a block away from here, too, and they've been brought up to speed on your requirements."

I nodded. That helped explain the special setup in the apartment.

"Tell me about the hospitals needing the room. That sounds bad."

The two women looked at each other, hesitant to say much more.

I sighed. "Ladies, I'm fine. Healing well. Honest and for reals. My memory of what happened to us is patchy, but coming back. I remember that we—with the sacrifice of Dixon and Grant—caused the underground complex to flood. I remember we fought like hell to escape, and made it almost to the ROM. After that, my memory gets wobbly."

My voice remained steady and calm for the most part. It only caught when I mentioned our two friends, who had sacrificed themselves for us. We all got a touch of that allergy again. Had to pause to wipe our eyes and blow our noses.

Gail looked at me and asked, "You sure you're ready to hear more, Felix?"

I nodded.

She sighed before replying. "We—all of us except you—were forced into the tunnel leading into the ROM. Mr. Thansworth and his people were there above us, firing into the werewolves attacking us." She paused as shudders ran through her. Quickly regaining her composure, she continued. "There was an explosion. We heard screaming, then there were no more werewolves attacking us. It was a ... a ... scene from a horror movie, Felix. Werewolves were howling and burning, the wind was gusting into the tunnel, and there was a horrible smell. Then Lee yelled your name and started running back out to the main tunnel. I followed her. Manderpootz came after us, and we all went out and found you."

Lee was sobbing at this point. Gail had tears running down her face. My own eyes were getting foggy.

"Stan and Jack showed up, firing into the mob of werewolves. We grabbed you and got you into the side-tunnel, somehow. Mr. Thansworth was there with some of his people, and they carried us up into the ROM."

Although Gail had tears rolling down her cheeks, her voice was firm. "The werewolves kept coming. Mr. Thansworth and his people kept killing them until there were no more. Then they moved the carved seal back into position and locked it in place."

Lee took up the story as Gail wound down. Her voice started out a bit shaky, gaining strength as she talked.

"There were men there with tubes of sealant and glue. They rushed in to caulk around the seal to prevent the water from comin' in. Worked well enough. We found out later it was never meant as more than a quick patch, and soon after they did a proper job with cement. Added steel bracin' to keep it

200

tight. Sealed and braced the door into the room, too. Behind the seal is a lot of water, so the room is goin' to stay sealed for a very, very long time."

I digested that condensed bunch of news. Sounded like Thansworth had believed us enough to get in touch with his contacts. Lucky for everyone.

Pointing at them, I asked about the bulges under their clothing, and the scratches on their hands and faces. Turned out everyone in The Group had gotten scratched up during the battle, although nothing too serious. Some of the scratches had gotten mildly infected, but those were being cleared up with antibiotics. Everyone still wore a few bandages, here and there.

"Any other casualties besides Grant and Dixon?" I asked. The two women looked at each other, back at me, and both nodded.

"The werewolves went insane, by all accounts," Gail said in a quiet voice. "Came out of all those exits around the GTA we saw on the map. Went on a killing rampage. Priests and Drones both, by the sounds of it."

"But Mr. Thansworth's warnings to the various police agencies allowed them to get to those exits before too many werewolves got out," added Lee. "I gather a bunch of people decided pretty quickly to plug those exits with debris, cement, and whatever they could find. Did enough to stop the worst of the werewolf attacks. And the worst of the flooding."

"But not all of it," I suggested. They both shook their heads.

"The GTA is under undeclared martial law," said Lee.

Gail added, "There hasn't been a werewolf sighting for a couple of days—at least, none reported. Lots of injuries, a few deaths. Enough to overwhelm the hospitals. You got extra treatment because Clio dropped hints to the right people that you were instrumental in fighting the werewolves. Otherwise you'd have been just one more werewolf victim."

More deaths on my conscience. Hadn't even thought of what would happen once we opened the floodgates. I sat there scrubbing my face with my hands—the parts that weren't raw, anyway. The right side of my face still felt kind of tender. I raised my eyes and looked at the two young women. They realized all too well it was our actions that caused the werewolves to spill out and go crazy.

"Hey. Hey," I said and waited until they were both looking at me. "If we hadn't flooded the complex and stopped that alien thing, there would have been a lot more deaths. Worldwide"

"You believe that, Felix?" whispered Gail.

"Yah. Still hurts, though. Can't help but. We made the right call. The only call."

"We know. That's the conclusion we all came to," said Gail, her voice soft and sad. I noticed a few gray hairs where none had been before, on the heads of both the ladies.

Lee noticed I was beginning to lean to one side, and interpreted it as a sign I was beginning to fade. She wasn't wrong, so I let the women fuss over me and give me my meds. They left the room, and I stretched out on the couch. It didn't take me long to fall asleep, and my dreams weren't too bad. All things considered.

CHAPTER FOURTEEN
Starting Over

The next couple of days were similar to my time at the hospital. Each day Gail and Lee went to work in the morning. I spent most of the time sleeping and eating. The magic ointment for my burns was clearing them up in jig time. Each day I felt stronger and more clear-headed. On the down side, each day I remembered more of what had happened during our encounter with the alien thing calling itself the True God.

By the third day I was feeling pretty good and had convinced myself I was back to normal. Normal enough to feel bad about intruding on my friends for so long. Normal enough to want a place of my own.

Going back to the farm was out of the question, of course. The rural areas were now considered no-go zones, and any survivors were being evacuated. There was still the odd report of werewolves skulking in the woods, the culling I'd barely survived was being uncovered, and looter gangs were roaming around.

The OPP was reeling from the discovery of its many murdered officers. Despite that, it was getting re-organized and beginning to restore order everywhere. It was going to take a while, though, so it was safer to stay away from those areas for the time being.

The undeclared martial law had been extended across the whole country, despite the fact that werewolves seemed to have all but vanished everywhere. People were strongly encouraged to travel only to work and buy supplies. Travelling around for pleasure or simple visitations was discouraged. Very strongly, judging by the arrest reports I heard about on the radio. So we had no further contact with any of The Group aside from a few brief text messages. The Internet was down, and phone service was spotty.

Within a week, the state of emergency was eased, Internet service was restored, and phone service was working. In a similar fashion, my memory was more or less back to normal. It was time to start asking questions and search for answers. Time to get my own place. Turned out there were quite a few places available, and at affordable prices.

During the past couple of years, people had been moving away to less werewolf-infested areas. Ofttimes without telling anyone—like landlords or the people who owned the mortgage on their now-worthless homes. After this last wave of attacks, Toronto passed bylaws allowing landlords and such to declare these vacant properties available for sale or lease. The only proviso was to wait twenty-four hours after posting a notice in a newspaper. The daily newspapers grew to size of telephone books for several weeks after that bylaw was passed. It wasn't quite legal, of course. However, when the banks threw their weight behind it, the provincial and federal governments rushed to change the required laws to make it so.

I found a nice condo townhouse across town. There was a decent medical clinic close by that met with Clio's approval. I needed regular checkups, and had a couple of stubborn infections requiring treatment. The area had a good broadband connection, which would be important when Internet service was fully restored. There was even a small back yard for a garden.

Not too many neighbours just yet, though I was sure that would change. The three of us drove out to take a quick look before I signed the papers. It all looked so lovely they were tempted to move there themselves. Alas, the lack of reliable public transit in the area meant the commute would have been horrific for them.

The area was a bit run down, but just from lack of

maintenance, not from being torn up by werewolves. I'd seen enough of that sort of thing to last a lifetime. All the empty townhouses I had toured were just dirty, as if the owners had left in a hurry.

The next day, Gail and Lee helped me load up the truck with my stuff. I insisted on driving myself out, though. The last time I had purchased property was when I got the farm, and involved weeks of dealing with paperwork and lawyers and bankers (oh, my).

Things were a lot easier this time. The sellers and banks wanted to make things as easy as possible. Especially when I was able to pay cash. Gotta love it when the banks get motivated to make money back from a losing investment. My savings took a serious hit, but what the hell.

Getting furniture and appliances turned out to be no problem. The stores sent reps to the bank. Right after I signed my papers, they took my order. To my surprise, they delivered and installed everything before the end of the same day. Heck, they even helped to carry in stuff from my truck. That sort of service wasn't going to last long, so I made a point of enjoying it while I could.

Still, it all seemed so unnaturally calm. No great panic, no great uproar. There was no real discussion about the werewolves, or their last terrible breakout. Just everyone going about their daily routine. The only difference being a bit less fear now it all seemed to be over.

The overall calm was strange, and a more than a little disturbing. Then I recalled the Control Plagues. It appeared the damnable things had finally served a useful purpose. Everyone was focused on the here-and-now business of cleaning up and re-building. It amused me to think that in years to come, people would no doubt look back on this calmness and attribute it to a superior Canadian pluckiness of spirit, or some such.

I still got tired easily. Now, though, I could nap in my own easy chair or bed as the mood took me. It was beginning to almost feel like a home. Sometimes I could even get television shows on the cable, which was a nice change for me. All repeats of stuff I'd seen before, despite not watching much television for years. Some things just never change. The radio stations all played happy-happy music, and the news was all upbeat. Don't worry, be happy. Your government was working tirelessly to get everything back to normal. Blah, blah, blah.

The cell and land line phone services usually worked well, with only the occasional failure. Better than the farm had been for quite some time, for sure. Thinking about the farm made me a bit misty and feeling tired, so I took a brief nap. I woke up feeling refreshed, so I fired off an email to the OPP enquiring about when they were going to allow people to go back to their farms. Then I got back to getting ready for the big visit later that afternoon. This was something I was quite looking forward to.

I had arranged for The Group to come up for a small get-together. They arrived as a group, in two cars. One car held Stan, Jack, and Clio. The other had Gail, Lee, and Manderpootz. It was a surprise to see him, and he looked a bit ill at ease. Not at all like the flamboyant know-it-all asshole of old. I gave them a warm welcome, and hugged them all with enthusiasm. Even Manderpootz, to his surprise. As we all walked into the house, he whispered a quick question wondering why the warm welcome. I whispered back that we had survived Hell together. The answer seemed to relax and please him.

Stan had brought a huge bag of potatoes and Clio had made a potato salad. I had obtained a large supply of hamburger meat (though no doubt it was a mixture of protein sources) and buns, so we ate damn well. They had brought beer and wine, and I had purchased some as well. We were all in fine spirits, laughing and joking and speaking only of pleasant things. Afterwards, we sat in the living room sipping on coffee. Real coffee, too, thanks to my grateful contact at the bank. Everyone expressed approval with it, and I took it as sign I hadn't lost my touch.

After a while, our conversation reached a natural lull. It stretched into an empty silence no-one wanted to break. Finally, I raised my cup in a toast, and said, "To absent friends."

They all just stared at me for a moment, before raising their own cups and repeating the words. None of us were dry-eyed. I'd put lots of tissues around the room, being sure the evening would involve tears at some point. Since moving here, I'd had my own share of them, as memories had surged forth unbidden.

"Uhm, I hate to bring this up," I said after we'd all regained our composure somewhat. "Has there been any sort of service for Dixon and Grant?" They all started to look around at each other, at the floor, and anywhere but at me. Sigh. They were still treating me like a brain-damaged invalid.

"Guys, the skull fractures have healed."

"Mostly," interjected Gail.

I favoured her with a glare before continuing. "And the concussion is cleared up."

"Mostly," interjected Lee.

She received her own glare.

"The point being," I continued, "I'm not a brain-damaged invalid. And there are things I need to know."

There was a silent discussion amoungst the Group.

Finally Clio spoke up. "Felix, it's not that you're not well. It's just..."

"You see, it's like this ..." continued Jack, before he stalled.

After a handful of heartbeats, Lee sighed and said, "We were afraid you would have broken curfew and heads if we had told you earlier."

"Told. Me. What?" I asked, a touch testily.

"They've been declared missing, not dead," said Gail.

I could only sit and gape at her, my jaw hanging open. I closed it with a snap, tried to say something, failed, then shook my head. That proved to be a mistake, so I stopped doing it pretty damned quick. Lee had been correct about the concussion.

"Felix, it has to do with events that came after we destroyed the underground complex. There were so many deaths and disappearances here in town. The discovery of the disappearances from the farms and small towns. No-one could prove if someone was alive or dead. Heck, there have been a lot of people in the past few years who have just packed up and moved on without telling anyone. So after some high-profile people got their knickers in a legal bind, the Feds passed an order-in-council saying death could only be declared if a body was produced. Period, end of discussion. No declaration by anyone would be accepted any more. Had to have a body. Otherwise, death can only be declared after five years. Period, end of discussion. Prevented some nasty succession wars that would have torn big chunks out of the business community."

That made sense, actually.

"Alright," I nodded, "but what about how the provincial legislature allowed the homes and such of missing people to be sold off after a declaration in a newspaper?"

Stan let out a dismissive snort. "Different set of big-money business interests."

"Fine, but where does all this leave Dixon and Grant? Neither has any family I ever knew of. Who's going to remember them, what they did, who they were? What about their apartments? Are their possessions just going to be tossed into a dumpster like they never existed? Like they never mattered?"

I was starting to get a bit steamed by this point.

"This isn't right. They died saving us and the whole damned world, and now the world is ready to toss aside their memory like they were nothing. That's just not going to happen." I was on my feet and yelling by the end of my little speech. My head was throbbing, but I didn't much care.

Gail stood up and walked over to where I was standing. She put a hand on my uninjured shoulder. "We'll look into it, Felix. But you've got to calm down." I shook off her hand and glared at her. Gail stood there looking sad.

Clio spoke up, the voice of reason as always. "Gail's right, Felix. Jack and I will contact their landlords. That was a smart idea you had, and I'm just sorry none of us thought of it before now."

"Why would you?" I muttered. "None of you had any reason to think about it like I have. That's how I got this place, remember?" I waved my hand to encompass the house.

Lee and Gail got me to sit down again. They sat with me, one to either side, each holding a hand. We began talking about our two lost friends, exchanging anecdotes and stories of how we had first met them. There were lots of tears and laughter, as every good wake should have. A good way to remember them. Even Manderpootz had a story to tell about Dix.

It turned out the lad had met Lee at work once when the Professor was there, and had managed to accidentally delete files when he stumbled against the Professor's laptop. Which hadn't been backed up in years, since no-one was ever allowed to touch it except the Professor. Dix managed to recover the files in less than a minute, after which he proceeded to write a script to do automatic backups. That was pure Dixon.

After finishing his story, Manderpootz looked woebegone and went silent. I thought it strange, since he hadn't known Dixon well. Remembrance came to me—his murdered colleagues.

"Professor, what happened your colleagues? Does this legal bullshit affect their status?"

He hung his head and wrung his hands for a few seconds. Finally he raised his head. "They, too, were declared missing. But the University has graciously agreed to pay out all benefits to their families." He hung his head again, lost in his own memories. Clio patted him on the shoulder, and he responded with a weak smile.

I figured now would be an appropriate time for dessert and coffee. Gail and Lee helped to distribute everything. In the privacy of the kitchen, they told me the University only paid out the benefits after Manderpootz had raised merry hell with them. His own high-ranking connections had saved his sorry ass from censure, and hushed things up after his misadventure. But the old boy surprised everyone by twisting arms and engaging in not-so-subtle blackmail to get the benefits flowing without delay. Burnt every bridge and called in every favour he'd ever had. Seemed much happier for it—or at least more at peace with himself.

The cake I'd baked wasn't too bad, considering the dearth of good-quality ingredients. I even managed to get some whipped cream made. There wasn't much of it, but enough that everyone got a bit. The mood was reasonably upbeat. Sort of a happy sadness, as we contemplated our lost friends. No-one seemed to want to discuss our adventure, or any larger issues. Which was fine by me, to be honest.

Things wound down shortly thereafter, and we decided to call it a night. Handshakes and hugs were exchanged all around. Soon I was alone in the house. Somehow it didn't feel quite so empty any more. Almost like a real home, in fact.

★ ★ ★

True to her word, Clio and Jack got in touch with the landlords of Dixon and Grant. Turns out both were decent people, and had been about to pack up belongings and put them into basement storage. They seemed pleased friends were available to do the task for them. And, oh by the way, could it be done within the week? There was a waiting list for each of the apartments.

I guess decency only went so far in Toronto.

After some debate, we decided to be somewhat ruthless when it came to their possessions. Clothes, furniture, utensils, and anything reusable would go to one of the charity stores, which were always in need of stock these days. Anything personal would get boxed up and stored. Since I had a house with a small basement, I volunteered to store it until we could decide on what to do with it. We were all weirded out about pawing through their stuff. Making final decisions on disposition was not something we wanted to do right now.

Both of the landlords said they'd take care of passing anything we left behind to the appropriate agency. For some reason, I decided to take them at their word.

Stan, Jack, and I managed to process both apartments in a single day. They still had boxes from when Jack and Clio and moved in with Stan, and Gail had some from her move, so we were all set. I knew both Dix and Grant were book lovers—hell, everyone in The Group was—but they both had an awful lot of them packed into their small apartments. We ended up just carting them down and dumping them into the back seat of my truck's cab. We would have run out of boxes otherwise. Some books we just left behind as they were just old college text books kept for sentimental reasons. We took computers, paintings, pictures, anything of sentimental value or looked like it might have sentimental value. After filling up my truck and Stan's, we headed back to my place and schlepped it all into the basement.

By the time we finished, it was late afternoon, and my offer to make supper was accepted with enthusiasm. Our conversation was of current news and such. Clio was spending long hours at her lab on some project or other. The two young men were busy with the reconstruction and rebuilding efforts. The pace of life in the city was quickening, they said, as if everyone had awoken from a deep sleep. Speaking of which, they had to leave shortly, as there was still job-related work to do when they got home. I could see they were eager to leave, so I shooed them out, and brushed aside their offers to help clean up.

It had been a long day. I was exhausted, and it felt good. Maybe it was a silly thing to do, saving all the bits and pieces of their lives, though I felt a lot better doing it. A bit foolish, too. I had so many years experience in feeling foolish it didn't really bother me much at all.

The next day I phoned their former employer, and spent some time explaining who I was and why I was calling. It turned out they'd gotten a brief email from the government about the status of the two men, and were at something of a loss on how to proceed. To my surprise, Dixon had listed me as an emergency contact—for lack of anyone else, perhaps. I was flattered nonetheless. Grant had listed Dixon as his own emergency contact. I spoke at some length with a nice young lady in HR.

Their workspaces had been cleaned up and personal items boxed. She hadn't had the heart to do more. Between us, we decided there wasn't anything of value worth my taking. Anything technical could go to the company library, and the toys could be distributed amongst coworkers. It pleased me to hear the two young men had been well thought of by their coworkers, and would be missed. The young lady was glad to hear both men had friends who would miss them, and who cared enough to take care of their affairs. I left my contact information with her in case they needed to get in touch with me for any reason.

After that, the days went by in a pleasant whirl. Somehow I managed to find enough to do to fill the hours. My burns and other assorted injuries healed well. I just needed physiotherapy to work out some of the kinks and stretch the healed skin. They encouraged me to do daily light exercise, which I expanded to include gardening as well as my morning walks. I planted the potatoes Stan had given me at the housewarming party. Additionally, I planted some garlic and hedge roses around the borders. My neighbours thought it was a damned fine idea, and they started doing the same. I suspected those sorts of plants were going to be popular for some years to come, even with the werewolves gone.

Everything began to stabilize and get back to normal. Shipments of all sorts started up again, as there were no longer any werewolves around to cause problems anywhere in North America. There were still periodic shortages. The difference this time was people would grumble about it. The power and communications utilities could affect repairs without werewolves damaging equipment and killing the service personnel. It wasn't that people were optimistic about things, but at least they weren't in a feral survivor mode.

Even better, brain cramps became a thing of the past. There had been a nasty flu going around everyone seemed to get. It only lasted twenty-four hours, and after some fever and mild nausea it went away. Everyone who got it reported feeling rather better than normal after it passed.

On the negative side, the water levels in Lake Ontario were down twenty centimetres or so. The tunnel network must have been more extensive than we realized. That affected everything associated with the lake—shipping, fishing, recreation, drinking water, sewage disposal, all sorts of things. Fingers were being pointed, government commissions were organized, businesses demanded bailouts and subsidies, and climate change was blamed. Some things never changed.

On the curious side, there were intermittent reports of strange lights, smells, and temporary illness reported along Lake Ontario. This was being attributed to the rapid and severe decrease in the water levels—nothing to see here, so move along.

The others in The Group were all busy at their jobs—the work of cleanup and reconstruction was kicking into high gear. Lee was welcomed back to the ROM, and the official story was nothing had happened except a minor professional misunderstanding. Again, nothing to see here so just get back to work.

We never managed to find a quiet spot on everyone's schedule to arrange another get-together, what with the overtime everyone seemed to be working. Gail came up for a visit one afternoon, though, which was a nice surprise. She reminded me to be careful what I said in emails and phone calls. Even though the undeclared state of emergency seemed over, the uber-watchfullness was still in full force.

That also explained why the news, such as it was, was filled with feel-good stories—the censorship bureaucrats were still active. Public transportation was working, though rationed in the on-going attempt to minimize travelling around except for business-related trips. Gasoline was going to be in short supply for a while—good thing I'd filled the gas cans when I left the farm. In spite of those minor issues, we had a great visit.

She brought me up to date on what everyone was doing. Everyone seemed to be so busy these days, especially Clio.

"What's she so busy with these days?" I asked in surprise.

"Not sure, to be honest. Something to do with the manufacture of medicines and such. What with manufacturing and transportation still screwed up, the government is finally getting serious about getting medicines manufactured in Canada."

"About damned time," I grumbled. "But what about patents? The multinational drug companies get damned nasty about such things."

Gail just smiled. "Guess someone in the corridors of power

213

finally grew a spine. Too many things are either in short supply or will be soon. It's been decided to get the job done, whatever it takes. In the national interest, don't you know." That made me snort in amusement. Having someone in government with the brains and balls to do the right thing just didn't seem natural.

"Speaking of government, kiddo, what was their reaction to all the stuff we brought back? The plague samples, and the pictures?" Gail looked down and the floor and cleared her throat. I sighed. "Just tell me. Please."

"There aren't any pictures. Not any of any consequence, anyway. Most of the cameras got ripped off by the werewolves in the battle, and the ones that survived just had shots of darkness or werewolves. And everyone's seen enough pictures of snarling werewolves." She paused, and looked down at the floor again.

"Well, shit. So, no record of anything," I said. "OK, what about the plague samples?"

"Uhm. Well. Clio took them all. For safekeeping. We kind of agreed not to tell anyone about those. Not right away. You know how governments love their bioweapons." I nodded, and continued to stare at her.

Gail sighed. "Well, anyway, Clio has access to facilities that can store them as well as anyone in the world can. And contacts with researchers who are second to none."

"And?"

"And that's it, Felix. Truth. I've only managed to talk to Clio once about this, security being what it is these days. She assured me the samples would be studied and destroyed."

The look on my face must have been quite something, because she started to giggle. I tried to say something, but couldn't find the right words. Finally I settled for a strangled, "What?"

Gail's face became serious. She was struggling with a decision. Finally she said, "Don't ask. Don't tell. Not ever. Not to anyone. Not to anyone in or out of The Group. This is for serious and for reals, Felix." I stared hard at her for a moment, then nodded.

"The samples were studied, Felix. To find a cure. The samples and research will be destroyed very soon now. End of story."

"Yeah, but..."

"No, Felix. End of story."

In a flash it hit me.

"That flu going around recently. Everyone got it, and felt a lot better afterwards. That was the cure, wasn't it?" Gail nodded.

"How did it get done so fast?" I asked. "Clio's amazing, but ..."

"But nothing," Gail interjected. "Clio organized it. She knows everyone who's any good, and there's people who've been studying the Change Plagues for years. I'm not in the loop. I can take a pretty good guess, though. Remember when I said we needed access to the base virus to understand the weaponized versions? Researchers knew a lot about the virus already, and with samples of the various payloads attached to it, it was easy to create a payload-free version."

"Ho-lee crap," I breathed. "They used the de-fanged version to provide immunity for any subsequent versions."

"Yes, indeedy," Gail said with a large smile. "And the only cost was enduring a mild 24-hour flu. The human race is safe, now." We grinned happily at each other. Alas, I had to ruin the moment by thinking too much.

"The research and samples. They can be used to create new variants. Or used as a basis of modifying different sets of viruses."

Gail nodded, now sombre. "Yes. That's why it all has to be destroyed. The samples, the research notes, everything associated with it. Even the specimens from my lab. And it will. Clio will see to it."

"They'll all be crucified by the government—any government—when this comes out," I said with sadness.

Gail gave a wry smile. "Funny thing...no-one seems to have taken notice of our little, uhm, adventure."

I could only gape at her, open-mouthed. "Heh. If you could only see your face now, Felix. After we escaped, everyone was busy sealing the tunnel and dealing with the werewolves running around. Now, the rebuilding and reconstruction have been soaking up everyone's efforts at every level of government. All anyone knows is we went into the tunnels, and a few hours later came running out. What happened inside is known only to The Group."

"No debriefing of any sort?"

"Nope."

"What about leaks? Clio's group? Someone's bound to talk."

"Unlikely. These are people who hate the Plague with a passion, and want to see it eradicated. They know how close to the edge of extinction we came, and won't allow that to happen again. Not on their watch. Not ever."

We sat there grinning at each other for a time, until her phone chirped an alarm. It was time for her to go, if she was to catch the train home. I drove her to the nearest subway station, gas shortages be damned.

Along the way, she tried several times to ask me something, but seemed at a loss at how to go about it. It wouldn't help to force it out of her, so I focused on driving. Finally she took a deep breath and asked, "Felix, do you remember when we gave everyone the anti-viral pills?" I nodded. My memory was back to normal. Or, rather, what passed for normal for an old man.

She licked her lips before continuing. "Dixon said something. He said he had to stay with the program. And then I saw Grant nod, as if in agreement, even though he took the pills. Do you know what that was about?"

I shook my head. "No. Now that you mention it, I thought it was strange at the time. There was so much else going on ..."

Gail made a soft snort. "I know what you mean. I've been thinking about, well, everything that's happened to us. Was thinking about Dixon and Grant, and it just sort of stood out in my mind. Don't know why."

We arrived at the subway station, and I parked along the curb. I turned to look at her, now able to give my full attention to what she was saying.

"Hmph. Good point. Don't forget it was Dixon who came up with the top secret database, too. A good kid—a good *man*—but he tended to hare off in strange directions. Grant seemed to be somewhat the same, though I didn't know him very well."

Gail nodded before replying, "Dixon brought him into The Group, and he was just in the background until this past year. Seemed like an OK guy—trustworthy, and helped keep Dixon from getting too far out of line."

I thought about she'd said for a moment. "Then there's how the two of them seemed more or less immune to the effects of The True God, while the rest of us got laid out flat on our backs. I dunno. They were the only ones to take the antihistamines and inhaler doses. Maybe that's what did it. Strange."

"Have you gone through their effects at all? Even a cursory look?"

"It's like I told you earlier, Gail—I just haven't had the heart to do it. Always seems to suck the energy out of me when I try."

She grabbed onto my hand with one of her own, and squeezed. We sat there and snuffled for a few seconds, before wiping at our eyes with our free hands.

"Don't force it, Felix. There's no rush for any of it," she said.

"Yeah, I s'pose you're right, Gail. So much has happened, and I'm just now starting to feel almost normal again."

I paused before bringing up something that had been bothering me for a while. "And that kind of segues into something I've been wanting to talk to you about. We've all been so busy with the here-and-now, cleaning up the messes and building for the future, what happened to us has gotten pushed into the background. Way into the background. This is the first time anyone has even brought up the True God, at least to me. Have any of you talked about this amongst yourselves?"

Gail shook her head with a sigh. "No. You're right about everyone being kept busy worrying about the here-and-now." She sighed again, and looked into the distance. "It all seems so ... unreal, now that it's over and done with. And, 'sides, it's nothing we can talk to anyone about, is it? Best to just leave it all in the past, I think."

"Sure, kiddo, sure. For the best."

We sat there in companionable silence for a bit, until it was time for her to go. She promised to get in touch with me in a week or so, once things settled down a bit more. The drive home was a quiet one. My thoughts kept turning to our conversation, and I had to force myself to keep my attention on the task at hand. When I arrived I was feeling somewhat tired, so I made an early night of it.

The next day the OPP got back to me regarding my enquiry. There was going to be a phased resettlement of the rural areas, as things got normalized. My area was scheduled for resettlement in eight to twelve weeks, at the earliest. I wasn't surprised to hear that, as the gangs of looters had proven to be as nasty as the werewolves, in their own way. Once the police had gotten re-organized, though, they quite efficiently began sweeping areas for werewolves. And in the process got rid of the gangs.

It looked like I was going to be stuck here for a while. Maybe until the fall, or even next spring. Which was actually fine with me. I had good neighbours and trusted friends close to hand. It sounded real nice to maybe have a winter without worrying about werewolves. A real nice change.

CHAPTER FIFTEEN
The Long Road Forward

I had settled in and prepared myself for a wait of many months before the OPP resettlement program allowed me back at the farm. I spent the time ordering stuff for my new home—some nice flowers for the garden beds, some bookcases, and a small freezer. I also bought equipment for a proper computer setup—UPS, kick-ass computer, large monitor, printer, that sort of thing. These were tools I needed to start working on answers—and formulating questions that no-one else seemed to be asking.

To be fair, everyone was busy at their jobs. The city, and indeed the entire country, seemed to be emerging from a sleep-walking state and was single-mindedly working to bring things back to normal. That left me to investigate what no-one had time to question. Like, what was that doorway doing in the ROM? What in hell was "the program" that Dixon mentioned? Come to that, where had he and Grant gotten those Glocks?

Thinking of Dixon got my eyes to watering, and I had to pause to wipe them and blow my nose. That gave time for thoughts to percolate into my conscious mind. The database that Dix had sent me was government-level stuff. Then there was "the program" thing. Combine all those with the fact that he had acquired a gun from "sources" made me suspect that he had gotten himself involved with some national security organization or other.

Grant's surprising attack on the True God, and Dixon's dash

to close the door and cut off the alien's baleful influence, spoke to the high probability that they knew what to expect. At least to some extent. And given that near certainty that someone in authority knew that the plagues were manufactured, that meant that some government agency or other would be tasked with finding out more. So why had it been left to our ragtag group to put an end to the True God's plans?

Speaking of which, was the damn shithead-from-space truly dead? Bloody unlikely, given how long it appeared to have been around. So what the freakin' hell was it, where did it come from, and where was it hiding? For that matter, how did the fucking alien sack-of-shit get those original bio-hackers to create the beginnings of the Change Plague? Or were those morons working on their own, and those original attempts used as cover by the True God to mask the release of the Change and Control Plagues?

Come to that, why was Toronto the centre of the alien thing's plans? Well, the small fresco that Manderpootz had spoke of a palace of creation in a land cleansed by ice. The underground facility could be considered a palace of creation, I suppose. And during the last Ice Age, glaciers had certainly scoured Canada as far the Great Lakes. Why was that important?

Then, of course, was the question of why the layout Toronto mirrored that ancient layout so closely. That was freaky strange, for sure. Then again, if the True God had settled here, then it's influence would probably make itself felt. Well, that fresco said that the True God would bring its blessings to the new land. Not much of blessing, though ... more of a curse.

So many questions, and now I had lots of time to work on them.

Later that afternoon, the OPP got back to me about my resettlement request.

The email message that arrived said to be at my farm the next day, at oh-nine-hundred hours, and don't be late or else I would lose my slot in the resettlement schedule. My resettlement authorization number was blah blah blah. I was to enter only as far as one car-length into the driveway, no earlier than fifteen minutes before the appointed time, and wait for an OPP representative to show up. Failure to comply blah blah blah. If there were any questions, contact blah blah blah. I was to bring a copy of this email to use as a pass into the restricted rural area.

The message was unexpected, and I didn't know quite what to make of it. I must have been gaping at the monitor, because I found my mouth closing with a "clack" that rattled my teeth. The reality of the whole thing began to kick in, and I began fretting about the logistics of moving again. That went on for some minutes before I got myself under control.

Taking a deep, calming breath I forced myself to re-read the message. Yes, it did indeed tell me to be at the farm next morning at a specific time. Yes, it seemed to be from the OPP resettlement office.

Time for a sanity check. First of all, I confirmed that there was, indeed, an OPP resettlement office. The contact information matched what their web page said, and matched what their adverts in the newspapers said. Alrighty then—the message seemed legit. Well, how about that? I must have sat there grinning at the monitor for over ten minutes before I got up and made myself a celebratory cup of tea. It was time for a serious think.

Thought one—this was quick. Why would that be?

Thought two—there were a lot of werewolf bodies around my old house, with obvious signs of battle damage. Was that going to cause problems?

Thought three—my security system was still active. Both active and passive defences. That could definitely be a problem.

Enough thinking, there was enough to sort out for now. The issue about the security system was the most important one, since I had left the defences under automatic control. Yes, there had been a major infestation of werewolves at the time. Despite that, if any human had been harmed by those defences my ass was going to get chewed.

I needed to get within WiFi range of the house and put the security system into standby mode. Could I go there now? No, I could not—OPP patrols were reportedly quite active and not inclined to play nice, what with the looter gangs roaming around.

That meant that I needed to get there before the appointed time. I might be able to push things by getting there twenty or twenty-five minutes early, rather than the stated fifteen. No, twenty minutes was all I felt it was safe to push things these days, with de facto martial law in effect.

Well, I could still leave here a bit early, and wait at a gas station or something on the outskirts of the Rural Zone, and get there a tiny bit early. Anyway, with luck all the active defences had been triggered and depleted by the werewolves.

As for the bodies all around, well, I could hand-wave that away by saying that I had to fight my way out. Depends on how fresh the bodies were, I guess. Or maybe blame the looter gangs. Nah, just say how I had to fight my way out, and if there were any other bodies I had no idea how they got there. Volunteer nothing.

That left the nagging question of why such a fast response? I wasn't a working farm, and those were reportedly getting priority. The more I thought about it, the more confused I became. Puffing out my cheeks with a sudden exhalation, I realized that the answers would only be revealed when I met with the OPP. There was nothing more to be done this evening. Oh, wait, there was. I needed to let The Group know about this. We'd begun to make plans to finally sort through the effects of Dixon and Grant, and had hoped to get together in a week or two. I emailed Lee and Gail to let them know about the message, and told them that I'd being heading out in the morning for the meeting.

With that email sent, I went to make myself some herbal tea. Regular seemed to keep me awake at nights, these days. While fussing with the kettle, the phone rang. The last time that had happened was a couple of days ago. Turned out to be a scammer trying to sell me some crap service or other. Some things just never changed.

I picked up the phone without looking to see who it was, and was greeted by Lee's voice demanding to know what the heck was going on. We talked about what a surprise the email had been, and how I felt about it. We didn't discuss anything sensitive, as one never knew who was listening in these days. I got the impression she was hoping that I wouldn't bother going. After a brief discussion I promised to give her a call as soon as I knew anything. With that, we wished each other a good night and hung up.

I'd been standing during the phone call, and felt the need to sit down again after it concluded, my tea forgotten. It was kind of nice to be closer to her and the others, I had to admit. On the other hand, the farm was my home. Or was it?

It was kind of nice to not have a big rambling house and yard to maintain. On another hand, there were a lot of wonderful memories at that old place, not just horrific ones. On yet another hand (I was running out of hands), my books and tools were there. Too many variables and not enough hands to juggle them all.

I sat there for a bit, just sort of lost inside my own head. Not thinking too hard about any one thing, nor worrying about the future. Just lost in a general buzz of what-if's and what-about's. After a half-hour or so of that, I decided that was enough wool-gathering, and went to bed. I had an interesting day ahead of me.

★ ★ ★

I sat in the farm's driveway at the designated location, with the engine idling. Although wasteful of gas, and not good for the environment, it was a damn fine idea from the viewpoint of security. As planned, I had arrived exactly twenty minutes before the appointed time. It was a matter of just a minute to log into the security system via WiFi and disable the defences. With that little task out of the way, I began to breathe a little easier.

The rest of the time was spent viewing the place through binoculars, and scrolling through the security system logs. From what I could see, things looked fine. The grass was pretty tall, and from what I could see the house and barn were intact and in good shape.

The only surprise was the lack of bodies or remains of any

sort. There might have been something on the other side of the house, but getting there was forbidden for the moment. I contented myself with looking through the security logs.

There had been an attack later in the day I left, which had depleted all the active defences. There were periodic incidents after that, and those had triggered the sonics and lights. The most recent incident had occurred two days ago. That was interesting, and made the resettlement notice all the more puzzling. Unless it was caused by the OPP checking out the house, which begged the question as to why they'd want me back so fast.

Speaking of the OPP, there was still no sign of them so I took a quick look at the control system's overall status. As far as the security system was concerned, everything was working. Or at least as much as it was when I left. There was still power being supplied by the batteries, although their level was a lot lower than I expected. It appeared that only a quarter of the solar panels were still supplying power, which meant that the batteries were only being partially charged during the day.

That was unexpected, and I was curious to see what had caused that. The solar panels were on the roof on the other side of the house from where I was, and should have been safe from werewolves. As expected, the mains power and all the communications links showed as non-operational. And yet the OPP said this area was now opening up for resettlement. Well, maybe the problem was at the house—it had taken a helluva beating from all the attacks. With all the wires run underground, it was impossible to see if they were intact or not.

Curiosity, and a growing list of unanswered questions, caused me to get a bit antsy. I was getting to the point of gnawing on the inside of my cheek, and was considering starting on my knuckles, when an OPP cruiser showed up. It slowly entered the driveway and parked behind me. Remembering the state of the world these days, I put both of my hands on top of the steering wheel and tightened my grip on it. No threats here, no sir. Just a harmless old man, coming here as ordered, sir.

Alternating looking at the side and rear view mirrors showed a uniformed figure getting out of the cruiser, putting on a hat, and walking purposefully towards me. In a few seconds the officer had reached the driver side of the cab, tapped on the window (which was still up), and asked me to step out of the truck. The voice was a no-nonsense woman's voice, and she appeared to be approaching middle age. Her hand was lightly touching the butt of the gun at her hip.

I got out, and stepped to the ground, holding onto the door handle as well as the courtesy handle on the side. Not only did that keep my arms wide and show that I was no threat, I needed both to get in and out of the truck these days.

"May I ask what your business here is, sir," she said in a no-nonsense but polite tone. It wasn't a question.

I identified myself and produced the printed copy of the email from an inner pocket of my windbreaker. She examined it with care before asking me for identification. I passed over my driver's license and expired passport, that being all the official ID I had. She compared the photo on the license and passport to my face. Frowning at the differences, she finally nodded and handed everything back to me. I stuffed it all into a pocket.

"Sir, are you prepared to move back into your home within forty-eight hours?" This was the pro forma question asked as part of the resettlement, and one that I was prepared for.

"Yes, officer, I am."

"Do you have any questions with regards to the condition of your home?" This was another pro forma question.

"Actually, officer, I do."

Her eyebrows rose a bit, and I thought that I could almost detect a slight smile threatening to form.

"Very good, sir. I have some questions of my own, if you don't mind." Again, it was a statement.

"Uhm, OK," I replied, becoming more than a little confused. "Did you want to ask yours, or should I ask mine, or what?"

"First of all, sir, I'd like to examine the outside of the house and barn with you. When I was here several days ago, the security system appeared to be active and let loose with a painful series of sounds and lights that only stopped when I retreated to about where we are here." She paused and looked at me expectantly.

I cleared my throat and explained that I had rigged up a security system for protection. It had worked against the werewolves for several years. When it became ineffective, I shot my way out and went to stay with friends in Toronto.

"Very good, sir. Were you aware that it is still active and preventing us from approaching?"

"Uhm, yes, officer. I disabled it while I was waiting for you."

Well, that got her attention. She enquired, with a touch of eagerness, how I had done that. She caught herself, and explained that doing so was not required and was not part of the resettlement interview.

Of course, I was happy to show off my technical brilliance. Grabbing the netbook, I showed her how the system could be armed and disarmed (being careful to avoid the menus for the active measures), and how it showed the status of power and communications. She seemed impressed. That led her to enquire about what measures I had for inside the house.

A tricky question, and my hesitation to explain was apparent. Oh, what the hell. I told her about the caltrops and bottles of drain cleaner and such that I'd left scattered on the various floors.

"I posted notices on the outside of the house warning about those," I said. "I just couldn't stand the thought of those fucking werewolves getting inside and trashing my home." She ignored my use of profanity, and nodded sympathetically.

"I saw those notices, sir, and they may have helped to protect your home from being looted. The bodies of the werewolves helped with that, too." All traces of humour were gone from her face.

That didn't phase me in the slightest, and I stared back with equal intensity. "I was fighting for my life, officer. I saw what they did to my neighbours, and I held on as long as I could. When worse came to worst, I let loose with everything I had and ran. I almost left that too late." I was getting a little heated by now, and allowed it to show despite myself.

We stared at each other for a few seconds, then the officer sighed and nodded. "Yes, sir, I understand. We've had to clean up a lot of bad things around here." For just a moment her eyes looked at something far away that only she could see. After a couple of heartbeats, her attention snapped back on me. "I'm supposed to escort you around the perimeter of your home. After that, if you are satisfied, there are papers to sign."

That suited me fine, so we got into our respective vehicles and drove around to the back. That's when the damage that I had left behind became clear. The ruins of the greenhouse, the generator, the windmills ... and the odd piece of skeleton poking out here and there. Nowhere near as many as I would have expected, until recalling how the werewolves treated any source of protein. I stepped out of the truck, and the wave of emotion that swept through me forced me to turn away and lean on the hood. The officer just stood to one side and told me to take my time.

I turned and took another long, slow look around me. "They came in waves for that last attack. Down the driveway, from the fields, and from behind the barn," I said in a dull voice. "I shot them. I killed them. They kept coming, and I killed more and more until I was almost out of ammunition. Then they retreated. After smashing everything."

After pausing for a moment to catch my breath I added, "Without the generators, without some way to grow food, low on ammunition ... I had to leave. To stay was suicide. I had to leave. This was my home, and I had to leave." There were tears running down my face by this point. I didn't care. I felt cold and weak. That weakness forced me to bend over and hold onto my legs for support.

After a minute, I regained control, wiped my tears, and forced myself upright. I had to use the truck for support at first, though. "This was a good place. A good place to call home. With good neighbours," I said to the officer, my voice once again clear and firm.

"Yes, sir, I know," said the officer in a soft voice. "This area is being opened up faster than normal to get people back on the land. To get things ready for production next spring."

"I'm not a farmer. Though you already knew that, didn't you?"

"Yes, sir, we did. Your neighbours depended on you for assistance, and to provide a home for lots of bees and birds. Those'll be necessary come spring, especially given the shortages of fertilizers and such. You also did a lot of technical support for them, helping to keep them up and running."

I nodded. Farm news was becoming a hot topic on the various media outlets these days, even in the cities. Imports of anything, much less food, were damned expensive and would likely stay that way for a while. At least a year, maybe more. "Still doesn't explain why you need me here. Why not just confiscate it and give it to a real farmer?"

It was her turn to nod. "Yes, sir, that was discussed. But you know this area, you know the land. More importantly, you know how to take care of yourself." She paused to glance meaningfully at the skeletal remains. "Weapons and ammunition will be provided, if you so desire. And a radio for you to contact us as required. You'd be expected to offer assistance to the farmers who will be taking over the working farms around here. Eyes and ears, if nothing else, so that they can concentrate on farming."

I nodded and said, "Point guard."

"Yes, sir. You helped set up those signal lights that we found on the surrounding farms?"

"Yeah. For all the help they were."

"I wouldn't be too hard on yourself, sir. It was a useful improvised system, and it did manage to save some people. I'm hoping that you can help us design a better one, something deployable to any of the resettled areas. As well, you come highly recommended as someone who can keep their head in a tight situation."

She smiled at the puzzled look on my face. "Detective Staff Sergeant Thansworth, sir. He spoke quite highly of you, sir. That was all the recommendation I needed." That still made no sense to me. I didn't know any OPP detectives ... oh. "I take it that you're referring to Mr. Thansworth, the head of security at the ROM?"

"Indeed, sir. He was most impressed with your recent ... ah ... actions." Oh, dear. I wasn't sure that I wanted those recent actions known by all and sundry. Although I was beginning to doubt that this officer was quite what she said she was. Nor, I suspected, was Mr. Thansworth.

I nodded to acknowledge the compliment. "The power's out. And the Internet connection. I'll be needing those. My solar panels aren't working too well."

The officer pointed towards the roof. "Someone fired some shots into them, I'm afraid. Perhaps looters further down the road firing at something and not caring where their bullets actually went. I couldn't see any obvious damage to the roof itself, although a closer inspection may show something. I might be able to find someone to help with cleanup, if you need it. As for power and Internet, those are turned off at the junction down the road. We only have those turned on for houses with people in them. That can be taken care of as early as tomorrow, if you'd like."

I looked around. There was a lot of work to get done. Useful work. Something that even a silly old man could do. "Where are those papers, officer? May as well get them signed."

She gave a broad smile at that. We spent a few minutes going over them, then I signed. Hell, I'd have signed without reading, except that she insisted on explaining what the paperwork meant. It all boiled down to that I was re-claiming my land and no-one could take it from me. Oh, and I promised to help my neighbours with their farming in unspecified ways. Fair enough.

The officer, Sergeant Janice Framsten, became a lot less formal after that. Smiled and everything. We arranged for me to come back the next day at the same time, and she'd arrange for the utility people to be here to hook everything back up. As she left, she mentioned how glad she was that I was going to move back. They'd been having some odd occurrences, and it was going to be nice to have an expert in such things around.

Before she left she affixed an identifying sticker to my pickup's windshield, and gave me a signed identification card. With that, she drove away. I was left in a happy daze, gazing about and planning.

The first task was to get back inside the house and clear out the nasty surprises I'd left behind. After going at it for almost an hour, I'd had gotten all the nasties cleaned up, boxed, and put off to one side.

It was time for a break, so I decided to make a cup of tea. The water out of the taps was pretty grotty, which was only to be expected after not being used for so long, so I let it run for a few minutes. I stood there watching it splash, when a thought hit me.

Sergeant Framsten had mentioned something about strange occurrences, and that she considered me an expert in dealing with them. It was only now that I began to wonder what she meant by that.

Oh, dear.

What had I gotten myself into this time?

About The Author

Brian retired from the software development rat race to take up the carefree life of an author. He lives with his wife and two cats in Ontario, Canada.

For the latest news about this and forthcoming books, the occasional commentary on life, or to leave a comment (we love feedback), check out Brian's blog at

www.BrianGreiner.ca

Books by Brian Greiner

All books are available as e-books and paperbacks
from :
> kobobooks.com
> amazon.ca
> amazon.com

The Ascending Darkness series
> #1   Darkness Creeps Forth
> #2   Darkness Comes Reaping

The Accursed North series
> #1 The Werewolves of Winter
> #2 The Final Doom

Darkness Creeps Forth

A terrorist attack that leaves Toronto's financial district in shambles and the country's economy vulnerable. An investigative reporter who uncovers a major national scandal and then dies of apparent natural causes before his story can be published. Investigating these seemingly unrelated events draws small-time private investigator Yancey Franklin and his friends into a century-old web of corruption and deceit that threatens the security and independence of Canada. In a desperate race against time, Yancey and his friends rush to prevent an attack by a ruthless opponent on an ageing secret military facility in northern Ontario that holds a deadly secret.

Darkness Comes Reaping

Small-time investigator Yancey Franklin has thwarted the plans of a ruthless enemy to unleash biochemical weapons in Northern Ontario. Now he is on the run and trying to uncover the secrets behind a century-old web of corruption and deceit that strives to eliminate Canada as an independent nation. In a desperate race against time, Yancey and his friends struggle to stay alive as they rush to stop their enemy's latest plan – the deadly "Harvest of Souls".

The Werewolves of Winter

The werewolves were created by the Change Plague—the result of ill-considered biotechnology. It was only their annual winter die-off that saved humanity. But every spring the Change Plague returned to create a new and more deadly crop of werewolves.

People adapted and managed to carry on despite the increasingly precarious situation.

One man, trapped on his farm north of Toronto, began to piece together hints of a deeper and more dangerous threat. With werewolves closing in, time was running out in a desperate race to uncover answers.

A novel of modern horrors, ancient prophesies, data analysis, and nerds who save the world.

The Final Doom

Felix Kurtsius discovered that the Change Plague was being dispersed as part of a deliberate attack. Toronto appeared to be the epicentre for the infection, which targeted Canada preferentially. He escaped to Toronto after werewolves began purging the rural areas of humans, only to discover insidious forces at work. In a race against the clock, Felix and his friends must use all their skills to unravel the forces behind the werewolves, and prevent the destruction of humanity.

A novel of modern horrors, ancient prophesies, data analysis, and nerds who save the world.

Preview - Darkness Creeps Forth

Book 1 in the **Ascending Darkness** series.

The Doll S7H heavy equipment trailer rumbled heavily down Highway 401. Its load was carefully obscured with padding to disguise the shape, and with tarps to protect it during transport. Nothing, however, could disguise the HET but it looked similar enough to normal low-slung transports that it would not excite any interest to any but the most discerning observer.

Secrecy was the watchword for this trip. It began at CFB Petawawa and was to end at a heavy equipment shop in Quebec. The route was not the most direct of routes, but that, too, was part of the security plan. Designed by experts and approved at the highest levels, the plan for transportation of the cargo was considered flawless. It was vital that security be perfect, to avoid any political fallout. The Minister of Defence herself was adamant that no protest groups learn of the cargo much less the route.

The cargo in question was an enhanced 2A6M Leopard tank. An excellent tank, proven in battle, it was en route from testing by the Royal Canadian Dragoons. Rightly or wrongly, the tank had become a symbol for wasteful military spending by a government committed to overspending on big-ticket military items. With the purchase of a new fighter aircraft to replace the ageing CF-18 bogged down with years of infighting and accusations of corruption, and the navy ship program grinding to a halt due to incompetent management, the Leopard tank upgrade program was the latest big-ticket item to come to public attention. To buy votes in Quebec, the government had ignored qualified firms in Western and Central Canada to give the upgrade order to an inexperienced firm in Quebec. Protesters of all stripes, from anti-war activists to budget waste protesters to anti-Quebec protesters to people just fed up with the whole venal collection of toadies and self-serving mercenaries in Ottawa, had zoomed in on this latest scandal-ridden boondoggle for all sorts of reasons. Oh, and national security played a small role in the security concerns, but only to the professionals. The politicians and bureaucrats were only worried about the protesters and political spin. Because of the overwhelming need not to draw attention to the trip the HET travelled alone with no escort, in the wee hours of the early morning to avoid traffic.

As the HET approached Highway 427, it suddenly signalled a lane change. It continued changing lanes until it was heading south on the 427. Surprisingly, this did not elicit any comment from Security Control who was monitoring the progress of the HET via a wireless communications link from the on-board GPS. This was, perhaps, not so surprising since the GPS and associated data link were actually on board a van that had been pacing the HET and was continuing eastward along Highway 401.

Soon the 427 came to an end and the HET continued eastward along the Gardiner Expressway. The HET was not seen as out of place, since with all the construction occurring such a transport was a common sight as they hauled large bulldozers and such from site to site.

As the HET approached downtown Toronto it began to gradually slow down, letting the sparse traffic pass it. Eventually it came to the Harbour Street exit, and it finally came to a stop with its flashers and tail lights strobing rapidly. A half-dozen men poured out of the cab and began slashing at the lines holding down the tarps, which were rapidly pulled off to reveal the Leopard within.

Suddenly, with a roar, the Leopard tank erupted into life. It spent a few seconds bellowing curses at the sky, then rolled off the HET and onto the roadway. From there, it accelerated down the ramp and onto Harbour Street. Picking up speed it turned north on Bay Street. Smoke began belching from the sides of the turret, and the *wumph* of the side-mounted mortars was heard at regular intervals.

A police car on a side street roared up with sirens blazing, but was quickly silenced by bursts from the 7.62mm machine guns.

As the tank passed Front Street, suddenly the main 120mm smooth-bore gun vomited with a roar of smoke and sound, and a split-second later the side of a building exploded into the night. Then another roar from the main gun and another building exploded. The main turret swung from side to side, periodically spewing destruction. The machine guns added a background chatter to the main gun, clawing away at buildings and vehicles.

Thundering past Wellington Street, King Street, Adelaide Street the guns of the tank raked destruction along either side of its path.

Onward past Richmond Street, then on Queen Street it slowed slightly as it jogged left then right and drove onto Nathan Phillips Square in front of City Hall. The tank fired one last blaze of destruction into the middle of City Hall, then fell silent.

A brightly-coloured orange helicopter noisily clawed its way from the sky and landed in the Square, off to one side of the tank.

The top of the turret opened up and out came the black-clad crew of the tank. They scurried into the waiting helicopter and were whisked into the night. A fountain of flame erupted from the tank as the incendiary charges left inside ignited. An answering eruption of flame answered from the Gardiner Expressway as the HET burned as a result of similar charges.

The helicopter made a powerful leap upwards and made a quick flip to fly south as it rapidly gained altitude to rise above the smoke and haze of the destruction wrought by the tank. It continued flying south until it got to the lake shore, then banked, flew down towards the water, and was lost in the waiting darkness.

The city was silent for a moment.

Then the screams of broken buildings and broken flesh split the early morning darkness.

Preview - **Darkness Comes Reaping**

Book 2 in the **Ascending Darkness** series.

It was the sound that got his attention when awareness returned to him. A soft meaty thudding that sounded vaguely familiar. Then came the feeling of a sharp twisting movement. It puzzled him at first, then he realized that the former always seemed to precede the latter. Following the movement came a sensation of pressure, building quickly to a dull pain that spread from the point where the pressure had occurred. He fit the pieces together and realized that all of the events were related, somehow, and the process of figuring it out gave him a vague sense of accomplishment. After some indeterminate time the process was repeated. Then again. And again. It gradually occurred to him that not only were all of the event related, but that they were happening to him. Something was hitting him. He tried to think, but the sounds and motion of the repeated blows made it impossible to hold together a chain of coherent reasoning. And he was tired. So tired.

The various sensations stopped, finally, and he felt grateful for the quiet and a chance for his thoughts to coalesce into something vaguely coherent. He became aware that something new was happening, something trying to get his attention. Voices. That was what they were, voices that saying something. He tried to focus his shattered attention on what they were saying - maybe it was important. Everything felt so thick to him, thick and disconnected.

"Mister Franklin" he heard the voice say, over and over again.

This confused him. He didn't know anyone named 'Mister'.

The voice continued its chanting, in a slow melodic manner.

He finally came to the realization that the voice was talking to *him*. With this realization came a limited return of awareness. He had a body, with a head and torso and arms and legs. He had forgotten about them, somehow. And he was lying horizontally on a hard surface, unable to move his arms or legs. The trickle of awareness increased, and memories started coming back to him. Memories of imprisonment and beatings. He was being beaten. Again. But he couldn't remember why. Everything hurt, and he was so tired.

"Mister Franklin" the voice intoned, "The Fist of Tolerance takes no pleasure in these activities. We only seek to guide you to The Path, but we require your assistance. Please, we beg of you, help us to guide you."

Yancey carefully shook his head as if to clear it, and opened his eyes as much as the swollen flesh surrounding them would allow. The bright light cut like a knife, and he quickly shut his eyes again and tried to move his head away. Strong hands firmly held his head, and a cool cloth was placed over his eyes. Yancey made a soft sigh that rustled through dry chapped lips.

"We have dimmed the lights for you, Mister Franklin" intoned the voice, "And we will try to make you comfortable, for a time. You must realize that coming to The Path is inevitable, for it is the will of God that we do so. Each and every one of us. This scourging of the flesh is necessary only because you resist the inevitable. All that is required is for you to confess. Confess and tell us everything that is in your heart. Tell us how you found this place. Tell us where your friends are. Tell us about the Shattered Palace. Confess. Confess and receive God's blessing and forgiveness. Confess and be comforted in body and soul."

Memories started to come back, like a broken mirror reassembling itself. Yancey remembered that he was in the hands of the Sword of Infinity Ascending. He remembered being captured. He remembered the interrogations. Most importantly, he remembered that his friends were now safely away from the

Sword. Nothing could force him to betray or endanger them. Nothing. He tried to form words, but his lips refused to cooperate. He felt a moist cloth against his mouth, easing the dryness. The cloth was removed and he tried again to speak. This time his lips worked, or at least well enough to form words.

"Fuck you."

Not many words, and not everything that he wanted to say to his captors, but it would suffice.

He felt the cloth around his eyes being removed, and then felt the heat of the blinding lights returning.

"You have only yourself to blame for this, Mister Franklin" said a deep sad voice, "The Fist of Tolerance exists only to guide sinners back to The Path ordained by God. You are a lost soul, and we will help guide you back to The Path. Remember that as we scourge the flesh."

The beating began again. And as before, his inquisitors were puzzled by the laughter that bubbled out of their captor's mouth before he lapsed into semi-consciousness. Yancey knew something they didn't, and the realization always made him laugh. He knew that the beatings couldn't break him. As a child he had grown up with similar sorts of beatings, and and from long practise knew how to retreat into himself to escape the pain.

Some things never change, he thought just before the kaleidescope of memories claimed him once again.

Preview - The Werewolves of Winter

Book 1 in the **Ascending Darkness** series.

I could hear them howling, hunting something or other. Hopefully not someone.

Howling or no, I had wanted to check up on my neighbours. The power, land-line phone, cell phone, and Internet had all been down for over a month, and I'd not heard from any of them in all that time. The signal lights I'd convinced them to rig up last year indicated that everything was OK. Still, it was past time to check up on them all—werewolves be damned--so I had kitted up my truck for the short trip to my neighbours.

The werewolves had begun to leave me alone these days. The beds of garlic, onions, and wolfsbane that I'd planted around the house helped. It didn't seem to do them any real harm, but hives, massive sneezing fits, and tearing eyes could be painful enough to be a useful deterrent.

My shotguns and rifles also encouraged them to stay away from the house. Enhanced healing was of little use when the blast of a 12-gauge shell filled with No. 4 buck hit them in the head or chest. A solid one-ounce slug or the bullet from a .303 worked well, too, although that required more precision when aiming.

So a truce, of sorts, held. Or maybe just a temporary cessation of hostilities. Whatever. They stopped attacking me, and I stopped shooting at them. I wasn't the best of shots, but thankfully the noise of the guns was usually sufficient to chase them off. Circumstances, however, had been forcing me to improve my aim. There were more of them than was normal for this time of year, so I had made a point of practising as much as my limited stock of ammunition allowed.

Alas, the truce, or whatever it was, only seemed to hold within the limits of my yard. As I drove down the road, I would sometimes catch sight of werewolves in the fields or brush. A few darted out to run alongside me for a few seconds before dashing off. Most lay or stood motionless, staring hard at me as I passed.

The back of my neck began to prickle as I began to wonder what would happen if I ever stopped. Or if something made me stop. Now that was an unsettling thought. Not a pleasant drive.

The looks in the eyes of the gathering werewolves was beginning to worry me. I'd seen them dash across the road ahead and behind me. Not often, and not too closely, although it seemed to be happening somewhat more frequently and a bit closer each time.

I caught sight of a couple of larger groups up ahead, trying to blend in with the scrubby spring grasses. That wasn't normal behaviour—small hunting packs were one thing, but this looked like an attempt at an ambush. At the first widening of the road I turned around and headed back home. Although the need to get back home almost made me stomp on the accelerator, I forced myself to keep the speed constant. It was important not to speed up or slow down too much or too quickly. Changes in speed seemed to trigger their hunting reflex, just like it would for any predator.

Sweat was beginning to trickle down my neck as I caught sight of my driveway up ahead. A look around showed nothing out of the ordinary as I made the turn into the driveway and drove towards the house. I glanced at the house and barn and saw that none of the alert lights were on. A good sign, but not foolproof. All that meant was that the motion detectors hadn't sensed anything recently.

The day was too warm for the thermal detectors to be of use, so those weren't going to be of any help. I drove behind the house, and up to the barn. Stopping just outside the garage door, I kept the engine running. The werewolves had learnt the hard way not to rush me at this point. Still, it was always best not to take chances.

I flicked a switch on the pickup's dashboard to arm the active defences, then another to increase the sensitivity of the sensors. Finally the third switch: the AHBL—All Hell Breaking Loose—switch. Sirens warbled and high-intensity LED lights strobed briefly. After a short pause, a different pattern of shrieks and flashes again cycled. With the sensors still showing that all was clear, I disabled the AHBL, and signalled the garage doors to open. At the first opportunity, I drove in and closed the door. Another check of the sensors showed that everything checked out OK.

Home sweet home.

With a heavy sigh of defeat I got out of the truck. There was no point in topping up the fuel tank, given that I'd not gone very far. On the other hand, adding some more gasoline stabilizer couldn't hurt. I was old enough to remember when gasoline could sit for practically ever and still be usable. With all the newfangled "enhancements" and "eco-friendly additives", gasoline now started to degrade within a week or two. I grabbed a bottle of stabilizer gunk and poured it into the gas tank. There was a limited supply of the gunk that I figured would run out at about the same time the gasoline did. Hard decisions were coming up later in the year. Another heavy sigh as I replaced the cap on the fuel tank and shut the lid.

With the vehicle's needs taken care of, I removed the emergency duffel bag and guns and stowed them in their appropriate storage locations. I turned to check the upper floor, then with a start remembered that I had yet to lock the garage door.

"Absent-minded old fool," I muttered under my breath.

Turning towards the garage door, I slid the locking bolts on both sides—top, middle, and bottom bolts. Yes, the garage door opener mechanism was supposed to protect the door from brute force attacks. However, when my life was on the line I preferred to err on the side of caution.

That chore completed, I continued into the barn proper. I had turned it into a general-purpose workshop and vehicle storage building shortly after I first moved here, some years ago. The bottom floor had about one third of it devoted to vehicles—the pickup, a medium-sized tractor, and a couple of snow blowers. The remaining space held small and medium-sized CNC mills and lathes for metal work, a laser cutter, a woodworking lathe, a small CNC mill for general wood carving, and a large CNC mill suitable for carving up full sheets of plywood. The finishing areas that had been used for painting and such, were now converted to storage and supplemental backup power.

Upstairs, where I was heading, was more or less office space. Once packed with computers and electronic gizmos, now it was a main hub for sensors and security. The uppermost loft also made a good sniper blind, with a field of view that stretched as far as several of my nearest neighbours.

I wearily climbed the stairs. This seemed to be getting harder every month. Much of that was just psychological, I knew. Not entirely, though—the advancing years seemed to take their toll, no matter how much I tried to outwit or deny them.

Reaching the top of the stairs, I headed over to the security system. It showed no untoward activity, and I decided to take advantage of that to start running a diagnostic. Although the system ran a diagnostic automatically every twenty-four hours, it never hurt to run them more often. Some of the sensors communicated via WiFi, some via cables running into serial ports, and some plugged into a hardwired network using CAT6 cable. A mixed bag of technologies that had evolved over the years and changed as technology changed. Now it was frozen into an as-is state, and as such it was a damn fine idea to run diagnostics to catch any issues or potential issues as quickly as possible.

It was too early for the thermal scanners to be of use, so there was no data from them. The motion sensors showed the usual random movements caused by wind, movement of the trees, and birds. I truly loathed the motion sensors, as they gave so many false positives. Still, once in a while they picked up something that the other sensors missed. Often enough that I didn't begrudge them the power it took to keep them working, nor the time spent in analysing their data. That didn't stop them from being an annoying pain in the ass much of the time. The video feeds were little better. Image analysis software was useful—although, like the motion sensors, it was prone to false positives.

Open source software was a god-send in setting this all up. However, with a workforce of one to do the programming, cooking, cleaning, security, and everything, well, it was hard to find the time to do it all properly. And, if truth be told, I wasn't the world's best techie. Talented enough to do some useful stuff, certainly, just not a super-tech. Not even in my prime, and I was somewhat past my prime.

With yet another heavy sigh I turned from the computer, went over to the gun rack, and selected the deer-hunting rifle. I slung it and headed up the short ladder into the turret. The turret was originally a cooling turret, of the sort seen on many barns, that I'd modified it into a nice observation post. Originally meant to allow me to easily view my property, it now served as a sniper post. The only blind spot was the front and west side of the house, but a set of video monitors showed me the feed from the cameras for those areas. Everything seemed quiet. It appeared that the truce was holding despite my brief sojourn.

I lifted up the rifle and sighted through its scope to scan the surrounding area. The binoculars racked on the wall would have served the same purpose, of course. However, the rifle was better for a quick wide-area scan. It was also better for shooting at hostiles than the binoculars were.

Everything seemed calm at first glance as I took a look at my neighbours, looking at the signal lights on their roofs. Green for all was well, yellow for out of the house, and red for trouble. Everybody showed green, which was reassuring. Alas, not everyone took security as seriously as I did, so that was as good as I was going to get without physically visiting them. Which looked to be out of the question for the time being.

With a sigh, I toggled my own signal lights from yellow to green. Although I'm not the most sociable of men, I enjoyed meeting with my neighbours more often than every couple of months. Things were better during the winters after the annual werewolf die-off. That was when things got back to a semblance of normal, and people tended to cram in a lot of social activities.

The rural areas had more werewolf attacks that the cities, and used the winter months to achieve a semblance of normality. At other times of the year people tended to stay home, venturing out only for the periodic swap and barter meets. Travel for those events was done in a convoy escorted by OPP cruisers. There was a strict schedule, and people had learnt the hard way to travel only with those convoys.

Normally we'd use the phone lines to keep in touch and arrange the meets. The phone lines, along with the power, cable TV, and Internet connectivity, were buried and theoretically isolated from the elements. In practise, alas, water would sometimes seep in and short out sections for indeterminate lengths of time. That had been a problem from the day they were installed, corporate propaganda and denials to the contrary. The outages got worse as time went on. In fact, everything had been out of service for the past few weeks. Hopefully it would clear up sooner than later.

It'd be nice to get the next meet arranged, and see my neighbours again. Also nice to top up supplies of spices and perishables. That assumed, of course, that there were any to be had at any price. The staples were usually available, but for the past year or so anything imported seemed to be sucked up by the big cities, with decreasing amounts for the rest of us.

For now, though, I was still on my own and everything looked to be shipshape. I took one last look around through the gun's scope, and one last look at the video feeds. Everything looked clear. No need to worry, silly old man. I climbed down, racked the gun, walked down the stairs and prepared to exit the barn and enter the house.

Oh, wait—another task I had almost forgotten. I walked over to the sink and grabbed the watering can, then went around the interior watering all the various plants. The ubiquitous garlic and wolfsbane were there, of course, plus a few others meant just for brightening up the place. As the ritual demanded, I said a few words of encouragement to each of them as I gave them their water rations. I don't know if talking to them helped the plants, but it always seemed to ease my own mind a bit. Sort of like a mindfulness exercise.

Whatever. It was a small pleasure in a world increasingly devoid of pleasures, large or small. When the watering was over, I returned the watering can to the sink and filled it up for next time. The plants upstairs had been watered a day ago, so they would keep for a while.

After a brief look around to ensure that I'd not forgotten something, I was ready to head back to the house. I walked over to the gun cabinet and selected the shotgun to augment the revolver that I always wore. I did a check of the shotgun (oiled just last week, and always loaded) and racked a shell into the chamber. Walking over to the door, I peered through the spy-hole to confirm that it was safe to exit. Even with fancy electronics, the old eyeball was still the fail-safe system of choice. A very good habit to maintain.

I toggled the door switches to activate the solenoids that pulled back the security bolts. When those clicked into place, I opened the door and stepped a couple of paces outside before halting. I continued only after hearing the reassuring clack of bolts shooting back into their locked positions.

Walking without haste towards the house, I took the stairs leading to the porch one at a time. Used to be that I'd bound up, taking two or three steps at a time, but not anymore. My footfalls made a solid thunk on the stairs. I'd built that stairway out of two-inch heavy oak, replacing the rather flimsier pine steps that came with the house. Stepping onto the porch made a similar solid sound—I'd replaced a lot of boards in the porch, too.

Finally, I stopped at the door. I pulled the electronic key out from an inner pocket of my jacket and held it up. The door gave a satisfying clack as its bolts were pulled back by solenoids. I pushed it open, stepped in, then pushed it shut again. The bolts immediately slapped back into place, securing the door from anything short of explosives.

A quick glance at the indicator lights sunk into the moulding showed that no surprises had been detected inside the house while I'd been away. With a contented sigh I opened the inner door and stepped into the kitchen. I ejected the chambered shell from the shotgun and put it back into the magazine before racking the gun in its slot in the kitchen. Shrugging out of my jacket, I hung it between the door and shotgun so no intruder could easily get at the gun. As always, the holstered revolver stayed on my hip.

The savoury smell coming from the slow cooker made my mouth water. A quick wash-up and it would be time for supper. There was a time when I'd sit on the porch to eat and sip tea, watching the natural world unfold as I unwound from the day's work. Alas, those times were long gone.

Fucking werewolves. They had ruined everything.